DEAD DANGEROUS

Adie Sturm Mystery

ANASTASIA AMOR

BRODT PUBLISHING

BRODT PUBLISHING

AnastasiaAmor.com

Copyright © 2020 by Anna Brodt

All rights reserved.

ISBN: 978-0-992134389

Cover art by Anna Brodt

Author photo by Kristen Wells

ACKNOWLEDGEMENTS

Thank you to all my friends and fans who encouraged me to continue the Adie Sturm Mystery series. Cozumel is a place close to my heart and nothing gives me more pleasure than capturing that glorious setting mingling it with romance and murder. Special thanks to my fabulous editor, Bruce.

Praise for **ANASTASIA AMOR**

A CORPSE FOR COZUMEL: ADIE STURM MYSTERY

"...hot sexy men... thrilling suspense... keep looking over your shoulder. You won't guess who the killer is until it's too late."
—*Night Owl Romance Reviews*

DAYS OF THE DEAD: ADIE STURM MYSTERY "...murder, hot romance, intrigue, and suspense...Adie is a modern-day, sexy Agatha Christie...charming and quite captivating...put together well!"
ReviewYourBook

"5 Stars! Detailed local color and flavor combine with intense mystery and intrigue as well as steamy romance ... Excellent descriptions, well-developed characters, and great action keep you right in the story, turning page after page to see what happens next. Sexual tension is high ...Adie Sturm is a wonderful character to help you enjoy another world from the comfort of your own home or beach chair. **Gripping story, hot characters, realistic dialogue and fantastic action!"**—*Melinda Hills, Readers' Favorite*

THE CURSE OF THE CARNAVAL: **ADIE STURM MYSTERY Epic Award Nominee5 stars** "Just when you thought it couldn't get any hotter..."—Michelle Stinson Ross

"Adie's back and it's hotter than ever, way hotter. And far more dangerous."
—*ChrisChat Reviews*

DEAD DELICIOUS: ADIE STURM MYSTERY

"*Dead Delicious made me a huge Adie Sturm fan*.... strong, sexy, and independent...Amor has incredible skill in how she unfolds the element of mystery while keeping the sensual atmosphere alivemaking us yearn for our slice of sun, sea, sand, and irresistible male company...the colorful band of tour group members who will have you laughing one minute and tearing your hair out the next....fun, fast-paced, drop dead sexy, and keeps your pulse racing in more ways than one. *Amor is truly the queen of steamy mysteries.*" —*Highly recommended!*—*Natalie G. Owens, An Eternity of Roses.*

DEAD DIRTY:ADIE STURM MYSTERY "...a splendid meld of mystery, murder, and sleuth...Dead Dirty is cunningly plotted and written with the deftness of a master's hand."— *Dzemo,Readers' Favorite*

Other books:

HAVANA HEAT: Sommerville Suspense Series...*a paranormal-fantasy romance*
"Havana Heat is a sensory experience. It's a sultry pleasure trip that rouses all the senses and won't let go.... Every chapter, every scene, thrusts you in a different world, a varied experience that transports you utterly into magical realms and otherworldly adventures. The story has many threads woven into the plot but they are seamlessly pulled into the finish line and tied together. The paranormal aspect is highly original and captivating. *Havana Heat makes you breathless.* ... Fast paced and drop dead sexy....the romance on these pages is something you won't soon forget." —*Natalie G. Owens, author of **An Eternity of Roses***

"Twists and turns in this tropical romance make it a paranormal reading adventure that will keep you on your toes until the last word!"
—*Barbara Huffert, author of* **Linked**

BOURBON STREET BURN: Sommerville Suspense Series
New Orleans is the perfect setting for a great paranormal fiction fantasy story and Anastasia Amor uses every bit of it to the fullest in Bourbon Street Burn: Sommerville Suspense. Amor captures the present ambiance of the city, along with the historical allure, with strong characters and an exciting plot. The blending of the two lifelines provides plenty of interest while keeping you guessing exactly what stakes each person has in the overall outcome of the adventure. A great read with excitement, intrigue, action and lust galore; you will be sorry to come to the end, wishing there could be more. *Melinda Hills Readers' Favorite*

EXPLORING IRRESISTIBLE...an erotic romance
" Exploring Irresistible is as decadent as fine dark chocolate and tropical drinks. Amor's vivid descriptions put me right there. What I love best is that I can come back and enjoy this story over and over again. This book is sensuous romance at its best. Hot sultry Puerto Rico. When Aleese sees sinfully irresistible Arman—a man like chocolate... the tiger inside her is unleashed! A fight for control over her life surges into a burning adventure of passion and erotic fantasy" —***Irresistible in every way! 5 Stars***—Michelle Stinson Ross

1

The text had warned him.

Your yacht is about to become fragmented. Can't wait to see it explode in a million pieces.

He had to stop this.

Bombs had been his business—building, detonating, and dismantling. He had used them in the construction industry in Canada for years and now here in Cozumel. Wolf Du Lac had been deployed in Afghanistan on a special bomb unit. Now he was on a mission to search for the instrument that could destroy his personal monument to his lady—*Adie's Storm*. The clock was ticking.

***

Dazzling bright sun sparkled silver on the crests of the waves. The Caribbean was a brilliant azure blue, the sky above, a soft cerulean blanketed with pillows of white. The sea waters lapped heavily on an elegant fifty-foot ivory yacht. It wasn't just any rich man's toy. It had my name in script next to the mermaid on the port side. *Adie's Storm*.

My phone chimed. I pulled out my iPhone and read the text.

Don't go on board! Keep everyone off the gangway. Will explain later. W

My glance caught a figure. I stopped in my tracks so suddenly my friend behind me, racing to keep up, tottered dangerously on five-inch stilettos. She bumped into me nearly falling backwards. Clutching her arm, I righted her, asking, "You okay, Carmelita?"

"*Dios mio*, Adelina! What is wrong with you?" Carmelita hissed out the last few words as her breath returned in gasps. "First you run like a demented person to get here and then you stop as if you've seen a ghost." She patted the skirt of her green silk dress in place. It matched her sparkling eyes exactly, intentionally. Carmelita, the designer knew what made her look outstanding and played it up whenever she could.

"Sorry, I was distracted by Wolf's text. He said we need to stay away from the gangway and the yacht," I muttered, my eyes mesmerized by the tall muscular man I saw standing on the bow in a black neoprene suit, mask and scuba gear. I paused, puzzled, "I don't get it. He's going for a dive?"

"So?"

"Wolf knew we were coming. He warned me to keep everyone away. Said it was dangerous and he'd explain later." My eyes shot over to the silver sheen of the Mercedes-Benz SUV parked at the dock. The windows were tinted, impossible to make out the interior but I would bet the seats were a soft black leather. It couldn't be his. Wolf drove a Jeep. "Why is he going now?"

Carmelita glanced at her shiny Cartier watch—a pretty thing encrusted with diamonds almost as bright in the daylight as the sun's rays striking the Caribbean.

"The Sea God is being overly dramatic. I'm sure it's just another surprise he has planned for you. Logically speaking, we are forty-five minutes early, chica. He isn't ready for us." She smirked. "Most likely he thought we'd be late after shopping. Probably thought we'd stop for drinks and snacks but, we were good girls for a change." She patted me on the arm, "And we found you a dress for your party. Not that your little wrap-around red print isn't cute but surely for the soiree you will wear a special outfit for the formal announcement."

"The aqua silk is beautiful but really you are mistaken to think—

Carmelita clapped her hands in excitement. "I think this must be the place he wants to make you a proposal and my bet is, he has decorators there working their magic as we speak."

I shrugged. "I told you, it hasn't gone that far."

She squeezed my hand. "I'm glad you two are moving slowly. You need to be sure. I know he's a hot guy but don't forget about the other fish nibbling on your line."

Carmelita nudged me. "Adelina?"

Ignoring my friend, I squinted at the boat. Wolf stood motionless for a few seconds before he shot backwards into the water in a perfect dive. He went under and then resurfaced again to clear his mask.

The gangway was in place awaiting our arrival. I debated shouting out to Wolf but I figured he wouldn't be able to hear me. There was a bench on this side that would do if we had to wait. I would take Carmelita over there when Wolf's text gave us an "all clear".

Marg might join us. Carmelita was Diego's sister and even though Marg got along with Carmelita, she was not keen on her brother, Diego. I texted Marg.

Waiting at the bench on the dock. Wolf said not to approach the gangway under any circumstances. Adie

I was worried about what Wolf considered to be dangerous. I turned to Carmelita to make sure she knew this was serious. "Wolf thinks something bad will happen."

"Oh? Has he been to see a psychic? She laughed at her joke.

"This is serious, Carmelita. I don't think he'd text me to stay away otherwise."

Carmelita pursed her lips in annoyance. "All right, I believe you." She swiveled her head. "So, what's a girl with a thirst have to do to get a drink?" She grinned. "I should have brought my new houseboy. He is excellent at making drinks, among other things. Did I tell you I have a hot one? Very nice on the eyes." Her tongue flicked over her lip reflectively. "My mouth feels as dry as a hot summer's day at El Cedral."

"Don't worry. I'm sure it's nothing that can't be fixed." I glanced around. "We could sit on that bench in the sun or head out to the beach club while we wait for an okay. Something may be wrong with the boat." I tapped my fingers nervously on the railing approaching the gangway.

Carmelita's eyes shifted to the ocean. The breeze was gently lifting her long brown locks off her shoulders.

Salt was in the air. I could feel it coating my skin. The ocean showed no sign of any impending danger, its waters a brilliant blue. Even as the ocean was gorgeous and the day was sunny, a knot in my stomach kept me wary. I had learned not to ignore my gut feelings. I surveyed the area at the waterfront worriedly.

Brushing a tendril away from her forehead, Carmelita remarked, "You know, chica, I love the sea. I would adore living in your Sea God's condo building. The view is terrific and the condos have more square footage than mine. I am so weary of my tired-looking place. There's no ocean view or beach. I'm so jealous of you. Even Diego has a fabulous view at his villa."

"They are lovely. Luxury condos with tennis courts and a pool."

"I should buy one," she mused. "Does he have any left?

"You have a few million to spare?"

Carmelita shot me a look.

"Of course, you do. Pocket change for a Bolivar Alvarez."

"No need for you to be envious. You'd have all that if you decided to marry my brother."

I sighed. "Wolf and I are trying to work things out."

"How many times have I heard that before? Isn't it better to move on if you have to keep trying to make it work, over and over again? Love should run smoothly, right?" Carmelita chuckled. "Not that I'm an expert but listen to me, chica. My brothers are both sinfully delicious, don't you think?"

I nodded.

"Well then. You need to reach out and grab one."

"The way you talk they could be chocolate truffles or incredible éclairs, not men."

Carmelita grinned. "All good-looking hombres are like chocolate. You've said it yourself often enough."

She was right. The handsome Bolivar Alvarez men were hot commodities but Wolf wasn't chicken liver either. "Come on, girl, let's go sit on the bench and watch the sea."

We were almost there when it happened. A yellow flash, a rumbling vibration and an ear shattering bang rocked the air. Fibreglass parts from the gangway went flying helter-skelter. I pushed Carmelita to the ground. She shrieked as the gravel tore into her skin. Carmelita collapsed in a heap with me halfway on top of her. My body shook with the secondary impact from the explosion and the missiles of debris.

***

In the parking lot a cell trilled. "So?" a silky female's voice purred. "Is he in a million pieces?" Her laughter was like the tinkling of a hundred tiny bells.

"The second explosive detonated. For some reason the first failed."

"Hm-m, it's good we had an alternative source. Now go ahead with the plan, mi amor."

***

Days earlier

Foliage from the tropical plants, subtly lit, surrounded the tables in the garden portion of the restaurant. Fuchsia tablecloths covered black wrought-iron patio tables, spaced out on the gray ceramic tiles. Behind us a bright blue wall was decorated with wine bottles. A flowering bougainvillea tree blocked the rest of the expanse.

A level up near the bar, the chairs were intimately placed for couples, while down below two or more chairs were situated at each table. We were on the upper level where soft music in the background set the mood.

Dusk was warm with a tender breeze ruffling my hair while it caressed my skin like a lover's lips. In fact, that particular special man was sitting across from me. I'd know him most of my life but had lost touch until a few years ago when I'd taken my tour group to Cozumel. The chemistry had sparked like an active volcano. It had been there even as a teen but nothing had come of it because our parents had objected and then later it was anything but smooth sailing. This time, we were in control of our destiny. The chemistry had morphed into a strong soul connection. Was he my person? Did I know if it was love?

My ex fiancé met my gaze. Was there still magic? Who was I kidding? He was the spark-master—his secret power enticing unsuspecting women.

"Babe? You didn't say. How about a Bahama Mama or a Mango thingy?"

I looked over at my ex. His hair was a bright halo of blond hair falling over a high forehead, he had a Norman nose, full lips and a significant chin. His contrasting black T-shirt displayed broad shoulders and muscular arms. He was Superman fit, and as sexy as ever.

"Sounds good. Maybe the Mango. Healthier." I grinned. "Should I look at the menu or do you have something picked out?"

"Are you in the mood for seafood? I heard they have ceviche. Let's start with a guac and a spicy pico de gallo."

I nodded absentmindedly, perusing the menu. The fish I could make at home and there were only a few I liked anyway. My choice was lobster or—I gave up. Wolf was looking at me. It was impossible to focus on food.

Wolf said something. The words coming out of his mouth came out as "blah blah blah", I was so intent on gazing into those sparkling blue eyes. Mesmerising. They reminded me of a freshwater stream flashing silver in the summer's sun on a hot still day. I was momentarily transported back to the French River where he had taken us in a motorboat to a quiet tiny inlet. It was just the two of us, quiet and still on a sweltering summer's day. This is where our story began, where I'd first felt his magnetic power. I knew he felt it that day. His skin glistened from sweat and his smile teased. Wolf was a guy on the brink of manhood and I was a teenage virgin—could be we both were but we were far from innocent.

Right now, I could feel beads of perspiration on my brow and moisture gathering in my armpits—something like I experienced before a karate sparring match. Nervous energy. I was transported to that weekend at his parent's cabin that culminated in smoldering glances, but no sex.

It ended abruptly when Agnes Du Lac snuffed out our excitement like the quick pinch of two fingers on a candle flame. She and my Pop decided we were not an item and would never be. We were told to put a lid on it. Pop was afraid Wolf would take my virginity while Agnes thought I would seduce her poor innocent son into an early marriage.

Her husband Jack had made it big time and she wanted a rich wife for her son. I had to wonder if I'd be a winner when it came to love this time. If Agnes Du Lac had anything to say about it, I would fold before my hand was played.

Life was a circle within a circle when it came to Wolf Du Lac. He was a man of mystery. I had been his fiancée once before until that blew up in my face. Too many complications. Now, we were giving it another try but what was up could be down any second on this ride with the handsome Sea God. He had layers like an onion.

"Babe?"

I knew so little about his life in those in between years. "I hope this isn't too personal but do you ever think of your time in Afghanistan?"

"I try not to." His eyes stared into the distance. "Bad times. Too many people dead on both sides. It's time to start living again." Wolf stroked my hand. "Right? We need to move forward. The past can't hurt us anymore."

"Memories can."

"Don't let them." Wolf's clear blue eyes met mine. "Can you do that?"

"I will try." I stared at the menu.

"Think about the food. What would you like?"

I sighed. "Yes."

Wolf gave me a quizzical glance. "Yes, to the apps?"

I nodded solemnly. "Sure."

He motioned to the waiter and ordered a mango cocktail for me and Dos Equis for himself. He still liked those best, I noticed. When the waiter asked about our food order he said, "We'll have the guac and the pico de gallo." He glanced over at me. You want the pollo de mole?"

I nodded. It was always good. Chocolate sauce coated the chicken. It had been my favorite from the moment I heard of it. The Mayans discovered chocolate, using it in entrees, desserts and strangely it was their currency when they first met the Spaniards.

Everything was better with chocolate. It releases endorphins in the brain, stimulating the pleasure principal. It blasted me away to a fantasy land especially if I was with a scintillating member of the opposite sex.

Suddenly, I felt a chill, the hairs on my neck stood up. Someone was walking over my grave. I shivered unexplainedly.

"And the fish of the day for me." Wolf said to the waiter before gazing at me curiously. When the waiter turned on his heel and trotted back in the direction of the kitchen, he grinned. "Chocolate anticipation is driving you wild or—?"

I shook my head. "No, it's nothing."

Wolf touched my forearm. "Something's up?"

"Just a feeling I'm getting."

"Tell me. Your eyes are a dark blue."

"That's the color they are."

"The Adie Sturm happy eyes are turquoise like the Caribbean. I know you're bothered about something."

I glanced at my ex. It was as if I was the fish on his line and he was slowly drawing me in. Sometimes, he could easily read my secret thoughts but this time he was off the mark. I didn't know if that problem would ever go away. So many events had interfered with us.

"It's just a bad feeling I have. Call it a premonition of something unforeseen about to happen. Something negative."

Wolf stared at me. "About what?"

I shrugged. "Nothing to worry about, I'm sure."

"Good. I'm hungry." At that moment the waiter reappeared as Wolf glanced back at the menu.

His white-blond hair fell on his forehead. I was tempted to reach over and push it back with my fingertips. Handling his hair felt good. But that would be too much stimulation, for me, maybe not for him. My temperature rose alarmingly every time I touched his thick mane. Wolf reminded me of a lion, his nose strong and slightly crooked from a sports mishap but he had a perfect profile with a significant manly chin. I sighed happily. He was like rich milk chocolate—creamy and sinfully delicious.

"What's up? Your moods are changing like the tide. One second your eyes are dark blue and the next they're turquoise. Have you been eating chocolate from a private stash in your handbag?"

I poked his arm. "Don't be ridiculous!" My hidden stash was in my suitcase.

Wolf looked back up, grinning. "Couldn't resist. Nice view."

"My shoes are awesome, right?" I was wearing strappy metallic sandals with three-inch heels.

"M-mm."

"What? You don't like them?"

"I think I need to give those stems a closer look."

A spark ignited in my brain and surged south, like a wildfire. It was steamy enough here at the table with the Cozumel humidity without Wolf's energy. I fanned my face with the menu.

"You okay?"

"Humidity. It's a hot September," I said softly. My fine blond hair was safely tucked into a ponytail. Hopefully, I looked okay.

"I like the red on you."

"My dress? It's not too short?"

"Nope. You have great legs. Nothing wrong with showing them off."

I nodded, agreeing with him but internally unsure. My dress was decent, just above my knees. Okay, I lied. It was a mini. Vertically challenged women look long legged in short dresses.

"Adie."

"Hmm?"

Wolf reached over to take my hand. "Tell me what you're thinking."

"I'm worried about seeing your mother."

Wolf nodded. "She's in Canada, remember?"

I pictured Agnes riding in on a broomstick, landing on the condo roof.

Wolf gripped my shoulder. "Listen to me, babe. I told her not to come. It's hurricane season."

Agnes Du Lac was a lot worse than any hurricane. She was scary crazy.

At that moment the server appeared with our drinks on a tray. My mango cocktail was a delightful orange concoction with plenty of ice in a large goblet.

Wolf raised his beer.

"Salud, to new beginnings," Wolf said in his husky voice.

I clicked his bottle. "New beginnings."

Wolf sipped his beer and then set it on the table.

"Have you told her?"

He shrugged. "You aren't wearing my ring."

Agnes Du Lac, was a contrary woman who had managed to intimidate my mild-natured mother. While Pop was freaking out about teenage sex, Mom was quaking in her boots at the thought of Agnes' rage.

"She doesn't like me."

"Mom doesn't like anyone I date, but let's cut her a break. Dad has only been dead a year. She's not thinking straight."

"I thought your parents didn't get along."

"They didn't. She's a bulldozer. My dad wanted to divorce her but he felt guilty leaving." Wolf looked wistfully at the darkening sky. "I wish he'd have lived long enough to see us together. He liked you. As for Agnes, no one will ever be good enough. You are not her problem. Besides, she has Heinz to worry about. He and Linda have a situation."

"Oh?"

"They're like fire and water. Always fighting."

I smiled. "We're both fire elements—Aries and Sagittarius. We should get along great."

"And we do. Fire flaming fire."

In my mind I saw skin against skin and heat from our kisses. I felt

9

that familiar tingle at my core.

Wolf smiled surreptitiously. "A woman like you does that to a guy."

I batted my lashes. "You charmer."

Wolf grinned. "I am a man of many talents."

True enough. He sparked my energy into a raging fire. "Seriously, what have you been up to?"

When the waiter set the apps on the table, I dipped my corn chip into the guacamole and took a bite while I watched him.

"Built the condominium and now I'm selling the units off to recoup my investment."

"How's that going?"

"Good, on the whole," Wolf said, somewhat hesitantly.

"Oh?"

Wolf dug into the pico de gallo bowl and scooped up the bright tomato salsa flicked with coriander.

"Is there something I should know?"

Wolf's expression remained inscrutable.

"Condos are selling?"

"Yeah, looks like it. Heinz is running the show. I've got another job I'm working on—renovating a building. It was better for Heinz to focus on managing the condo sales. I let him invest in the project."

"That's great. But you're frowning," I said, noticing the downward turn of the corners of his mouth. "Something happened?"

"He moved here with his wife, Linda, thinking they would be in nirvana. Linda was seriously religious, remember? Not any more. Linda's gone hippy. She dumped him."

"Really? Agnes' perfect daughter-in-law?"

"Yup. I think she's stoned every day. She hasn't seen the inside of a church in years."

"And what about you and Heinz?" The brothers had conflicts. Their personalities didn't mesh. "I thought you quit working with him years ago."

"I should have but I felt like I had to help him out."

I hadn't seen Heinz since I was sixteen. I remembered he took after Agnes Du Lac—kind of stocky, chubby even, like his mom, but unlike her, he was pleasant. Back in our teens, when my family was visiting their cottage, he had taught me wakeboarding in no time.

Wolf was different. I was lucky if I could pry any information out of him. He was more enigmatic than a secret agent on a mission in the Middle East.

"Tell me about the condo project."

"There are more partners. You don't know most of them." He frowned.

I swept my hand dismissively. "How about you tell me anyway." I had this feeling these people were the source of the furrowed forehead.

The waiter had our entrees on his tray. "Pardon me," he said placing the orders on the table in front of us.

I checked the pinned-on name tag. "Gracias, Estefan."

"Enjoy!"

The browned chicken was smothered in a chocolate sauce. Ever since I first came to Cozumel it was my favorite dish.

"I'm sure I will." A furrow creased Wolf's brow. "Tell me about the investors in this condo."

"Leon Luis Ruiz Del Socorro, Texas oil money, Ed Marion, from Florida, a wealthy high-profile criminal lawyer, gets off anyone guilty or innocent, and then there's business owner Orlando Keene, has a string of bars, from Cancun originally. We also have a woman, Perla Bravo Gonzales, owns art galleries dealing exclusively in Mayan, South American and Mexican art. She's attractive and successful." Wolf paused reflectively. "Single too."

What a stupid thing to say. I reached out to pinch his bicep but his muscle was too hard.

"Get off me, woman," he said, brushing my probing fingers away impatiently.

"She's not your type, cowboy."

Wolf's eyes twinkled mischievously. "Why?"

"Has she got the crazy gene?"

"No." Wolf grinned. "Too boring?"

"You've got that right. Anyone else involved in the condo building?"

He laughed dryly. "This wouldn't be Cozumel if your buddy, Alvarez didn't have a piece of the pie."

"Diego? He's involved in your condo deal? My bet is he's put in

11

a huge amount so he'd have a say."

Wolf nodded. "He did, but so did the other investors."

"So, you figure this way he can't run a solo show."

Wolf looked away at the patrons dining. A couple sat besides us. They weren't talking. Married too long. They ran out of chit chat. I hoped Wolf would never be like that with me.

"There's something else, isn't there? What aren't you telling me? Has Diego pulled a fast one already?" It was a well-known fact that Santiago Francisco Bolivar Alvarez, known as Diego to his friends, was the island's godfather. His family had a powerful position controlling the city and the police. Whatever he wanted he got. Everyone succumbed to his bribes or threats sooner or later.

"Not yet. At least, not that I know of."

"What aren't you saying?"

"There is another investor. She's made a killing in real estate and wanted part of this circus."

"You sound disappointed by the condo deal."

"I am a bit."

"And this woman? Do I know her?"

"You do. It's Daniella."

My jaw dropped.

"Daniella had the money and was willing to buy up a parcel of condos. She brought her friend in on it."

I brushed a tendril of away from my cheek, trying desperately to wrap my head around this one. I didn't exactly hate Daniella Consuela Puntez de Fuego but I wouldn't trust her as far as I could throw her. Daniella was an insidious man-eater—python like, capable of capturing and poisoning them with her acidic saliva. She swallowed them whole, but in her case, rats were not her game. She liked rich spicy men. Was she making a play for Wolf, again?

"What's wrong with you? You know she's only out for number one."

Wolf laughed. "Don't like her, do you?"

"Who's her friend? Diego?"

"Nope. Not this time."

"Who then? What's this sucker's name?"

"The Texas billionaire, Leon Luis Ruiz Del Socorro. Seems nice enough."

"What's in it for him?"

Wolf shrugged. "He's having a good time?"

"I feel sorry for him."

"Not really my problem," he stared pointedly at me, "or yours."

"No worries. I won't get involved with Daniella and her affairs."

"He could be just a friend."

"Sure, and the ocean is yellow."

"It can be at sunset." Wolf grinned. "Let's forget about Daniella and do as the waiter said. Enjoy dinner."

I did as he suggested. Food was one of my favorite things, surpassed only by one other activity. Forking up a piece of chicken, I allowed myself to get swept away in the heavenly flavors. I was a big fan of chocolate mole. I savored the spicy sauce on my tongue, allowing the chemicals to hijack my brain— pleasure endorphins danced wildly out of control. I stared at Wolf. He was so in control—so chill.

Wolf handed me a key card. "This is for you."

I tilted my head up. "Explain."

"It's a master key. I've given you the condo adjacent to mine, 302. It also opens the door to any condo in the building including mine, 301. Beyond that one is Heinz's new place since he moved out of the cottage with Linda." He winked. "Make that one your home when you feel like it." I wasn't sure if you wanted to move into my man cave right away. I think you need space to get your head together. You need to be sure. Besides, my place will need redecorating for you to feel at home, but this way, we can work things out faster with you staying next door. Of course, when you are ready you can move in to my place anytime or," he smiled, "just visit."

"But all my stuff is still in the condo near the Museo—the one Diego gave me." Seeing his frown, I continued rapidly, "I haven't used it. I gave the key back to Diego and he gave it to Carmelita."

"No worries, your things have been moved into your new condo."

"How?"

"You remember my housekeeper? She arranged it with Maria, Alvarez's housekeeper."

"Awesome! They did all that? You must thank them for me." The clothes were designed by Carmelita Bolivar Alvarez, Diego's sister. She had her own design house in Cozumel. Every article was uniquely fashioned as well as being well-made with the finest materials. All of the outfits fit me like a glove and made me feel fabulous. "Is that all right with Diego? He let me take the wardrobe?"

"He doesn't care. Alvarez likes you in expensive clothes so other men will admire you. He likes to show you off like a trophy. He thinks we will break up again and then he will snap you up."

"Sounds like I'm a fish."

"You are. A tasty angelfish. Now, Alvarez, on the other hand, has shark DNA."

"Not true. Diego is really sweet. I know you don't get along but try, for my sake."

"Sure, if he keeps that engagement ring locked in his safe and never takes it out for you again. You are my fiancée not his."

"I told him I wasn't ready to think about marriage or moving on with him."

"Alvarez isn't a good listener. He hears what he wants to hear. You know that."

I nodded. "True."

Wolf frowned. "As long as the godfather plays nice and leaves you alone, we'll get along great."

"I'll make it happen. Diego and I are friends and we'll stay friends."

"Friend-zoning Alvarez is good. He's not part of the plan."

"You have a plan?"

Wolf laughed. "For most things, no, but for you, yes."

"I'd like to hear it." I stared at him inquisitively. "I think it has to be something fun, like strawberries, chocolate—"

Wolf smiled mysteriously.

A cell phone pinged.

"Sorry," I said. "I didn't know it was on."

"It's mine. I'll make it short." Wolf reached into his black jeans. "Hey," he said, into the cell. "What's up?"

The person on the other end did all the speaking. Half a minute later, Wolf pushed the icon to close the call.

"Bad news?"

Wolf stroked his chin thoughtfully. "No, not exactly, but I have some business that needs my attention right now."

"So, no dessert?" I sighed with disappointment.

14

Wolf's eyes danced. "There's always dessert waiting for you, babe."

Wolf Du Lac had a way of kissing that set my mouth on fire. If that wasn't enough, I could count on his lips to explore the secret places of my body. "I'll take a taxi. You can text me when your business is done if it's not too late."

His blue eyes looked regretful. "Thanks, princess. Sorry about this."

"No, I get it," I said, placing my fork on the table. "Work first. I'm the one on vacation this time. No tour group to distract me. You don't need to entertain me. We'll do this another time."

I stood. Wolf threw down some bills and got on his feet.

"Loved dinner," I said softly, hugging him close, "and being with you."

"Missed you, babe." He pulled me close and drew me into a steamy kiss, promising more as he moved his mouth between my lips. When I kissed him back, I felt like I was floating on a cloud of light. I had a sudden flashback, his arms around me, caressing every curve of my body. Our contact was sizzling. I knew he felt it too, when he kissed me once again. Reluctantly, I withdrew from his embrace and the longing in his eyes, yet by the time I ventured out the gate and paused to wave goodbye, his eyes had taken on a distant look. My hunch was correct. There was something else he wasn't telling me.

2

On the way out I checked my texts.

Can you come to Hemingway's? I need male attention. Let me know. Waiting here for you. Carmelita

On my way. Adie

Carmelita was an easy drunk. I had to hurry.

Hailing a cab, I jumped in. A few minutes later I strode inside the restaurant-bar. Hemingway's had seating under a roof and on an outdoor patio. I glanced around.

The band hadn't started but it wasn't quiet with all the people milling about.

The glorious sunset Hemingway's was known for was gone but slashes of pale pink and yellow in a powder blue sky above calm teal blue water made my heart swell. Sunsets always affected me this way but this one was exceptionally beautiful. In the distance against the pastel sky I saw a boat silhouetted, most likely the pirate cruise ship—a well-known excursion, organized by a local tour guide, where there was a pirate show along with dinner and drinks galore.

Taking in the expanse of the sea and the sky, I paused, allowing the energy generated from nature to enter my aura. Sometimes, that was all I needed to release my stress. I shouldn't have any considering I had just had a wonderful evening with the mysterious Sea God. He was as magnetic as always but I had sensed something—a negative vibe cutting into our evening. He was worried about the condo project. I had to find out what I could about this.

For now, I would tuck those thoughts away. Carmelita needed me and admittedly, I missed the single scene ever since I started seeing Wolf again. Tonight, I would make the most of it.

Carmelita had been a special friend to me since the moment we'd met. She was a free-spirited designer, a willowy fashion model with bouncy brunette waves down to her waist, of which I was exceedingly envious. She had a pair of mischievous emerald green eyes. Carmelita was also the sister of the richest man I knew, Diego Bolivar Alvarez. When I came to a cluster of sofas around a coffee table, I saw her. She waved me over, we exchanged cheek kisses, and then I slumped down on the couch next to her.

Carmelita motioned the waiter and ordered margaritas. "Just in time to see the freaks arrive."

"Huh?"

She motioned with her chin at an anorexic disheveled long-haired guy, dressed in black spandex with a young girl on each arm. "Local musician."

"Popular man," I commented, dryly, thanking the server who brought us two huge goblets of frothy green liquid.

"Oh, yes, but that show-off is not the only one. Take a look at the bar. See anyone you know?"

Glancing past Carmelita, I noticed a shapely brunette in a clingy canary-yellow mini dress, legs crossed, her large butt resting on a barstool. She flicked her hair back in conversation with a tall exotic blond man. He looked European. They laughed, almost intimately.

On her other side was the tall blond's competition. An arm slung around the nasty skank, almost out of habit not intentionally, a swarthy man, in a white outfit like Mr. Clean, drank a beer out of a long-necked bottle. A third man was with them. Blocking some of my view, a massively built dark-haired man leaned in attentively to the woman who had a talent for ruining my evenings.

I sighed. "Why does she have to be here? Daniella is such a beotch."

"The more important question is why does that *perro* get men while I sit manless? What's wrong with me? You know, chica, I am so tired of being on my own." Suddenly, she perked up, a sly smile on her face. She studied the men at the bar. "Listen, I have an idea."

I sank down into the couch, making it my protective shell. Carmelita's bright ideas often ended up in disaster. I should discourage her, talk her down and get us out of here fast.

"Look at those hombres. Which one should I go for?"

My glance swept over the men, once again. The tall blond had a bit of a foreign look, his face sculpted, cheek bones so prominent he could have been a fashion model and his hair cut in a fade, long blond strands hanging over his forehead. He was dressed casually in a long-sleeved blue shirt rolled up to the elbows and gray Italian designer jeans, bare feet in leather slip-ons. Good taste and not a bad looking dude.

The second was a lean edgy bad boy rocker type, flashy Versace mirrored sunglasses, and his hair a statement piece, a carved high-top like a rooster's crown and a fade on the sides. He was clad entirely in white, an ensemble of a long-sleeved white cotton shirt and tight ivory pants. I got a wealthy slimy vibe out of him.

The last man was built like a brick shithouse—a bodybuilder with broad shoulders, giant guns, a tattoo sleeve in black ink, wearing an oversized red floral shirt hanging loose enough to hide a concealed weapon in the small of his back, and loose dark blue jeans, tucked over into a pair of white slip-ons. When he turned, I saw his face. Black-framed sunglasses perched on a long straight nose, an oval face, high cheekbones and a beard-moustache combo. His hair was braided over the top and at the back and sides. He was interesting but not as hot as he was pretending to be.

Suddenly, a slender redhead appeared at the entrance, turning the heads of the males. Her long straight hair swung with the breeze. She managed to flick it in the air with a one finger salute. Dressed in a flimsy green print mini dress she headed straight to the group at the bar. She knew her power.

The tall blond man blocked her path. Those two were tight or my name wasn't Adie Sturm.

I was close enough to overhear some of the exchange.

The redhead was angry. "Are you friggin' crazy? You can't say no to them."

The blond lifted an eyebrow. "I am keeping us out of trouble. You don't seem to realize what we could lose—"

"What do you mean by us? I thought we were divorcing? This is our big break, doofus. Our jackpot! You need to go for it or we both lose out."

"We're splitting up or have you changed your mind?"

"I'm coming out of this with a payoff with or without you."

So, they were married, not happily. I could see that relationship ending.

The redhead's end of the conversation was confrontational, hands gesturing wildly, green eyes darting arrows. The blond man's lips formed a thin line. Try as I might, I couldn't hear them, just a word here and there. There were too many people and the music started up. I continued to watch them.

When he tried pulling her towards the couches near us, she jerked his hand away. His cheeks flushed red in anger. Seeing this approach was not working, the redhead started cooing and stroking the tall blond man's arm suggestively. Coolly, he shrugged her off like someone shaking off an irritating ball of cat fur blown into his eye. Apparently, he wasn't having any of what she was selling. The auburn beauty's wide mouth twisted into a grimace. She waved at Mr. Clean and Brick Shithouse like she knew them before she sauntered off.

Carmelita poked her finger, slightly indignantly into my side. "Who is that puta?"

"Ouch," I said, feeling the tip of her shiny pink nail-polished forefinger. "Stop poking me!"

"*Perdon.* I was not in control. The margaritas are getting to me. Forgive me."

"Sure. Just watch where you stick those claws."

Carmelita laughed. "You are so funny. But seriously, never mind the redhead." She tilted her head. "I've seen her around. I don't recall exactly where. Some party, I think. She is sexy but I am Carmelita Bolivar Alvarez. No competition, no worries."

"She knows the blond dude. He doesn't like her much."

"That could be it. I've seen them together. Must have been at Diego's," Carmelita mused. "I should know her." She twisted a tendril thoughtfully. "Seems to me they were a couple but not a happy one."

"The redhead has Mr. Clean and the weightlifter dude in her sights. Did you see how she checked his guns out?"

"Never mind her. She's not a contender. Pay attention to the men. Daniella is picking an hombre for her bed right now, I'd bet."

"Maybe. Who knows what the snake is up to? I bet she'll go for the dude with the most money."

"I concur." Carmelita curled her bottom lip. "I say we foil her plan. That puta deserves to be manless."

Carmelita was biting at the bit to stick it to Daniella. That was fine by me. I've never liked the cobra especially after she appeared at Wolf's hotel room, a bottle in hand gung-ho to seduce the Sea

God, knowing full well I was his girlfriend. She was an annoying manipulator that needed a come-uppance. I wasn't interested in hooking up with Daniella's admirers but I did want to help Carmelita find her man and if that meant flirting, I would do that.

"What are you thinking?"

"I say we entice those hombres away from her." Carmelita's eyes glittered dangerously. "She doesn't deserve *any* man. Are you up to it?"

"How?"

Carmelita rolled her eyes. "This coming from the chica that has the Bolivar Alvarez men on her hook not to mention the incredible Sea God? You know how it's done. Fluff up your hair, flutter your lashes and touch the hombre frequently."

"I suppose I can—" None of the men appealed to me but this was for Carmelita.

"If all else fails, show cleavage, chica."

Carmelita was so pumped, I grinned. With a last sip of my margarita, I nodded. "Let's do it! Take whichever guy you want. I'll try to distract the others."

"Splendid!"

Daniella had been making her plays so intently she hadn't noticed us until we pushed the guys aside and greeted her with cheek kisses. Carmelita turned her back to Daniella and eyed the men and said, "We are here to rescue you," grinning slyly.

"I feel honored," said the blond man. "Gorgeous ladies are always very welcome. Never mind these guys." He waved his hand in the direction of the Brick Shithouse and bad boy Mr. Clean. I am at your service. What are your names?" he said, eyeing both of us with interest.

"Carmelita, and my friend is Adie. Nice to meet you."

The blond looked at me searchingly. "You look familiar. Have we met before?"

I shook my head, confused. "I think we have, but I can't think of where."

"You enjoying your evening?" Brick Shithouse said. His eyes flit over our bodies before returning to our faces.

"Getting better by the second," Carmelita said. "What a night. So hot!" She leaned forward, her head back. Her silver dress was cut low to the waist. A trickle of perspiration appeared on her chest, dribbling between her breasts.

The blond guy's gaze travelled down to her cleavage generously exposed by a deep V-plunge to her waist. Carmelita, pretty as she was, was a former fashion model. With that kind of figure there wasn't much flesh to be seen unless she had implants, which she didn't. A boob job was detrimental to a model's career—larger breasts made a dress gape at the buttons.

He quickly turned to check out my body. My dress had a sweetheart neckline revealing enough to pique his interest.

Brick Shithouse had a not-so-subtle leer on his face. "I like your dress, girl," he muttered to me, "and what's in it."

"Thanks." What a loser line. "I like to stand out in a crowd." I winked.

"You do, gal. I'd bet you stand out in any crowd. I'm Ed. And you are Andie?"

"No, it's—"

Before I could correct him, Daniella piped up, "Her name is Aggie but forget about that one. She's engaged, almost married, I'd say."

"No, I'm not," I protested, "and FYI, my name is Adie."

Carmelita butted in, closing in on Ed. "And what gets your motor revving, big guy? I would love to know." Carmelita's voice was slightly slurred.

Brick Shithouse ignored that question and motioned for drinks. "Margaritas for the ladies, Jose, and beer for us boys." He gazed at her. "Ed from Florida, originally."

"I'm Carmelita from Cozumel."

He grinned. "Cozumel has great looking women and I have the feeling you are the best."

She fluttered her lashes. "You are very perceptive, cariño."

"I'm a lawyer. I can read people. Now, if you ever get into a situation," he reached into his shirt pocket and pulled out a card, "it would be a pleasure to be of assistance or even if you have no situation, I can relieve your boredom."

Carmelita glanced at the card before tucking it away in her clutch. "I will remember your offer but I have some services of my own to extend to a worthy man."

Ed smirked and placed his arm around her waist. "Are you from around here?"

Whatever Carmelita replied was lost in the music of the band.

Was Brick Shithouse her chosen man? I tried to catch her eye but she was busy flicking her hair and stroking his arm.

I, on the other hand, focused on distracting the other two guys, brushing against Mr. Clean, for a split second as I reached for the margarita goblet. He grinned encouragingly, sidling up closer. My smile was frozen into a permanent fake grin. Gently, I kicked Carmelita's foot. "Girlfriend, have you made a decision?"

Startled, she hissed, "Watch it, amiga! I have sensitive feet." She lowered her head to regard her pink high-heeled sandal. "I don't want smudges on this adorable shoe either."

Mr. Clean handed me my goblet. "Drink up, honey. I'm Leon. I'd like to hear all about you."

"I'd rather hear about you." I let him run the conversation. When he started talking about his silver Mercedes and how it drove like a dream, and the technicalities of the engine, I zoned out. Mr. Clean prattled away while I thought about Wolf, wondering what he was so worried about. When could I make a discreet getaway? A trip to the washroom and then a sprint to the exit?

This second drink was as potent as the first. Knowing how little tequila I could tolerate; I was on borrowed time. I hoped Carmelita appreciated my efforts because I was wasting my time with this substandard dude, in danger of falling asleep listening to Leon's monologue about the finest roadster ever, the S-Class Cabriolet. Yes, it was a fine car but it needed a hot driver—not him. I was up to the task but didn't have his kind of money.

"Hola, chica," a male voice called out. "I found you! I should have looked here before."

A muscular buff guy wearing a navy T-shirt tucked into pale blue jeans appeared before us. He sported a head of wavy brown hair and an over-grown beard. Pushing past Ed, he gripped my arms, staring intently at me with a pair of clear gray eyes. Did I mention the scintillating smile he had pasted on his interesting face? Cy Bolivar Alvarez edged forward, knocking Mr. Clean back into a rotund brunette swaying with the rock band's beat.

Cy laid a couple of kisses on my cheeks.

"Hey! Watch it, bud!" Mr. Clean's cheeks blotched red.

"Sorry," Cy said offhandedly and grin on his lips.

"I am talking to this lady," Mr. Clean said in warning, stepping forward and putting his arm around my shoulders. "We are having a *private* conversation."

I squirmed uncomfortably. His breath smelled slightly of onions. I shifted away.

Cy positioned himself between Mr. Clean and me. "Adie and I go way back," he winked at Mr. Clean, "if you know what I mean."

"Hey, Cy. What a surprise." I should have been irritated by Cy's interruption but I was so glad I had an out. One more second of Mr. Clean and I would scream. He would be a bad choice for Carmelita anyway. Besides, I think she had a thing for Ed, the lawyer-weightlifter.

"Nice of you to come, finally. I've been waiting so long. This is—" I waved my hand at Mr. Clean, not at all sure what his name was.

"The name is Leon," Mr. Clean hissed between clenched teeth. "Leon Luis Ruiz Del Socorro."

"I'm Adie Sturm," I said, too flustered to remember if I had already introduced myself. "And my friend is Cy." I marvelled how Cy had returned to Cozumel so quickly. I was sure he was diving somewhere, in the Red Sea or some little-known location in Malaysia.

Cy grinned, a Hollywood smile, a Bolivar Alvarez smile. Like Diego he had symmetrical features and charm when it came to personality, but they led different lives. Diego ran the family-owned Imports and Exports company, while Cy preferred the adventure and challenge of a scuba diver's life. Both brothers played the field, although Diego had turned over a new leaf lately, making marriage overtures to me.

Cy glanced at Mr. Clean. "If you've got somewhere to go, I will take care of Adie, no worries." He leaned over my shoulder and peered at the woman swinging her leg. "Well, if it isn't Daniella, what's up, girl?"

Daniella tittered at Mr. Clean's angry expression. "Hemingway's needed me. The women here are too mundane for these awesome guys."

Mr. Clean turned to Daniella with his game face back on. He moved in beside Daniella. I could see his brain churning trying to come up with something witty to say.

Daniella was amused. It was like looking at an iguana on a

broiling tiled rooftop—biding her time to attack her victim. The skank crossed her leg, making sure her dress rode high on her thigh.

Cy saw Carmelita all over Brick. "Hey, sis. What's goin' on?"

Carmelita's hands were stroking his chest and abs. She didn't answer, she was too occupied laying kisses on him.

"My sister is ignoring me."

"She's on the hunt. Wants to find a man."

Ed did not seem her type at all. Carmelita was wasted. Alcohol had blurred her vision and clouded her mind. He was not at all her type. Brick could have been one of Diego's security men he was so huge, arms like a gorilla. Maybe, Cy could save Carmelita from herself. Surely, she didn't want to have sex with this dude?

"Come." Cy grabbed my arm, guiding me away from the bar.

"No!" I protested. "I'm staying here. I have to make sure Carmelita's okay."

Cy heaved me into an empty couch. "Never mind my sister." He slid in next to me. "Let's talk."

"About?"

"I have a condo in the Erizo del Mar."

"That's Wolf's building. He gave me one too. Do you like it?"

"It's fine, but there's more to this. Diego wants me to be his eyes and ears."

"Is something going on?" Could this be why Wolf looked so worried?

"The investors are under scrutiny."

"Why would you say that?"

"Diego is—"

"Suspicious?" I laughed. "That's not like him, is it?" I giggled. "Diego is such a trusting soul."

Cy squeezed my arm. "Snap out of it! The deals are in cash."

"Isn't that done a lot in Mexico? People have to use cash."

He nodded, and whispered, "But it could mean more. Those people," he said, indicating Daniella and the men, "may be into something illegal."

"Really?" This was a strange wrench in the mix. I doubted if Diego did anything above board himself. "You're kidding me. Diego is concerned about something illegal?"

"Yeah, this time he is."

"You can tell him there is no need to worry. Wolf's brother, Heinz, is managing the sales and stuff."

He stared, his eyes on the man at the bar beside Brick. "That Heinz?"

"What do you mean?"

"I mean the tall blond hombre with Daniella and Carmelita. That's Heinz Du Lac, brother of your boyfriend or is Du Lac now your ex?"

"Ex? No, he's not. Wolf and I are working it out. What do you mean? That dude is Heinz?" Omigod, he'd slimmed down from the stocky teenager he was ten years ago! "He doesn't look at all the same as I remember. I didn't recognize him." I couldn't get over it. Heinz was handsome in a sculpted way. This guy had the cheekbones of a model. He was almost on par with the Sea God.

"Diego thinks Heinz is dirty."

I pursed my lips, thinking. "Why?"

"No reason. You know my brother. Diego can recognize another dirtbag."

"Heinz? Seriously, Cy, he was such a good boy. Always did exactly what his mama said. That couldn't have changed."

"It can if he needs the money. Heard he's getting a divorce. Life can change a good boy into scum."

Could this be why Wolf was worried—his brother was a wheeler dealer or worse?

Casting my glance over to the bar, I could see Carmelita smothering Brick with attention. She was holding her goblet with one hand and with the other stroking his butt cheeks between giggles.

Cy took a look at the activity at the bar and frowned. "She's worse than that puta Daniella. I should drag her out of here before she gets a nasty disease from that *cabron*."

"I'd better talk to her," I said, remembering the girl code. "Say, look! Heinz seems to be packing it in for the night."

"Well, I have to get to the bottom of this. I'm following that hombre." With a determined set to his chin, Cy sprang up and headed towards the bar.

"I'm going with," I said, tagging behind him.

"And Carmelita?"

"She wanted a new man. I guess she's got him." I waved to

Carmelita to indicate I was going. She nodded and waved back. "Do you want to come?" I mouthed.

Carmelita shook her head and motioned for me to go.

"I hope she'll be okay," I said, stopping dead in my tracks. "She's hammered."

"She sure is. Carmelita is a danger to others when she gets like this."

"Do something, Cy."

"Wait here. I'll make sure, he leaves her alone." He strode over to Carmelita and Ed. The conversation was brief before he returned to my side.

"We can go now. He won't hurt her."

"How can you be so sure?"

"I mentioned she was a Bolivar Alvarez."

"Would he know the name?"

"He lives on the island. He'd have to be batshit crazy not to. I don't think he wants to lose his *cojones*. He has only one pair."

I nodded. The Bolivar Alvarez family was way too powerful to mess with. Even Brick Shithouse would not be so stupid.

Cy grabbed my hand. "Let's go. My Jeep's outside."

3

Heinz hailed a taxi and headed south along Rafael E. Melgar. We were right behind him.

I checked my cell. It was 12:30 am. What does a boring dude like Heinz do after midnight?

Cozumel is not an active place, like Playa del Carmen. Some of the bars have live entertainment but it is not unusual to see an empty bar with a lone guy tipping back a beer. Too many people have to get up early for a dive. When the taxi slowed down, we were in front of Wolf's condo building, the Erizo del Mar. It towered above us, at least twelve stories high—an ivory edifice, luxury condos for the privileged.

"This is where he's lived since his separation. Wolf gave him a condo." I put my hand on the door handle.

"Stay," Cy said, like he would order his dog, if he had one. "I want to do this alone."

"Well, that's too bad. I don't take your orders or anyone else's."

"Maybe, it's time you started."

I glared at Cy. "I have an interest in this too. My ex needs to know if Heinz is involved in nefarious activities."

"You are a difficult female." Cy sighed. "Diego gave me a condo to keep an eye on everyone. Listen to me. I'm just saying, we need to be on the same page, Adie, if we're going to find out what he's up to. We have to follow at a distance and it would be safer if you stayed in the Jeep."

"Either he's going to his condo or visiting someone else."

"True, but you should still stay in the Jeep."

I glanced over at his broad shoulders and athletic body. "If it's not safe for me, it won't be any better for you if a gun is involved."

Cy smirked. "I can't see you in hand-to-hand combat with Heinz. Now me, on the other hand—"

"I'm sure it won't come to a fight. You've seen too many action-packed movies." The building lobby looked quiet.

"Heinz must be past the lobby by now. I'll see where he's gone." Cy shrugged. "Then if he's gone to bed, our work is done."

"I guess we could go to bed too." Then realizing what I said, I added, "Separately, of course."

Cy grinned. "Of course. We wouldn't want to ruffle Du Lac's feathers, would we now? Are you two getting it on?"

"That's none of your business. Wolf gave me my own condo. I need to see if we are good together. After everything that happened, we need our own space. Wolf sent for my clothes from the other condo."

"That was the place Diego gave you."

"Yup, but I gave the condo back and I refused his ring. I don't owe him anything. I admit I liked the clothes that came with it— Carmelita's designs. Diego insisted I keep the clothes. Wolf's housekeepers should have brought them over." I smiled thinking of the clothes. I felt like a princess wearing them.

"You sound like a kept woman."

"I would be happy in a hotel with my own clothes but since Diego owns the building—"

"Along with a group of investors."

"And Wolf, remember? So, let's stop arguing and get in there," I said. "We have to find out if he's gone to his condo. Follow me, I know where it is."

"Sure," Cy said, stepping down from the Jeep. He waited for me to get out and when I took too long because of my heels and dress, he held my door open and gave me a hand. My exit was not graceful but I was on terra firma, hurrying to the condo with Cy behind me.

When we entered the lobby, the young concierge was dozing on a chair.

"Let me do the talking." Cy nudged the teen awake. "Where did the hombre with the blond hair go?"

"Huh?" The boy's eyes had sleepy crusty bits at the corners.

A text pinged in my purse. I had a quick glance. It was from Diego.

Taking you out tomorrow morning for breakfast. Be ready for nine. D

No, thanks. I'm sleeping in. A

Please, Adelinita. It will be incredible. D

Ok. Pick me up at the Erizo del Mar at 9:30. I can't get up any earlier. A

You win. See u then. D

I glanced over. Cy was still talking to the boy in the red vest. The kid shrugged, shaking his tangled black hair. He muttered something in Spanish. It didn't sound encouraging.

I strode up to Cy and tapped his arm. "What did he say? Where's Heinz?"

"He doesn't know. He can't tell us anything. It's a privacy issue. He's not allowed."

"Heinz most likely went to bed."

"Alone or with a friend?" Cy grinned wickedly.

"Since Daniella was not available, he is most likely alone."

"Or, he might have a mistress waiting in a black teddy holding two glasses of champagne in his condo." Cy chuckled as if imagining this scenario for himself.

"When he was a teenager he never drank."

"He was throwing those margaritas back tonight, no problem."

"True. He has changed." I looked at the elevator door. "Let's go."

"Where? You figure him to be in his condo?"

"I do, and I know which one is his." I strode over to the elevator doors and pressed three.

Cy stepped in after me. "Are you psychic? How would you know?"

"No mystery. Wolf told me."

The elevator lurched as it started up. When the doors opened on the third floor, Cy headed out and stopped at 304.

"It's 303. Why are we stopping?"

From his jeans' pocket he took a card key and inserted it in 304. "I want to see my condo. I'm curious."

"This one is yours? Wait, I thought the idea was to check on Heinz?"

Cy opened the door. "I can't see what we're supposed to do about him. Knock on his door and ask him if he's up to something? From my condo, I should be able to hear any activity going on inside his."

"Holding a glass to the wall, are you, or did Diego equip you with spy tech?"

"Diego doesn't give me orders. I am merely helping 'Imports and Exports', the Bolivar Alvarez company."

I followed him into the condo and examined it. The panels were a

29

bright teal, ironwork sculptures of sea creatures accented the walls, and white leather couches surrounded a twisted metal coffee table. On the wall near the door, black wetsuits hung on a rack.

"Nice place," I said. "Diego does love his brother. Did he give you the wetsuits too?"

Cy's lips twisted. "He said they were my birthday gifts. Well, if you ask me, he has to pay for the investigative work and the hours I put in. It's probably his paranoia going overtime anyway."

"Not that you need the money, of course." The Bolivar Alvarez family was wealthy and powerful. I was envious. "Your share of the Bolivar Alvarez estate is extensive," I said, sweeping past Cy to take a look at the dining room. Modern white leather chairs with chrome stands and an ironwork table. At the bedroom, I did a quick turnabout and clicked my way back in my high-heeled sandals. My feet were getting sore. I had to take these babies off before I needed ice packs.

"I hope mine looks as good as yours." I sat down on a couch and took off my heels.

"You staying? I bet I have a comfortable king-sized bed. Plenty of room for visitors."

"Fat chance, Alvarez. Look at my feet. They can't take the humidity. No wonder all the women here wear flipflops." Holding the silver sandals, I padded to the door.

"Leaving so soon?" Cy drawled.

"Yup, have a good night. Text me if you find out anything." When I saw him unbuttoning his shirt, giving me a quick view of an impressive chest, I made a quick exit.

Stopping momentarily at Heinz's door, I put my ear to the door to listen but no sounds carried out to the corridor. Going further along the hall, I reached 302 and pushed my key card in the slot.

I felt vaguely disappointed. It had always been one of my dreams to be an investigative reporter or a cool private detective, instead I became a tour guide. Having taken all the college courses I needed to certify, I usually enjoyed the travel and put up with the irritating tourists, looking at the positive aspects of my job. Sleuthing came naturally to me and Cozumel and the crimes I encountered provided the opportunities.

In the past I ran into disreputable characters, deception, and murder. Death is devastating. It leaves people drained when it happens but solving the murder gave me a feeling of satisfaction, knowing I helped the friends or family of the victim.

My frequent run-ins with murder had been explained to me by a shaman. I was born on December 6, the Day of Death, according to the Mayan calendar. As such, I would encounter death more than others.

As I entered, I was entranced by the coral walls decorated with bronze and shiny blue sculptures of angelfish and dolphins. An enormous green turtle sculpture safeguarded the dining room with its magnificent presence. Both rooms were similar to Cy's condo with white leather furniture and plush leather stools on chrome stands facing one another across a white table in the dining room.

Excited to see the bedroom, I carried in my sandals and switched on the light. The walls were a soft coral hue, the bedding lightly printed to look like a coral reef. The closet was immense, and I was pleasantly surprised by the array of clothing and shoes. I placed my sandals on the rack to join the army. I'd guess there were at least twenty pairs of various styles, all of them expensive.

Rapidly, I leafed through the clothing hung according to color and arranged from day to evening wear. I was being treated like a celebrity by Diego but I owed Wolf for the luxurious condo. I should have felt guilty but I didn't. Maybe Cy wasn't the only one with a commitment issue.

After leaving my purse on the bedside table I eagerly made my way to the balcony. The sliding doors opened to a stunning night view of the Caribbean. The water sparkled with lights from the cruise ships and from the balconies of the condo below.

Cozumel was called the "Place of the Swallows" in Mayan. The island is only twenty-eight miles long and nine miles wide. It's a diver's Mecca. Tourists came for the fish and to scuba dive and snorkel the second largest coral reef on the planet, Palancar.

Centuries ago, it was the destination for women to pay homage to the fertility goddess in the hopes of getting pregnant. They would row from Playa del Carmen to Cozumel to leave presents for Ixchel, for her blessing. Some of these young women would never arrive, bad weather snuffing out their short lives in the rough waters of the Caribbean.

A narrow strip of beach backed onto the condo grounds. I let the stress leave me as I breathed in the fresh sea breeze. The palm fronds swayed with the wind and cast shadows on the sliver of sandy beach. The figures of three men were illuminated by the light of the full moon.

The tallest one was a blond. The other two looked darker. They were of medium height built like heavyweight wrestlers, gorilla-like in their stances. Their voices surged and died with the beat of the waves banging on the shore. The calm ocean had been replaced by a rough sea, white tipped crests crashing on the coral rocks.

The quarrel escalated and one of the brawny men threw a punch. The blond blocked it but the other guy kicked him in the knee. The tall man crumpled with the blow. They circled to kick him again.

Two against one isn't a fair fight. I had to do something. That guy could be killed before the police would arrive and the skinny boy in the lobby wouldn't be much help either. In fact, it occurred to me, the tall blond could be Heinz. I couldn't let him get hurt. Wolf would expect me to help. Quickly, I grabbed my purse and pulled out my iPhone.

Meet me at the elevator. Now! A

I pressed send, and ran to the door shoeless. Pushing the down-button I waited for the elevator. The doors opening immediately. I got in and held the open-door button.

Cy appeared almost immediately clad in jeans, shirtless, revealing a tight six-pack. "What's going on?"

"On the beach. A guy's getting beat up. We have to help." I motioned urgently. "Get in."

It was a long ride to the elevator with my nerves making each second seem like a minute. In the lobby, the young guy was still sitting on a stool behind the desk, just beginning to nod off again.

"What did you see?"

"Two big dudes beating up on a guy. It might be Heinz."

"I'm not sure what I can do. It would be best to call the police."

"No time for that. He might be dead before they arrive to help. Look, there," I said, spotting the beach entrance down the hall.

The door opened automatically and we were outside. The guys were booting the blond curled up in a fetal position. Otherwise, the beach was deserted. Where were the security guys? It was their job to make the condos safe.

"I'll take the big hombre. You stand back," Cy yelled out, his voice thrown back by the sea breeze.

I ignored him, sprinting out to the smaller guy, and gave him a sound roundhouse kick to the back of his knee. His leg crumbled but he righted himself and tore around to fight. I slashed my hand, knife-edge down on his forearm as he swung out with his fist. I made contact. My karate training was paying off. When his head came down, I grabbed his hair and kneed him into the kidney. I thought he was done but I had underestimated the man, leaving myself open to a punch to the gut. It was strong enough to carry me airborne and drop me backwards into the sand a few feet away. I was too light to withstand such a blow. It would have been totally correct to run after the initial technique, especially for a woman of my height and weight.

When I looked up, he was gone and Cy was racing after the big dude. I got up to check on Heinz who I discovered prostrate on the beach. He groaned as I touched his head.

"No, I won't do it," he muttered, oblivious that I was beside him and not one of the muggers.

"Hola!" a man shouted from a distance away. "I am security. What is your business here?"

"A man has been hurt. Two thugs attacked him. Come help!" In the opposite direction I could see Cy returning without the attacker, limping slightly.

"Adie, you okay?"

"Got hit. Did something happen to your leg?"

"Yup." Cy bent down to check out Heinz. "Looks like he got a good beating."

The security guard in a black uniform trotted up. He pointed at Cy. "Help me. You take his other arm and we'll bring him inside." I followed the men into the lobby.

"Hold the door for us, señorita, por favor."

They picked him up and dropped him on the couch in the lobby. The young skinny guy woke up and shouted in Spanish, gesturing wildly. I could smell tequila. So, that explained why he'd been asleep earlier.

Apparently, we weren't the only ones here. Another security guard in a black uniform came in from down the hall. He was rough looking—angry black eyes and hair. He snarled something in Spanish. The little doorman got up and then decided against it, sinking back into the office chair.

33

My Spanish was too limited to get the gist of it but he obviously thought we had injured Heinz. I doubt he recognized him as a resident. Cy calmed him down, explaining the man owned a condo. The security guard shouted he wanted to call the police. Even I understood that much.

It looked bad. Heinz was bleeding from a cut to his forehead, his skin splotched by wet sand. He seemed disoriented from the blows. I didn't blame the doorman for not recognizing any of us.

Cy shouted out rapid-fire Spanish. The security man persisted until Cy showed him his driver's licence. The Bolivar Alvarez ID satisfied the security guards. I breathed a sigh of relief. Together a security guard and Cy gathered up Heinz and transported him into the elevator. The doorman watched as the doors closed.

"Let's take him to his condo, okay?"

The security guard questioned Cy in Spanish on the way up. He helped drag Heinz down the hall. My key opened the door. Heinz was deposited onto the couch. Apparently, the security guard was satisfied with Cy's answers and left the matter to us.

The condo walls were in hues of turquoise. A large fish tank, about six or seven feet long, four feet or so, wide and with a depth of about four feet was the central focus of the living room. Bright red and yellow fish darted in amongst the fake coral and seaweed. I thought these condos were set up the same but mine didn't look at all like this one.

Ivory leather couches surrounded a heavy oak coffee table. I had the same white couches, although my pillows were green and aqua and I had a metal coffee table.

Once in the condo, we managed to drag him to the couch, setting a blue cushion under his head. It took a lot out of me.

"What's wrong, Adie?" Cy said, when I groaned involuntarily.

"It hurts to move."

Cy looked worried. "Maybe you need a doctor to check you out?"

I shook my head. Gripping my abdomen, I said, "He caught me off guard with that punch."

"Could be bruised or broken ribs. You are a delicate petite girl."

"I trained in karate. I've had worse."

Cy lifted an eyebrow. "He punched you."

"I'll get over it." Heading into the kitchen, I found two tea towels. After wetting one, I said, "Can you get me ice?"

Cy opened the freezer door. He got out an icepack and herded me back into the living room. "This should help. Sit down." The dog command again. Cy really wasn't used to talking to women. "Put this on your bruise." Cy was totally uncivilized, more biker than billionaire with his bushy beard. Too many years under the ocean scuba diving to behave like a gentleman, but I did as he said, resting on the edge of the couch beside Heinz.

Heinz was a swollen mess but he managed to sit up. I got to work dabbing at the blood seeping from the broken skin. Heinz winced and waved me away.

"You are cut and bruised."

Heinz held up his hand in a stop gesture. "Leave me alone."

"At least hold this to it." I handed him the other tea towel. "That should stop the bleeding."

Heinz muttered, "Who made you the boss?"

"I did. We saved you, remember?" Ungrateful idiot. He had some nerve when I was the one making an effort to help him. I snatched back the tea towel. "You're missing it all," I said, scrubbing some dried blood off his chin. When it looked like the mess was cleaned off, I placed the tea towel on the coffee table and remarked casually, "So, who are those men, Heinz? Why did they beat you up?"

"Don't know." Heinz shook his head, in confusion. "Listen, thanks, but you'd better leave. Both of you."

"Don't be a fool man," Cy said. "You are in need of a doctor. You could have a concussion."

"I'm fine."

I peered at Heinz's forehead. "Give him an ice pack."

"Hold on to this," Cy commanded, handing Heinz another ice pack from the fridge. "Keep it on your forehead. I see that bump getting bigger by the second."

I stared at Wolf's brother. He looked like a truck had crushed him. Heinz, slumped down, his head on the pillow, feet stretched out. He stared at me through the slit of one swollen eye. The other was closed. "Say, do I know you?"

"We met earlier at Hemmingway's and yes, you do know me. I'm Adie Sturm. Our parents are friends. I met you at your family cabin years ago when my family came for a visit. Remember?"

Heinz scrutinized me with the good eye. "I kept thinking you looked familiar back at Hemingway's, but you're a woman now and fancier. That was eleven years ago. You and Wolf, can you believe it? He told me how you met up accidently. It's hard to believe. Our dads went fishing together years ago, remember?"

"Did Wolf speak to you about what happened between us?"

Heinz shook his head. "No, just that he was involved and it was starting to get serious." He grinned painfully, his lip bleeding with the movement. "He thought I'd let your name slip. Probably didn't want mom to know. She was not keen on you two being an item."

"She might have to get used to it." I examined his bruised face. "Those guys did a number on your face. Want to talk about it?"

Heinz shook his head. He moved the ice pack to his cheek which was particularly red and swollen.

Cy took a spot on the heavy oak coffee table beside me. He stared at Heinz. "Who were they?"

Heinz leaned forward his head in his hands, muttering, "Don't know." His one normal eye opened and he gazed past us at the fish tank. "The housekeeper feeds them. Don't know why they put that tank in my condo. Wolf is the one who likes fish."

I exchanged glances with Cy. Heinz was amateurishly avoiding the subject. "Maybe you'd like to explain who those guys were."

Heinz looked back at us with a frown. "No, not really. It's nobody's business."

"We're not leaving until you tell us," I said steadily.

"I don't know," he groaned. "Let it go, okay? Now, both of you leave. Thanks, for the help but we're finished here."

"Okay, have it your way. Come on, Cy." I stood up and went to the door with Cy on my heels.

At the door, Cy spun around. "If you're in trouble you need to tell me the story," the scuba master said, his voice low and threatening. "I won't allow this condo project to be at risk."

"And just who do you think you are?"

"I am Amancio Bolivar Alvarez, Diego's brother. Imports and Exports has a vested interest in this deal."

"You know what I think of your vested interest?" Heinz held up his middle finger.

I rolled my eyes. "You forget I *know* you. You're Agnes Du Lac's perfect son. Does no wrong, right? We'll talk tomorrow and you'll tell me the whole story." Before closing the door, I turned back. "Hey, Heinz, you want a painkiller? I have some in my condo. It will reduce the swelling."

"No!" Heinz roared. "Now get your little butt out of here and take Diego's dickhead brother with you!"

As I stood there giving him a grilling stare I reserved for uncooperative bad boys, he mumbled, "Did my brother ever tell you what a big pain in the ass you are?"

I paused at the door and grinned.

4

A huge black cat stalked its prey. Wide slanted green eyes, the black centers narrow slits. He crouched, ready for the attack. Letting out a roar like a jungle cat, the feline flung itself on me, digging sharp teeth into my neck to make the kill.

A buzzer sounded. It snuffed out my dream. I was still alive but haunted by the image of the cat tearing into my neck. Almost trance-like I placed my fingertips on the tendons of my neck. My pulse beat quickly. Why did I have this dream?

I loved animals. Seldom has a cat not liked me. At home, in Canada, I had three rescue cats, cared for by my niece while I was away. Not a single cat was black, the closest being my tuxedo cat, Zee, a hunter of mice and birds but an exceedingly lovable cat. Call me superstitious but dreaming of pitch-black felines was a warning of impending danger.

Again, the buzzer sounded. What the heck? At first, I thought it was my cell alarm but that couldn't be. I hadn't set it. I gritted my teeth. It was like an electroshock treatment to my weakened brain. Margaritas and Heinz. Neither of them were pleasantly rewarding the morning after.

Awkwardly, like a newly awakened zombie in the apocalypse, I crawled out of bed and made for the door where the noise resonated.

"Hola," I said, into the intercom.

"This is Jorge from the lobby. Señorita, an hombre by the name of Ernesto is here to pick you up. A chauffeur. He says he works for señor Bolivar Alvarez."

I remembered Ernesto. He was always polite and accommodating. "Tell him to please wait. I just woke up."

"He wants to know when you will be ready. He said señor Bolivar Alvarez is anxiously waiting. You are late."

I grimaced. Breakfast. Who needs it, especially on vacation? Sleep is what I needed.

"When, señorita?"

I felt like banging his annoying head against the wall but it wasn't his fault he was a pain in the butt. Wouldn't you know it, Diego and his breakfasts. He was up early and in an obsessive mood.

"Really, I don't know. Soon, I guess."

The young man's tone was sharp. "You must tell him when, por favor, or señor Bolivar Alvarez will be angry with us all."

Taking pity on the kid, I said, "Twenty minutes or so."

I regretted saying it as soon as I said it. How the heck could I get ready for Diego in twenty minutes? No need to panic though, I was confident I could do this. After all, it wasn't a party, just breakfast.

After I showered, I coated my body with sunscreen, brushed my teeth and styled my layered locks before enhancing my face with lip gloss and mascara. My cell phone told me I had ten minutes to spare.

Not bad, I thought checking my image in the mirror after donning low silver sandals which matched the blue print romper. At the door I grabbed my cross-shoulder bag, and headed out.

When I stepped into the lobby the chauffeur was waiting.

"Buenos dias, señorita Sturm," Ernesto said. He had been chatting to Jorge, the doorman, but when he saw me, he straightened up, swept off his chauffeur cap, and bowed.

"Buenos dias, Ernesto. Long time no see."

"It is an honor, señorita Sturm. You have made quite a name for yourself as the crime stopper of Cozumel, besides being a tour guide, and I heard an excellent one, so described by señor Bolivar Alvarez himself. He sings your praises."

I was not a detective but was intrigued when it came to a good mystery, eager to put my foot in where no man, nor sane woman dared to tread.

Ernesto held the door open for me, letting in hot humid air. "The limo is cool. You will find it enjoyable for your journey."

"Journey?" I repeated, walking beside him to the black Mercedes. "Is it far?"

Ernesto put a finger to his lips. "I was sworn to secrecy, not to reveal anything. It is a surprise." He grinned. "But I can say this— you will like it."

When Ernesto swung the door of the vehicle open, I sank into a plush tan leather seat. I had plenty of leg room. Fluted glasses were arranged on a table next to me, a bottle of champagne sat chilling on ice.

"Señor Bolivar Alvarez wishes you to drink the wine."

I shook my head. "Not first thing in the morning, Ernesto. Too early for me."

Ernesto nodded his head wisely. "Quite right too. Of course, after you consumed those margaritas last night."

"Oh, who told you that?"

He twisted his head back towards me and shook his head.

"You can tell me." I said sweetly, but was fuming like a live volcano about to explode. *Who was gossiping about me?*

"Señorita Bolivar Alvarez mentioned it when I drove her to her home last night. She said she wanted a condo just like yours."

"Oh?" So, Carmelita did not sleep with Brick Shithouse. Ed did not get lucky. Good. Maybe I could nip this in the bud.

"Señorita Bolivar Alvarez must have enjoyed the margaritas."

When I looked up into the mirror, a big smile was plastered on Ernesto's face. "You too, señorita?"

"I did. Hemingway's is a great restaurant with quite the view."

"It is popular." Ernesto's face became more serious. "I don't know if you realized that Señorita Carmelita had a difficult time these past few years. I am pleased that she ventures out again."

"Yes, it is good but only if the person she sees is deserving of her."

Ernesto frowned. "Sometimes she chooses not as well as señor Bolivar Alvarez would like. Hopefully, she will find a suitable gentleman for marriage. We all wish children for her."

"I would like her to be happy."

Ernesto nodded. "Yes, certainly, we want that for señorita Bolivar Alvarez."

While we spoke, we passed the shops going north on Rafael E. Melgar until once again we were in the hotel district, the ocean glimpsed only occasionally between the palms. The traffic thinned as we veered away from the center of town.

On the right there was a golf course, emerald green grass, busy with avid players, trying their luck in the morning. At ten o'clock it was already hot, the air heavy with humidity, the morning sun wreaking havoc on the pale arms of the tourists. All the golfers wore sunglasses and caps pulled low over their foreheads and the customary shirts and shorts along with golf shoes and gloves. It was a game with little physical activity in the way of walking as golf carts were the mode of transportation for the golfing enthusiasts. When I saw them sweating it out while swinging their clubs, I was determined to have a better experience. Snorkeling would be more refreshing and give me that inner peace I craved.

By now, I was extremely curious about our destination. The road ended in a circular parking area. There was nowhere else left to drive.

Ernesto pulled the car over and announced, "We have arrived, señorita Sturm."

I was puzzled. There was nobody and nothing on this parking lot. Why was Ernesto coming to my door to help me disembark?

For a moment I stood there looking around. At this point I was ready to shake Ernesto to get some answers when a loud whirring noise brought my eyes to the sky where a speck was rapidly increasing in size. The helicopter's landing brought my hair swirling around my head, the blades creating a wind tunnel as the aircraft landed in a cacophony of noise.

Jumping to the ground was a man as devastatingly handsome as a Calvin Klein model, sporting a long-sleeved white shirt and well-cut tan trousers. His dark hair curled over his ears and his lips wore a Cheshire Cat smile.

"Adelinita," he shouted out over the noise of the helicopter. "Are you hungry?"

Diego strode over, kissed my cheek and took my hand leading me to the helicopter. "Your carriage awaits, mi amor."

Most women would be astounded to have this type of transportation but my host was known for his flamboyant gestures. Diego was like an actor on stage and his stage was Cozumel.

He reached out to hold my hand as I gazed apprehensively out the window, the helicopter lifting in the air. Soon we were far away from civilization flying over the northern part of the island, the sea on either side of the thin strip of land. A narrow dirt road wound north. The terrain spotted with shrubs on either side of a coral road wound near a pristine ivory beach and crystal-clear vivid turquoise waters. If there was a heaven on earth it was this stretch of sand.

"This is amazing," I called out to Diego, gazing at the scenery below. "I was on a tour on that road once. It's a rough ride."

"Fourteen miles of hazardous driving. I thought the helicopter would make the trip smoother." He squeezed my hand. "I want this experience to be extraordinary, cariño," he said, as the helicopter dropped down for a landing. "Did I tell you how lovely you look today?" Diego's eyes swept down my body skimming my legs fleetingly. "Is that outfit one of Carmelita's creations?"

"It is. Thank you for making the wardrobe available for me."

"No problem. I want you to wear only the most flattering apparel and," he chuckled, "someone as lovely as you can only help promote my sister's designs. Am I right?"

"Carmelita is talented. If wearing these outfits makes her more notable, I am happy to wear absolutely all the designs."

"Good. You are almost family but I am hoping for more."

I shook my head. "I don't want to encourage you to believe there is a future for us."

Diego placed his finger on my lips. "Don't think about that. Whether you promise yourself to Du Lac or not, I will always protect you."

Before I could protest, he pointed to a white structure ahead. "See over there. That's the Punta Molas lighthouse. Usually, it is only available with a Jeep tour or a boat excursion."

"Cool."

The pilot swung us around after we closed in for a closer view of the red and white lighthouse and then flew south a short distance before slowing down.

Cozumel has a notoriously flat terrain. It is difficult to find any sort of hill on the island but Diego had scouted out a location with an embankment that overlooked the ocean. The view was breathtaking, the crests of the waves crashing on the sandy white shore. This is what was called the "wild side". It was the most secluded area on the island as there was no traffic here, only an occasional Jeep tour. Regular vehicles were not covered with insurance traveling on the rugged coral road. It was the first time I was here with Diego on the north part of the island.

A while ago, Wolf had leased a house for us on the east coast. We'd go there to get away from all the drama and submerge ourselves in romance. Wolf was my wild man. I almost married him once but there were obstacles to overcome. Our romance had been thrown off course by manipulative forces beyond our control.

Today, I was here with the other man who had asked me to marry him. I cared for him as a friend but didn't know to what depth these feelings extended. Could I have a future with him? Only time could tell. There was no time to ponder that further as the helicopter lowered to the ground.

Upon disembarking, I noticed the huge spread Diego had arranged for us. His minions had been hard at work providing a cozy blanket, a sturdy umbrella and a huge hamper full of tasty items—bread, cheese, meats, pâté, and a bottle of red wine.

"I must apologize for the cold repast, mi amor. I thought if Churo cooked for us, although the food would be fabulous, we would not have the opportunity of enjoying each other's company with the perks of privacy."

I raised an eyebrow. "And you think we have matters to discuss requiring secrecy?"

Diego smiled surreptitiously. "Perhaps. Certainly, an audience is not necessary." He opened the hamper, took out two crystal glasses, set them down on the lid of the hamper as a make-shift table and proceeded to uncork the wine. The ruby-red wine sparkled with the sunlight filtering in under the umbrella when he poured it into the glasses. No acrylic glasses for Santiago Francesco Bolivar Alvarez. He liked to have the best wherever he went and could afford his luxuries anywhere in the world without batting an eyelid about how much he spent.

After pouring the wine he gave me a glass and said, "To intimate moments!"

I hesitated. "I wouldn't want you to presume too much."

Diego sighed. "Yes, I know, you are still deciding if you want to commit to anyone but forget that and toast this moment."

"I don't know if I can trust my instincts to know what I want or need."

"That's because life is complex and," he stroked a tendril of my hair, "you are a many-faceted woman, like a clear-cut diamond—a quality woman. Let us drink to life and love!"

I grinned and clicked his glass. "Life is good and love is elusive."

"Why not celebrate the elusive aspect?"

I clicked his glass and swirled the wine, stuck my nose in to breathe in the aroma before taking a small sip. I let the wine caress my tongue. "Nice."

"So?" Diego stared at me expecting something more.

The taste of the fruit in the wine resounded clearly. "Berry. A smooth finish. A good wine."

"It should be at that price, mi amor." He held up the bottle of deep red wine, the label a drawing of a naked lady against the background of the sea and the sky. "Blackberries, spice and currents." He examined his glass. "Excellent bouquet. Do you taste the essence of hazelnut?"

"I do," I said, breathing in the scent before swishing the wine and taking another sip. "The aroma is marvelous."

"Sorry, it's not a shiraz. This blend is Chateau Mouton Rothchild, 2010. a cabernet sauvignon with six percent merlot. It's a favorite of mine." He surveyed his glass for the color before tipping it back. "I know you love a good shiraz but I thought you mentioned your admiration for an excellent Merlot or Cab?"

"True. I like them, as well."

My stomach growled and Diego smiled on hearing the sound. "I think we must eat." He opened the hamper. "Your choice of lamb, beef, spiced pork in the Mayan style, pâté or cheese along with bread. There is a gluten free bread for you."

"You remembered?"

Diego nodded. "I will take care of your sensitive stomach as well as your other needs." Taking out a serrated knife he sliced the bread and with a butter knife spread the butter. "Which would you like to try first?"

"I think the spiced pork."

"Mustard? I find it brings out the flavors. My chef encourages me to try it. He makes his own."

"Sure. Thank you. If he prepared all these, he is talented." I was impressed with the chef's way of turning a boring lunch into something distinct. Usually, I avoided sandwiches because they are deadly to my digestive system but Diego had found me a gluten free bread.

"It's all palatable for a plain lunch but I wish to indulge you more, with dinner perhaps?" Diego shot me a look. "I believe it's time for you to meet another member of my family. It's important for you to get along with Mama, don't you think? Especially, moving forward."

"What? You want me to meet your mother?"

"Of course. I have always wanted that."

"I thought I was made it clear when I told you I was trying to spend more time with Wolf. We were engaged, remember?"

"For less than an evening."

I looked out at the waves crashing on the shore. "It was a stressful time but it's over. We want to build our relationship so there are no doubts."

"There will always be drama with Du Lac. He is like a hurricane, gathering force as he nears you until he destroys what he creates. I can't believe he is your man." Diego took my hand. "Tomorrow night. I'll text you the time."

"I can't make plans."

I might be delusional but Wolf was the one. He awakened a deep visceral sensation inside of me that had been dormant for years. I caught a hint of sadness in Diego's eyes. "Sorry, Diego, but Wolf is the one for me but I just want to know for sure, so I postponed the engagement. I shouldn't be wasting your time but I thought I should explain in person." I patted his hand. "You are a good friend."

Diego took up my hand and kissed the inside of my wrist. "I can be more than a friend. I think we have desire and pleasure waiting for us if you give it a chance."

"And love?"

"I don't really think you realize how dear you are to me."

"Really, I'm dear?"

Diego chuckled. "It would be somewhat cheesy to admit to being in love, wouldn't it?"

I shrugged. "No one's perfect."

Smiling, Diego pulled me close and whispered in my ear in a husky voice, "You are it for me, Adelinita. As soon as you discard Du Lac, I want you to think seriously about me."

A shiver escaped with Diego so close, his lips on my shoulder. No matter how I tried, I wasn't oblivious to his chemistry, but did I love him?

"Let's just see what happens, mi amor. There is no need to rush this. I want you to be sure."

For a while we sipped wine in silence. We ate, gazing at the beauty of the Caribbean crashing on the shore. From time to time Diego fed me an occasional chocolate coated strawberry. It was a lovely escape but I had an agenda to consider.

"Why has Cy been sniffing around?"

Diego frowned. "I don't want to be paranoid about this condo project but there are rumors."

"What have you heard?"

Diego shrugged. "It is better you don't worry yourself over such matters. We are here to enjoy our brunch."

Ordinarily, I would persist and pester him but I had quite the buzz on that comes quickly to me with two large glasses of wine. Presently, the most intense danger was not the evil forces at work at the condo but finding myself alone in the middle of nowhere with an intensely sexy man.

Digging out my cell phone, I pretended to see a text. "I have really enjoyed this, Diego, but I must be off. Can you get the pilot to pick us up?"

Diego dove in for a kiss but I jerked away to avoid his lips. "Are you sure?"

I took a deep breath and whispered, "Yes, I am. I should go back. Thank you for lunch."

The green of the waves and hills mixed together in the beer-like brew of his eyes.

***

I had barely thrown my tote on the table, and slipped off my sandals when there was a knock on my door. Peeking through the peephole I saw Wolf.

What was he doing here? Surely, he wasn't jealous about my breakfast with Diego, and how did he hear about it anyway? I opened the door slowly bracing myself for Wolf's disapproval.

He shot in the room like a whirlwind.

"What's up?"

"Did you forget? Grab your snorkeling gear. We need to hit the road now."

"Snorkeling? You didn't tell me about this last night."

Wolf frowned. "I must have forgot. Sorry. Oh, well," he perused me, "guess you're dressed and ready."

"I can't go like this. I have to change."

Wolf dropped his lanky frame into a leather chair, swinging his long legs on an ottoman. "You look great for this thing. Don't bother to change."

"Maybe something more casual and I have to locate my mask and fins. Where are we going?"

"We have a Humane Society fundraiser. You can meet the investors on my condo project. They should all be there. We'll kill two birds with one stone—a snorkeling excursion on the reef and we get to spend time together. That's a perk, right?"

"It is. I wouldn't miss it." Fleetingly, I studied the athletic man waiting for me on the couch. He was so magnetic he gave me a sweet that ignited my core. I was in danger of starting some internal fire if I did more than look. "Give me a minute. This won't take long. I'll hurry. Promise."

I raced into the bedroom, pulled off the romper and searched the drawers of the pine dresser. Someone had neatly stacked the casual clothes. I found a bikini, and shorts and a tank top which I hastily tugged on over the bathing attire, pausing to lightly touch the blue bruise on my abdomen. I winced and withdrew my hand. It would be better in a few days. I sighed and strode to the closet. When I gathered up my snorkeling gear—my mask and fins and tossed them in a net bag, I was ready to roll.

Trotting into the living room, I called out, "I'm ready. Let's go!"

"Okay, babe. I texted you an hour ago. Didn't get anything back. Where were you?"

"Oh, sorry about that but," I said, picking up my sunglasses, "I was having breakfast and didn't look at my cell."

Wolf opened the door for me to go through. "Your phone wasn't on?"

I met his eyes. "I guess not. I was up late last night. Not enough sleep to think clearly."

"Too many margaritas, eh?"

"Not really. Lots of excitement last night. Heinz was attacked."

"You mean my brother Heinz? You must be kidding?"

"No, not at all. Cy and I went out to help him or he'd be in a worse state than he was. There were two thugs out there knocking him around."

"Who were they?"

"I don't know. He wouldn't tell me but I think he knows."

Wolf sat silent a moment. "I trusted him to manage this deal. He must have stepped on a few toes."

"He sure did. We rescued him but I wouldn't put it past him to get roughed up again. Maybe you need to ask him why. He wouldn't tell us who they were either."

"Always more shit." Wolf wiped his forehead pushing his hair back and looked worried. "Are you hurt?"

"A little sore."

"Sorry about that, honey."

"I'm okay, really." I patted his arm reassuringly. "Just don't give me any tight hugs."

We set out in Wolf's Jeep, heading south out of town on Rafael E. Melgar. After a while we passed Chankanaab, a recreational center loaded with tourists and drove south on Carretera Costera Sur. This area is known for the fabulous snorkeling. The coral reef is sensational all along this section of shoreline.

Eventually, we stopped at Skyreef, a club just south of Playa Corona. I was excited, no longer caring who attacked Heinz.

No further thoughts about the investors entered my mind. It was like a dream come true to be at this idyllic spot and get the opportunity to snorkel again. This whole stretch of coast line was known for its reef. To me, this was paradise.

The investors sat around several patio tables under umbrellas by the sea. The sun dazzled and the Caribbean shimmered like glass on the crests of the waves. Water lapped softly off the pier onto the cement steps below. A warm breeze caressed my skin and I had that chill feeling that makes a person jump into the nearest hammock. The effects of the wine mellowed my disposition to such an extent that a languid wooziness came over me as I took a plastic chair beside Wolf, prepared to listen. I'm afraid I zoned out mid-sentence.

Don't get me wrong, I love animals and have rescue cats myself, but the guy speaking was muttering information about neutering more into his margarita than to the members and if I was being honest, I'd say he was wasted. He wore a pink shirt to match his rosy sun-splotched face and light blue jeans. High blood pressure I'd guess. I wasn't the only one with glazed-over eyes. When he ended his speech, the other members started talking amongst themselves making plans for the real work involved in aiding the animals. I was happy the members took this seriously. There were too many homeless animals running around the streets.

Glancing around me, I knew some of the guys. Brick Shithouse, as buff and broad as ever in a Hawaiian print shirt, loosely hanging over relaxed jeans, his sleeve tattoo of showgirls visible by daylight. A flex of a bicep put on quite the dance show for the women assaulting him with their eyes. Beside Ed, his buddy Mr. Clean was there. He dressed down for this event, entirely in white, but this time wearing a white muscle shirt and tan shorts. He waved to one of the ladies and gave her a sleazy grin.

Over towards the steps to the sea, Heinz Du Lac, happily sucked on a straw embedded in a frothy green margarita, the liquid disappearing rapidly. A florid brunette sporting a few excess pounds hidden by an orange empire-waist floral dress was seated at his white plastic table, tequila shots lined up in front of her, eyeing him from under a straw hat. She tossed one back and then handed a glass to Heinz. Wolf's brother was keeping a low profile, a straw hat tipped over the abrasion on his forehead, a hand held over his bruised cheek while dark sunglasses guarded his eyes, the swollen one hidden. His injuries forgotten, he clicked the brunette's glass and gulped it down.

My eyes drifted back to Ed, now flirting with the lithe petite Latina, ignored by a bored Mr. Clean. Leon sat beside him tapping his fingers nervously with one hand while chain smoking a cigarette with the other. Carelessly, he let the ashes drop to the ground.

Closer to the beach there were some serious looking emaciated dudes, one gray fuzz-topped and the other cue ball bald. Both had thin lips, lined foreheads and jowls. I'd put them in their seventies or on the bad side of sixty. Regular sun exposure left a parchment surface of wrinkles besides the regular lines that came from laughing and frowning. One wore Dolce sunglasses, the corners shiny with rhinestones and the other aviator wire rims. Their gravelly voices were raised antagonistically as they discussed different views on neutering cats and dogs. They were trying to round up island residents to participate, unsuccessfully so far. The men were eating something that resembled pulled pork in a rust-brown sauce and drinking Coronas. Several empty beer bottles were lined in a row on the plastic table in front of them.

"Pardon me, for my tardiness," a familiar voice said softly. Diego smiled like a fox coming out of a hen house. He was duded up in a chartreuse shirt under a safari jacket and pleated off-white trousers. He tossed his Panama hat on the table directly in front of Wolf and took a plastic chair. "I had something to attend to earlier." He scanned the ocean and sky. "Those clouds are our warning of the hurricane. Did you know this one is called Pandora? She will unleash the evils of the world." He laughed. "Some would say they are already unleashed, right, Du Lac?"

"Where there are beautiful women there is only good."

"Well said. I didn't know you had become a Latin philosopher." Wolf's eyes twinkled.

"If the hurricane becomes a category three, I would hope you would consider staying at my villa."

"No need, but thank you. I have a cottage in town that is well above four feet high. I had it specially constructed in case of a hurricane."

Carmelita, stood at the restaurant entrance. Her gaze flit around until she suddenly spotted us. In a luminous sea foam beach dress covering her shoulders and thighs, she trotted to our table. The silver bikini she wore underneath was clearly visible through the thin material. "Diego thought I should get out more, so I came too. Hope it's all right?" Carmelita leaned down and air kissed my cheeks and then bestowed the same on Wolf.

"Always a pleasure, Carmelita," Wolf said smoothly.

"What's this about a hurricane?" She tossed her long brown locks as she surveyed the sea. "No sign of it yet."

I forced a smile. "I hope they are wrong." I glanced at Diego. "What a surprise to see you." I was pretending that I hadn't seen him earlier. I hoped he picked up on the hint.

Carmelita grasped my hand and squeezed. "*Ay, caramba*, last night was an eye-opener! We have to talk, amiga. *Mierda!*" She placed her fingertips at her temple. "Those margaritas knocked me out."

Diego sat back in his chair and lazily eyed Wolf. "My sister and your ex-girlfriend were out carousing last night. I thought you were interested in renewing your relationship with the entrancing Adelina or is it finally over?" He paused to smile condescendingly. "Perhaps she has found clarity and discarded you?"

"True, she has found clarity," Wolf said, with a smile. "Adie wants to fix things between us." Wolf stared challengingly at Diego.

I put my hand up in a stop gesture. "Swords down, guys. I am not committed to anyone at the moment but," I said, directly to Diego,

"Wolf and I are working on our relationship and FYI, no carousing was going on. I was merely assisting Carmelita in the exploration of the local talent. She wants a new man."

"I am so pleased you are getting to know my family so well, mi amor," Diego said. He signaled the waiter. "Margaritas for all," he said, lifting an eyebrow. Wolf shook his head and said, "Dos Equis, por favor." The server nodded.

Diego lifted an eyebrow. "You are friends with my brother, as well, mi amor?"

"We are good buddies. Cy was my scuba master."

"My brother seems to be unaware of your attachment to Du Lac or to me. I had hoped you would have friend-zoned him by now. Let him down easy. The poor hombre has been through enough."

"Seriously, Diego, I had no idea he liked me."

Wolf smothered a laugh under his breath.

"Well he is busy with an active single life. Always with one woman or another." He shrugged. "Who can keep track?" Diego reached for the margarita the waiter set down. "Cy needs to settle down but Adelina is hardly his type."

"That's not fair, Diego. He's not an open book, but," Carmelita said, grinning wickedly, interested in egging on her brother, "I know Cy likes Adelina. He's mentioned it to me."

"Did you tell him to come today?" I asked.

Carmelita sighed. "I suggested it but he wasn't sure if he wanted to be here. I think he wants to date you, Adelina and is rather depressed about your lack of enthusiasm."

"But, Carmelita, doesn't he know Wolf and I are together?"

Carmelita shook her head, her long brunette tresses flying in the breeze. "He figures, no ring, nothing serious. He wants to pursue you." She turned to Diego. "And by the way, Adelina didn't accept your ring either."

"You Alvarez boys need to find your own women." Wolf reached over and taking my hand, gave it a squeeze.

Carmelita glanced over at the restaurant. "*Perdon,*" Carmelita said suddenly, heading to the ladies' room.

Diego glanced over to the other tables. A pretty brunette waved at him indicating he should join her. "Sorry, I must go. Business. I have a house for sale on the east coast with a stunning view." He smiled at me his teeth flashing white. "We shall speak later?"

I nodded, handing him a goblet. "Take this margarita to her. I can't drink anything right now." I was glad he hadn't mentioned our breakfast. Wolf disliked Santiago Bolivar Alvarez way too much to accept the idea of me having a helicopter outing with the godfather. Hopefully, Diego would keep his mouth shut. I didn't need any more stress with these two.

There was something more important to be thinking about than my love life. Heinz hadn't been upfront about the men attacking him last night. If I wanted to figure it out, I'd have to keep a sharp eye on him, finding out what I could as quickly as possible.

"I saw Heinz and his wife last night. Didn't have a clue he was your brother or she was his wife, at first. They were arguing. I overheard them. She's a looker."

"Attractive on the outside but not a nice person."

"Temperamental, but she can't be that bad."

Wolf laughed. "I think she is."

"Really?"

"Be careful with her. She's devious."

"How so?"

Wolf leaned back in his chair. "Linda did our books when Heinz and I had a partnership back a few years. She embezzled $40,000. It was all gone by the time I discovered it. My mother covered for her, paying it back into the business."

"That's awful."

"It was worse for Heinz. She had affairs." He shrugged. "Not that he didn't. But she was so angry with him, she shot him in the arm in our Cozumel office."

"Was she arrested?"

"No. We didn't want the bad publicity."

"And they stayed together?"

"They got through it, found religion again and moved back to Canada for a few years. Now he's back and they are about to divorce. It's always been on again, off again." Wolf tipped back his beer. "Linda wants Heinz's money."

"Divorce is an equal split."

Wolf lifted his forefinger into the air. "Not the business though. Investments can be split but if she's found a man to latch onto, the better it is for Heinz. She won't look like she needs the money when the judge looks over the papers. Also, she's young enough to get a job."

"And your brother, does he still have feelings for her?"

"Unfortunately, yes. It's like she's a maggot under his skin, eating away at him."

"Darling, how nice to see you!" a melodic voice said from over my shoulder. The sun was in my eyes but I made out a curly mass of red hair, carelessly contained by an elastic. She was long and slender wearing a loose gypsy print top and skinny pale-blue jeans, ripped at the knees and the thighs, an appliquéd "bad ass" on her butt which I saw when she spun around to check out the men. And beads, did I mention beads—lots and lots of colorful beads, around her neck, arms and drop earrings to her shoulders. Her eyes were heavily lined black, eyelash extensions fringing her narrow slanted green eyes—blue shadow on the lids.

Wolf gave a lazy glance. "Linda, how are you?"

"Great, now that I've seen you." She tossed her hair, her green eyes sparkling mischievously.

Wolf studied her. "Have you decided to invest in the condo project?"

"Soon. I have cash flow problems until the divorce is settled. Heinz and I are separated though." She turned to me. "And this is?"

"Adie Sturm."

"I knew it! You looked familiar." She smacked her forehead with the palm of her hand. "Ah, yes, of course. Years ago, at the Du Lac cabin on the French River. We shared a room. You were the little teeny bopper Wolf liked."

I did a double-take. This was the plain freckled girl with the scraggly red hair who dated Heinz about ten years ago. She had clearly wanted a breeding program for them–six kids minimum and although a religious Lutheran, had no trouble making out with Heinz in the bedroom we shared. I lay there in the other single bed, feigning sleep waiting indefinitely for them to quit kissing and leave.

I had no idea she had stuck it out so long with Heinz. More importantly, this was the amazingly devout Christian girl who had managed to please judgemental Agnes Du Lac, mother of Wolf and Heinz. Something I had not managed. It was hard to believe she had been such a straight arrow, especially now, looking at this modern-day hipster.

"So, you and Heinz—"

"Dated for years and are separated but that doesn't mean you can have him."

My eyes widened. "I wasn't thinking—"

"Well don't! I know your type. The Du Lac brothers are out of your league."

Wolf saw my astonished expression and said, "No, she's not. Adie is my fiancée."

Linda chortled. "Are you serious? You two? If you do, it won't last. I give it a week, maybe two." She fluffed her long auburn tresses. "Heinz and I were perfect but now he wants me to leave the island and go back to Canada. Who the hell knows why?" She glared at me. "And don't get any ideas about Heinz. He has a considerable amount of money. He doesn't need to be with the likes of you."

Diego overheard Linda on his way to our table. He took a seat and growled. "Control your tongue, Linda. There is no need to insult Adelina. She has better choices than Heinz Du Lac." Diego's security guards, Churo and Luis took their positions behind his chair, feet astride, hands behind their backs.

Linda giggled. "Hey, how about that? Diego Bolivar Alvarez has a thing for this one too."

"It might be best if you leave," Wolf said abruptly, getting up and taking her arm. "I will escort you to a taxi."

I put my hand up in a stop gesture. "Listen, it's okay, Wolf. The drinks are strong. She's had too many."

"Even more reason for her to go," Diego said.

"Are you guys for real, listening to this little squirt?" Linda pushed Wolf's hand away and shot me a look. "I am warning you. Stay away from Heinz." She scanned the tables. "Is that Daniella? What is she doing here?" Her words came out as a hiss.

"She's an investor in our condo project, Linda," Diego said softly. "Perhaps you should go. One of my men will drive you back to your cottage." Luis, his security guard took a step forward and whispered in his ear. "Excuse me; there is some business I must attend to. Luis, make sure Adie is not bothered again."

Anyone threatened by that massive man was likely to run but not Linda. She retorted hotly, "I have a right to my opinions. Anyone that trusts Daniella is in for a rude awakening."

Scornfully, she added, pointing a forefinger at me, "And watch yourselves around this one, boys. She's a gold digger."

"What?" I couldn't believe this woman. Where was she getting this from?

Wolf took hold of my hand and whispered, "Let it go. She's a whack-job."

Seeing everyone glaring at her, Linda shrugged her shoulders. "Okay, okay, I'm going already!" Luis, Diego's security man steered her away from our table. At the last second, Linda twisted about and added, "Anyway, I don't care what Heinz wants. I like the island life. There's nothing better than Cozumel. I am here to find someone new and move on." Her eyes scanned the tables, and rested on Mr. Clean.

"Why don't you go for it," suggested Wolf. "These tables are reserved for the Erizo del Mar condo group, a fundraiser for the Humane Society. You can sit anywhere but no more drinks, eh?" When Luis led her to the area closer to the main building, Wolf turned to me. "Are you okay? She's—"

"I know, crazy. But Wolf, something is not right. You need to speak to Heinz about the guys who beat him up last night."

Wolf gazed over to his brother's table. He shook his head and studied me in concern. "What about you? Are you hurting?"

I pressed my fingers to the bruise below my ribs. "Still sore where the dude punched me in the ribs but otherwise, I'm good."

"I'm so sorry, babe. I shouldn't have gotten you involved. Why didn't you call security?"

"No time."

"Tell me what happened."

"I saw three people on the beach fighting. It was dark. Two dudes against one. I didn't know it was Heinz. I texted Cy and asked him to come down with me. We tried to stop the thugs. When I questioned Heinz, he wouldn't tell us who they were." My lips curled into a frown. "Heinz has changed. He was rude."

Wolf grinned. "You tend to bring out the worst in a man."

I put my hand on his arm and slid it down to his hand. "And the best?"

"That too. That's why I keep you around." Wolf motioned to the waiter.

"Cy thinks Heinz is involved in something illegal."

"What's it to him?"

"Diego gave him a condo so he could investigate your brother's activities." I checked out Mr. Clean's table. He had taken his shirt off and was more hard-muscled than I had imagined. Linda was rubbing sunscreen evenly on his back like she was spreading olive oil to pan fry a fish.

"Alvarez doesn't know goody-two shoes Heinz."

"He wasn't all that nice last night. He gave me the finger," I said resentfully.

Wolf grinned. "You must have really pissed him off." He patted me on the shoulder. "That's my girl."

After taking an order at the next table, the server came over. He was about twenty, tanned, had dark brown hair and big coffee-colored eyes. He wore a white T-shirt and black trousers cinched with a decorative leather-embroidered belt. His name tag said "Emilio".

"What do you think you'd like? Are you hungry?"

"No, not very. I ate a while ago. I think guacamole will do."

"Sounds good. Two," Wolf said to the waiter.

"And to drink, señor?"

"Dos Equis, por favor and for the señorita—?"

"Water, please. I'll have something later, after I go snorkeling."

I watched the young man with the ready smile disappear into the restaurant as Diego came back.

"Did I miss anything?" Diego slouched down in a chair beside me.

I indicated Heinz with my chin.

At this moment Heinz was in a heated conversation with Brick Shithouse and a tall Latina girl at a table overlooking the sea. "Who is that woman speaking with Heinz?" The woman that captured my interest held her head high and surveyed the guests as arrogantly as a queen would her nobles.

Carmelita rejoined us, a margarita in hand. "Who is that woman, Diego. I've seen her before."

"Hm-m," Diego responded quickly, "that's the gallery owner. What's her name, Du Lac?"

"Perla Bravo Gonzales. She's sharp. Makes a practice of taking a sizeable profit from her art deals. Native sculptures and paintings from here and South America."

Eyes on Perla, Diego delicately lifted the margarita glass, his pinky ring glinting in the sunlight. The family crest signet, a black cat walking, set in a square of gold. "She's invested a great deal of money into the condo project. I didn't think the art business profited so highly but she has Mayan glyphs and a few South American artists. I bought one last week."

Carmelita peered at the tall athletic brunette, long wavy tresses and, a skimpy sky-blue one piece with cut-outs visible under the open sheer aqua cover-up. Her face was turned away. I couldn't be sure if she was attractive or not. "Smart and trim. Could be a woman for our brother. Is she pretty?"

"Too much like a boy," Diego commented sourly. "Nothing to hold on to."

Carmelita stared. "I meant her face. In my opinion she is no different than my models. Well proportioned. Good legs. I can't see her face though."

"I doubt if he likes his women that tall or that powerful," Diego said critically. "That one is a giraffe. Six feet one for sure. Look at that neck! She could easily feed on the grass at her feet."

Wolf grinned. "She does look strong."

"Since when doesn't Cy like tall women?" Carmelita argued. "On the other hand, recently, he finds the petite ones hot—like Adelina. Tiny and sexy too. Maybe a small woman brings out the protective male in him."

"I'm sure it does. Let's face it, Alvarez, Adie has it all." Wolf squeezed my arm. "She's a firecracker. This lady is a tiger in the—"

"Please!" I stopped him with a hand gesture. "Too much information, Du Lac!"

Wolf leaned over and kissed my cheek. "Sorry, babe." He turned to Carmelita. "Besides, your brother is a scuba diver. He's hardly interested in art, is he Carmelita?"

"Interest in the partner's job is not a requirement for a lover, Wolf. My lovers dress well but hardly wear designer clothing." She surveyed the gallery owner. "That one has the clothes and the money to be worthy of a Bolivar Alvarez. If Cy comes, I'll introduce him to Perla. He needs stability. As for me, I'm window shopping."

"Well, there were some men you liked—none of them keepers."
Wolf tipped his beer up. "After that last scumbag there was the
washed-up fashion model, a big fan of De la Renta or was it
Versace?" Wolf grinned. "Luckily, for you, those tools are out of
the picture. Maybe, it's time to forget the past and find yourself
someone new and different."

"It's true. I make deplorable choices when it comes to men. I
don't know if that will ever change." Carmelita sighed. "Yet, I
have to find a man. I can't be a nun forever."

Diego laughed. "I can no more believe you are a nun than I can
believe you have been canonized a saint. No one expects you to be.
We have standards as a Bolivar Alvarez, to be happy and if
possible, marry money. The hunt is up to you."

"It's not that easy, my brother. I never know if they want me for
myself or to get their greedy paws on my share of the fortune."

Seeing Carmelita's mouth turn down at the corners, I hastily
changed the subject. "What about Mr. Clean out there talking to
Linda? He looks familiar. Does he interest you?"

"Don't you remember, chica? We met him last night." Carmelita
smiled sweetly as if reliving a warm moment. "It was a fun time at
Hemingway's, wasn't it?"

"Oh, yes. I forgot." I gazed at Wolf. "We did meet these guys
briefly at the bar."

"We did, until Cy came along." Carmelita explained, to the two
men eyeballing her. "He ruined the night, taking Adelina away.
We were checking out the guys." She added hastily, "For me, not
Adelina."

For the life of me I couldn't remember Mr. Clean's name. Those
Hemmingway margaritas were powerful. I squinted my eyes. "I
think that dude's name is Leonard or Loewy."

Wolf shook his head. "You must have been wasted, babe. It's
Leon."

"I was personally more interested in the strong powerful hombre,
his friend," Carmelita purred. "He works out. Buff bod. That is hot
in a man. I've met him before. He seemed interested. I told him to
speak to me if he appears at this event."

Diego grinned. "Apparently, that fellow needs to tune up his
skills with the ladies, dear sister."

"Why do you say that?"

"I gather you spent the night alone at your own condo."

Carmelita rolled her eyes. "Ernesto has a big mouth."

Diego grinned. "He knows who signs his paycheck." He tilted back his margarita. "I'm glad you held off. No need to give the man milk unless he wants to buy the cow."

"*Dios mio!* What sexist crap, Diego. I am not a dairy cow."

"You are more a thoroughbred mare, I'd say," Wolf interjected. "Ed will need to catch you before he can race you."

"Not you too!" Carmelita glared. "I am a woman not a horse!"

"And a desirable one at that," Wolf drawled. "Let the man chase you before you give in, eh, Alvarez?"

Diego nodded. "Truer words were never spoken. My sister has no need to act like a cheap tart. That's something Daniella would do. You are far superior to that woman."

"This coming from my brother who dated that puta." Carmelita glanced over at Ed who took a table near the water. "I need to speak to him. Excuse me."

"Is Ed a good choice for Carmelita?" I was worried about the way the man checked out my friend, like a hungry cat eying a fat juicy mouse. I had a bad feeling about him.

Diego sighed. "He's not stupid, at least. He's a criminal lawyer from Cancun. Seems he's employed by cartel types. He gets them off, no problem."

I watched Carmelita's head tilt back, her tinkling laughter carrying over with wind. She was flirting, her body language intimate, her chair pulled up so that Ed's thigh touched hers. Something about that dude's profile reminded me of Federico, her last husband. His nose was pronounced. He had squinty eyes some women found attractive. Small eyes are narrow windows to the soul, I say. Ones I would rather not open.

"Is it just me or does he look a bit like Fede?"

Wolf checked out Ed. "Yeah. I can see it. Looks like a shark. Fede's doppelganger, all right."

I turned to Diego to see if he noticed the resemblance.

Diego didn't say anything for a moment as he narrowed his eyes. "Let's hope Carmelita uses her instincts when dealing with this lawyer from Cancun."

"I'm sure I'm worrying for nothing."

"You are a good friend, Adelinita. Carmelita is lucky to have your concern." His gaze was disconcerting, the adoration in his hazel eyes making me slightly uncomfortable.

"Perhaps, you will attend my soireé tomorrow night, Adelinita?" Diego glanced at Wolf. "It's for the condo project. All the investors are coming. Shall we say eight?"

Wolf nodded.

Diego took up my hand and kissed the inside of my wrist. "Will you enhance the party with your beauty, mi amor?"

"I would love to." I beamed at Diego. He was such a sweet guy. Always a compliment. In my present mood it made me feel so much better.

"Should I send the limo to pick you up?"

"Thank you, but no. I'll come with Wolf." I tilted my head in question.

"Of course. We'll go together." Wolf squeezed my hand. "By the way, Alvarez, we need a brief meeting of the investors."

"Why not have that meeting at the party in my villa? You can text everyone involved?"

Wolf nodded. "No problem." He glanced at me. "You'll be okay on your own for a while? The meeting won't be long."

I nodded, only partially listening. My mind was on Carmelita, playing with Ed's hair. She fell too deeply too quickly. Please don't let him be another bad apple in the barrel. I needed a good man to treat her fairly with respect. She didn't need another unsuccessful relationship. Carmelita was too emotionally fragile.

I excused myself and found my way through the restaurant to the washroom. It was clean but unfortunately, that redhaired harpy was leaning into the mirror when I entered. She swirled around and glared. "You need to mind your own business. You'll get us all killed."

"Pardon?"

"Heinz has his lotto ticket. Do you understand? I will be flying like a bird when they fork out our money."

"You and Heinz?" I wasn't sure what she was getting at. Heinz had made winnings somewhere?

"It would all be good but Heinz is having doubts. He was just seeing reason and then you came along—"

"I don't know what you're talking about."

"Don't play stupid. I know you rescued Heinz on the beach with that Alvarez brother. If Heinz doesn't do as he is told he will have more than a few bruises."

"Look, Linda, I hardly know you. I have no idea what Heinz told you but—"

"You know me. I was Agnes Du Lac's dream daughter-in-law. Remember? But that's not what this is about. You need to leave Heinz alone. He has a monkey on his back that won't get off."

"I didn't do anything. Really."

"I've heard about you interfering."

"You're wrong. I was trying to help him."

"Listen to me!" Linda lowered her face to mine and hissed, "If we have to pay for your stupidity, I'll see that you are gone. You hear me? Gone!" Linda swung around and dashed out the door leaving me more puzzled than ever.

***

The sun felt hot on my body until I immersed myself in the salty warmth of the Caribbean. My mask was clear and looking down I could see pale yellow brain coral over a branch of green staghorn coral. A bright blue angelfish crowned by a bright golden patch passed a few feet away. A mass of sergeant majors, round yellow-striped fish surrounded me before swimming by in a school, eying me for bread crumbs but seeing I had none, swam to Wolf.

Wolf had decided the meeting could go on without him. I agreed and was just as eager to immerse myself in the Caribbean for a while and enjoy the snorkeling. He was a few feet ahead of me but that was fine with me. Finally, I was at peace, not a care in the world when the ocean hugged my body. The bruise on my tummy was green but didn't hurt as much anymore. I was accustomed to injuries during karate workouts, having had several broken fingers and toes. Bruises tend to hurt more though.

Bright blue tang fish shot out from the purple fan coral waving with the current. Below a wide flat flounder appeared bright blue, its pattern rapidly disappearing as it camouflaged into the sand surrounding it.

Wolf motioned me to the right. I caught a glimpse of a long narrow needlefish before it darted off past the brain coral. Nothing beats the joy of the sea waters. I wasn't a strong swimmer but I had buoyancy with the mask and fins that kept me afloat and confident. I felt fins brush my skin as a trunkfish and I took the same turn. They are friendly fish with no malicious intent. It was my fault for invading his restaurant. Before I could figure out how to apologize to the jostled fish I was distracted by a red squirrel fish swimming past, his pointy fancy fins setting him apart from the others. This time I directed Wolf to come and see. At least here, in the sea, we were free to enjoy each other with no conflict and no one to interfere. It was a sanctuary where love could grow.

All was well until the current pushed me towards a mass of plastic bags. Only they were not garbage. Jellyfish! Big ones with pale-white air sacs and gossamer tentacles that could cling to your neck and thighs like a swarm of wet yellow jackets. Contact with just one of them was like touching a live electric cable. I back-pedaled in the water and twisted around, veering away from them.

The sense of foreboding danger I had above the water had transcended to the depths of the Caribbean. Wolf and Diego's apprehension was point on. I couldn't help but feel Heinz's attackers had something to do with it. That instinctual feeling of foreboding was overwhelming.

It was then that I started to feel a chill, the water although not cold, hovering around eighty degrees Fahrenheit, was cool for me. I didn't have enough body fat to stay warm. Crossing my arms, I indicated to Wolf that I was done. He nodded his head and we swam to shore.

As Wolf headed to the outdoor shower, I decided on a washroom trip. On the way, I encountered Emilio, the server. He smiled and asked if I was okay. When I looked confused, he said the redhead was trouble and, in his opinion, I would not be her only target today. When I tried to question him further, he shook his head. I grabbed his arm to stop him.

"She likes the rich ones but *caramba*, she has a bad temper." He then rushed off to the kitchen. I was right on his tail. He stopped and shook his head.

"*Por favor*, please," I said, "You know something else."

He indicated with his chin the group at the railing overlooking the sea. "See how she shouts at senorita Bolivar Alvarez? She is," he pointed his index finger at his temple making a circle, "She is *loco*—crazy."

I couldn't help noticing the similarity to the other night. It was almost a repeat of Hemingway's—Daniella, Mr. Clean, Brick Shithouse, and Carmelita. One major difference, Linda was taking my place with that group. Reading her body-language told me she was zooming in for a man.

***

A cell phone trilled.

"Diga," the woman said into her iPhone. When she heard his voice, she snapped, "Why do you call me now? You know I am not alone. Surely, this could wait?"

"You are my eyes and ears, correct? This plan can go wrong without my input, woman."

"Sí, it could anyway, with or without your annoying phone calls," she hissed, angry with his disrespect. "What do you want?"

"I am being vigilant, unlike you. Are they all there? Do they suspect anything?"

"How would I know?"

"Find out. Don't just sit there and fill your belly. A lot of money is at stake, chica. Make sure the packages are all delivered. There is much to be done."

"I know this already. I will be a billionaire soon."

"It's not just about you," he said slowly.

The woman's voice was flat with disdain. "You gain because of my plan. Don't forget who made this happen."

5

"Shower?" Wolf said on the elevator, leaning close. His lips swept the nape of my neck setting off a familiar sensation. I pressed into the unbuttoned shirt to kiss his chest. He tasted like salt and smelled of ocean breeze. My fingers worked quickly to undo the rest of the buttons.

At the open doorway of my condo I paused to undo his belt. My swimsuit cover-up slipped to the floor. His big hands, stroked my breasts, lingering on my perked nipples under my bikini top. A moan escaped my lips.

Using the side of his foot Wolf slung the door shut. Faint light, hues of pink and purple came in through the wide windows and sliding doors of the balcony. It was perfect lighting for us—not too bright and just right for me to see his eyes. My excitement was mirrored in his blues.

Wolf picked me up and laid me on the white leather couch. It felt smooth to my naked skin. His eyes sparked like a match ignited. I pulled him closer to feel his shapely lips against mine. He kissed me slowly, sparking a fire within me, growing rapidly in strength as I sucked his lower lip. My fingers threaded his hair, nibbling his full lips gently—not hard enough to draw blood but forcefully enough to send me reeling into a heady state of ecstasy.

Clothes fell on the floor. We zoned in on new territories discovering each other with our lips and hands until he rolled over with me on top. I quivered from his touch. It was like an out of body experience when a person faces near death and ends up walking into white light—enraptured euphoria before an electrifying finish. I shuddered and cried out. Wolf groaned his pleasure as we lay entwined together in our rapture.

***

I awoke suddenly, not knowing why. I recalled how we had been possessed by adrenaline madness, flinging ourselves on the couch to work our magic. A warm shower washed off the love juices. His hands loaded with body wash stroked each contour of my body while I did the same, massaging his hard, muscular form. His moan told me everything. Nothing felt better nor more satisfying. The chemistry was still there as strong as it always had been.

"Are you sure about this?" My Logical Voice whispered in my brain. "He's let you down before. That's true. He's exciting but can you count on him?"

Hormone Voice shushed Logical. "You said it before. He's a Sea God. No man is equal to him."

I shut both voices off and concentrated on Wolf. He was everything I needed.

We dried each other off laughing, stress released, and the Zen feeling I had from the aftereffects of pleasure was more than any mortal deserved. From sheer exhaustion we headed to bed, this time to sleep. I watched him succumb to dreams. His unusual features had a perfect profile. He muttered softly. He twitched as if a massive spider was crawling across his face. His arms flailed as his body thrashed. The dream must have been highly disturbing. Sliding my hand along his arm to calm him, he slumped into a deep sleep. Ultimately, I dosed off too, wondering what was on his mind.

Voices. Shouting, shrieking and loud thuds vibrated through the walls of the next condo. What was going on? The noise was coming from Heinz's condo.

Startled, I reached out across the soft sheet in the king bed to wake Wolf but found the space empty. It was very early. My cell by my bed said 5:50. Where was he?

Jerking up in a sitting position, listening to the jumbled voices next door. I knew I shouldn't get involved but since so much had happened to Heinz, I had to check. Were those men after him again, this time gaining access to his home in their attempt to take him out?

Quickly, I dressed in leggings, and a sweat shirt, not bothering with a bra and underwear, I slipped on my sneakers. Grabbing my master key, an umbrella for protection and my cell, I raced to Heinz's condo. My ear glued tightly to the wood I listened at the door. The earlier clamour had subsided. It was quiet.

Should I go in? Would Heinz get angry? I didn't want to widen the rift between the brothers but my instinct told me he was in trouble.

I pulled out my cell and texted Wolf.

There's something's bad going down in 303. Meet me there asap.
Pushing the key card into the slot, it clicked as it unlocked. Still I hesitated.

With a kick of my foot, the door creaked open. At first glance, everything was as it should be. The sliding doors to the balcony were open wide and a breeze drifted in. The furniture was in place. It looked unoccupied.

Dropping my umbrella by the door and with my cell back in my sweatshirt pocket, I advanced further into the room. At the coffee table a man lay face down, his arm stretched out. Rushing over, I knelt on the floor and turned his head. It was Heinz. Carefully, I skimmed my hand over the back of his head. Blood had clotted in his hair. Glancing around, I saw a metal statue lying on the marble floor. It was a bronze angel holding a tiny bird, covered with a sticky red mess of hair and skin.

Before I could check out the rest of him, he let out a loud groan.
Thank you, God! Heinz was alive!

"Heinz?" I whispered. "Can you sit up?"

"Adie," he said through bleary eyes, "where's Linda? She was here."

"I didn't see anyone."

"We argued. She wants more money." Heinz seemed disoriented. "I think she hit my head."

"Linda came at you from behind and hit you?" I looked at the angel statue on the floor, blood dripping on the ivory floor from the base of the statue, not believing him.

He shook his head in confusion. "I don't know. Maybe not. She was in front of me. Linda was so angry. This doesn't make sense, does it?" Heinz looked over my shoulder. He froze. "Oh, no!" The words came out like a soft moan.

Spinning around I saw what gripped his attention. In a dream-like state I headed slowly to the aquarium.

Foot-long flaming-red seaweed flowed in rhythm with the tank's aerator pulse—swirling about touching the green coral and the gold marble angelfish. Only something was wrong. This was not seaweed. It was long auburn hair attached to a human head, the rest of her body hanging over the side of the tank. I stood my eyes transfixed on the dead woman partially submerged in the water. Her flat black pupils stared lifelessly at the ceramic pirate's ship decoration on the surface of the gravel at the bottom of the tank.

My hand shot to my mouth, gulping down the vomit that threatened to surface. It took supreme willpower to circle the gurgling aquarium and the body. She was dressed in a clingy strapless black dress, bangles on her dangling arms, one hand lodged in the aquarium, fingers inside a fake skull statue. The murderer had pushed her upper torso in but the rest of her hung slack over the side of the glass. Blood dripped from a wound on the base of her skull.

Her shapely butt stuck out, legs pale, long and slender, one silver sandal remained on a foot resting on the floor but the other had dropped off, the stiletto heel pointing upward towards the ceiling. A puddle of urine sullied the marble floor where her bladder released as she died.

I tried to make sense of what had happened. Either Heinz had faked the wound and murdered his wife or the more plausible theory was Heinz had nothing to do with the killing and there were two intruders. The killers had knocked them both out and dumped Linda into the tank to die.

The breeze from the balcony was stronger now, damp with humidity from the open balcony doors. It had started to rain. I padded over to the sliding doors. The rain whipped into my face. The Caribbean was gray fading into a dull sky. A tendril of my hair thrashed against my cheek like a slap from an angry lover. Taking the door handle in both hands I pulled it until the door shut out the hostile weather.

I glared at Wolf's brother. "Heinz, what happened? Did you kill Linda?"

Heinz shook his head. "I didn't do this, Adie. I swear. Believe me. I told her to stay away from those people."

"The same people that beat you up did this?"

Heinz shook his head. "I don't know for sure. Could be. I was threatened. They said I'd regret it if I didn't do as they said. They'd hurt my family, which meant Linda, but I told them I wouldn't do it." He glanced down at the fish tank. "I made a big mistake. I could have prevented this."

"Who are these people? What did they want you to do?"

Heinz pushed on the bleeding wound on his head. Bright red blood dripped down his arm. "They said I had to take their money and deposit it in the bank. I'm not proud of what I did. Now Linda's dead."

"Who are these people?"

"Mexican mob or cartel." He stared at Linda's head in the aquarium. "I did love her, you know."

I patted his hand. "I believe you but this is bad. I should call the police."

Heinz jerked up. "And tell them what? These people are dangerous. They'll make sure we die before we tell the police anything about the operation. Besides, your fingerprints are all over the place, just like mine. The police will question us. What can we tell them?"

He was right. If I called the police, they would likely haul us both to the police station and throw us into a jail cell to rot. Maybe, I was wrong about Mexican prisons, but I had read horror stories enough on the subject to think I was in deep water.

From my pocket I pulled out my cell and texted Wolf.

Come to 303. Now!

It had been at while since I sent the last text yet there was still no answer. Now what?

"Who're you texting?" Heinz mumbled from the floor where he now sat his back resting against the couch.

Checking my contacts, I ignored him and decided I had to phone. He would know what to do.

On the second ring, a sleepy male voice murmured, "Diga."

I breathed his name softly, "Diego."

"Mi amor, what is it? You sound distraught."

"Sorry to wake you. I have a situation in 303 at the Erizo."

There was a pause. "Don't say anything. I'll bring Churo and Luis. We will be there shortly."

"You called Alvarez?" Heinz frowned. "Shouldn't you have contacted Wolf?"

"I tried. He didn't answer my texts."

"What can Alvarez do?"

"He knows Cozumel. He'll help us."

A knock on the door sounded. I turned to Heinz. That couldn't be Diego. It would have taken him longer to get here.

"Look out the peephole," Heinz whispered faintly, as he sunk back on the floor. He was close to passing out.

It was a distorted Cy peering up at the ceiling as he waited.
I opened the door a crack. "Cy?"
"Adie."
"Diego called you?"
"He did." Cy edged in past me. "He wanted me to secure the scene."
"How exactly would you do that?"
Cy shrugged. "Depends. What happened?"
"There's been a murder."
Cy's eyes landed on Heinz slumped against the couch motionless. "He's dead?"
"No." I took Cy's shoulder and rotated him to face the aquarium. Cy's jaw dropped. *"Pinche!"*
"It's Heinz's wife, Linda. You may have seen her before."
"No." Cy's eyes narrowed. "Did he kill her?"
"Hell no!" Heinz muttered. "I didn't touch Linda."
Two sharp knocks on the door announced the arrival of yet another visitor.
I raced to the door hoping it was Wolf but what if it wasn't? I peered out through the peephole. They were two massive men with faces only a mother could love—Churo and Luis, Diego's bodyguards. Wide like bulldozers, and strong as bulls. Behind them, stood the head honcho himself—Santiago Francisco Bolivar Alvarez.
I opened the door to admit the bodyguards, Churo and Luis, dressed as usual all in black. They marched in, followed by their boss, casual in jeans and a green T-shirt. What was different were the shadows beneath his eyes. Diego rushed to take me in his arms.
"What has happened? You sounded distressed."
Before I could answer Churo motioned to the aquarium.
Diego hardly blinked. "Who is she?"
Cy spoke up. "Heinz Du Lac's wife."
"You know her. It's Linda," I said. "She was at the Skyreef."
Diego nodded. "She was the one making a scene, correct? Extremely unfortunate for her and for us. This is poor publicity for our condo sales," Diego said seriously. "Were you thinking to finish her off in your own apartment, Heinz? What's wrong with divorce?"
"But-t," Heinz stuttered. "I didn't. I really didn't. I've been set

up!"

"By whom?" Diego's eyes surveyed the room.

Heinz shook his head.

Cy crossed the room to the balcony doors. "These are unlocked."

"They were wide open when I came in," I said.

"And you closed them?" Diego asked.

"It was raining in. The floor was getting wet."

Diego nodded. "An intruder could have entered and escaped from the balcony, leaving the doors open. Now, tell me, what were you doing with Linda? Were you two having a sexual interlude?"

Heinz's jaw dropped. "Are you shittin' me?"

"Watch your language. There is a lady present." Diego added, "It would be understandable if you did. Linda was gorgeous. You might have had regrets about your breakup. Were you planning on continuing the marriage? Is that why Linda came to see you?"

"We were separated. I had no idea she was coming here. Linda told me she had a text to meet me at the condo."

Cy stared at Diego. "Sounds like Heinz is right. It was a setup. This man is stupid but not a murderer."

"Shut up, Alvarez. I am no more stupid than you are. Linda came here uninvited."

"You need to come clean and talk," I said.

"I have nothing to say. I didn't *do* anything."

A smooth voice from the open door called out, "Hey." Wolf checked out the occupants of the room. His forehead furrowed when he saw Diego, Cy and the bodyguards. "What's going on? Are you okay, Adie?"

"I'm good. Talk to Heinz."

Wolf strode into the room and headed for his brother who was seated on the marble tile floor, his back leaning against the couch, and a hand pressed against the back of his head. "What happened?"

Heinz's eyes swept to the aquarium situated behind Wolf. Puzzled Wolf did an about-face. He took in the aquarium with Linda's head and upper body in the water. His jaw clenched. Calmly, he approached the fish tank and took a closer look saying nothing as he peered at the red hair swirling in the water.

"I didn't kill her, Wolf. Linda came by making demands. I said the lawyers can sort it, but she kept going on and on."

"And then you hit her," he spied the figurine on the floor, "with that?"

Heinz shook his head.

Wolf knelt down and saw the blood on Heinz's head. "What the hell?" Did she club you with something?"

Heinz shrugged. "No, I don't think so."

Wolf shot him an incredulous look.

"I don't know what happened. I really don't."

Wolf turned to me. "You okay, babe?"

"Yes. Where were you? I had to call Diego for help."

"There was a crisis at the construction site." Wolf gave Diego a nod. "Thanks for coming." He took my hands in his. "You look so pale. Come sit down." He led me to the couch and I sank into the soft leather.

Diego spoke softly, "No need to involve the police, Du Lac. Any bad publicity would discourage buyers."

"A murder will do that."

"We need to talk," I said to my boyfriend.

Wolf gave me a warning look. I understood that he didn't want Diego or the others to know anything that affected his family. "We will, later. For now, this mess is the priority. Alvarez?"

Diego nodded. To Churo and Luis he ordered, "Find a tarp, rope, towels and a box. You men will need to wrap her and put her into a box to carry outside."

"There should be some things in the storage room at the end of the hall," Wolf continued, "and maybe a mop to get rid of the excess water when the body is removed."

"Good thinking. No trace must be found. Is that understood?"

"Sí, señor Diego," Luis said quickly, hurrying to the door. Churo followed rapidly on his heels and made his way out.

"Thank you, Diego," I said, coming up to him.

Diego's hazel eyes gleamed. "My pleasure. There can be no mention of your visit here, mi amor, or what transpired within." He picked up my hand and kissed my wrist. "I think you need to get back to bed. Rest. You look tired."

I glanced down at my shapeless-gray sweatshirt. Someone should call the fashion police. Without mascara I was downright plain. I grinned inwardly. Diego would not be so keen on marriage now, having seen me at my worst.

Wolf nodded. "I'll let your men do the cleanup. I'll take Adie

71

back to the condo."

I bristled. "Sure, it's not every day I see a woman drowned in a fish tank but I am perfectly capable of walking down the hall by myself. I want a full report of everything," I said, staring at Wolf and Diego.

"And you shall, mi amor. Amancio, it would be cavalier of you to escort Adelina back to her apartment."

I picked up the umbrella I had thrown on the floor and opened the door.

Stopping, I called back. "Don't forget Wolf."

Wolf nodded, as Cy steered me out.

I shook Cy's hand off in the hall. "Stop this macho stuff! I'm not an invalid. I just saw a murd—"

"Ss-h, Adie. Someone can hear you out here. Give me your key card."

6

I woke up with a splitting headache. My brain was being hammered unmercifully by Thor, god of thunder. From the bedside table I picked up a bottle of Tylenol and extracted a pill, swallowing it with the water I kept handy. Picking up my cell phone at my bed, I saw it was just past ten. I clicked on my texts. One new message.

Can we meet for lunch at 11:30? Marg
Sure. Java. See you there. A

Marg was my Canadian friend. We went way back, sharing our lives since skiing lessons at a local resort years ago. The ski group consisted of six girls, coincidentally all having wide downhill skis with a chicken on the tip. Marg liked to call it the sign of the chicken because of our panic near the mogul hills. When the ski season ended, for some unknown reason we became besties.

Internet dating had never been Marg's thing. Tingle was way too brash and bold for someone of her timid nature. Even the three-date rule was too trashy for her. Not that she disliked making out, in fact, she was hot to trot. Raised a conservative woman, Marg wanted to know the guy before she became intimate. She lived at home for years before she married that weirdo Boris, a sociopath with serious obsessions.

By the time she had a child with him she realized he was weak—a power-hungry man trying to control her life with verbal and physical abuse. At that point she found a lawyer, and started divorce proceedings. Fortunately, after she lost her house in the divorce, she came into an inheritance that allowed her to send her only daughter to a boarding school and move to Cozumel.

When Libby decided to live with Boris, Marg began her single life. She met Manni on an island tour and embarked on a relationship with a man who appreciated her, or so she thought at the time.

Lunch was at the Rock'n Java down the street from my condo building. It's not easy to forget seeing a dead woman. After a horrendously stressful night, it was a relief to wander past the hotel lobbies and gift shops, window browsing on the way.

In Canada, they have a law prohibiting the capture and sale of dolphins. Not so here. I passed dolphins kept in a large pool. If a person liked bloody cockfights and traditional bullfights, Mexico was the place to go.

The island needed change. I thought this once again as a horse-drawn buggy passed on Rafael E. Melgar. It was a sweltering humid day yet the carriage was filled with overweight tourists pulled by one tired horse.

I wiped the sweat from my brow as a guy ran out of his shop, a bracelet in his hand.

"For you, señorita. You are so beautiful. Please wear this bracelet I made." The man was casually dressed in khaki trousers and a white golf shirt. His brown eyes sparkled as he smiled brightly. "It is for the ankle. Can I put it on for you?"

"Yes, gracias," I said, presenting my foot. The turquoise bead string tied on easily yet his fingers lingered at my ankle. "My name is Josef. And yours?"

"Adie. You can call me Adelina."

"A pleasure, Adelina!" Josef grinned winningly. "Will you come in? I have turquoise and diamond jewelry inside." He gestured to the shop door. "Earrings, necklaces and bracelets."

"Another day, gracias. I'm meeting a friend at the Java."

"Do you have a novio? If not, perhaps you would consider—"

"Sorry, but I have someone in my life." I smiled, not meaning to sound too abrupt but I hardly wanted to get into a discussion about my relationships. I didn't want *another* guy.

The slim dark-haired man flashed me a white smile. "Have an enjoyable day, señorita, and if you find your novio unsatisfactory, please come back. I am told I am a charming dinner companion."

"I am sure you are. Nice to meet you, Josef."

"Hasta luego, Adelina."

"Adios!"

A block further, I saw the sign out front for the Rock'n Java and entered the restaurant. A counter for baked goods had tasty buns, pies and cupcakes for sale. I had to walk around the lineup in front of the cash register to get to the tables. Marg was seated by the window overlooking the Caribbean. I'm glad she decided to sit at a table with a view. Since the Java was situated next to a naval base it was plus to be able to watch the sailors disembark from the navy ships.

It had been a while since I had last seen my friend. Marg's hair was the way I remembered it—brown shoulder-length, streaked with red in a layered style. Before I took her to Alejandro, she sported a boring blunt cut that covered her face most of the time hanging like a drab curtain over her cheeks. He improved her appearance massively. Marg was looking attractive without the heavy square black-framed glasses that usually dominated her narrow face. Instead, she wore contacts but kept blinking as if there were foreign objects in her eyes. Her eyes were wide-set and gray, noticeable with the contacts. She wore a denim jumper, mid-calf length, a blue T-shirt underneath and dreary navy-blue clogs.

"Marg," I said, giving her the customary double cheek air kiss when she rose from her chair. She was more precise with these air kisses than I was, but understandingly so as she'd been living here for a few months now. "How's it going?"

"If you're asking about Manni and me—don't! I'm done with him!" She groaned, "I am so sick of men. They're so kind at the beginning, full of compliments but once they win you over, they expect a slave in the kitchen and never say anything nice."

"But look at the bright side, you're here in Coz in the tropics."

"Yup, I like the weather just fine but," Marg tossed her hair defiantly, "I've got to move out of my rental and get a house. Can't stand the neighbors."

"Oh?" Distractedly, I picked up a menu but already knew I'd go for the eggs. Lucky for Marg, she was way better off financially than I was. She could afford a condo in the Erizo del Mar.

"I've decided I'm changing my life." Marg studied the menu. "My mom passed last year, Libby is in boarding school and spends vacations with Boris, so I am free as a bird."

"You haven't repaired your relationship with Libby, have you?"

"Libby says she hates me."

"Teenagers hate everybody."

"Apparently, the divorce ruined her life." Marg waved the menu as if she was swatting away an annoying wasp. "I'm giving her space. I can't take all the temper tantrums, always blaming me. She visits her dad and doesn't see his anger management problem."

"Libby likes staying with Boris?"

"No, not really, but most of the time she stays with Ellen when she has a holiday."

"Isn't she too old for a babysitter?"

"Ellen is like a grandma to her since my mom died. She's respectful to Ellen."

"She is?" Libby used to be a great kid once, but she changed from a nerdy techie to an entitled princess with a gutter mouth.

The waiter came over and asked if we wanted coffee. It was the magic word. Marg had a serious coffee addiction. She nodded vigorously.

Coffee was okay and necessary to prop my eyes open but my addiction was chocolate, and men who were creamy delicious, like chocolate. They didn't have to be rich, just gainfully employed. I didn't need anyone leaching off me, to live in the custom they dreamed of. I needed an independent male that could hold his own.

"For you, señorita?"

"Coffee, orange juice and I'll have the eggs over and hard with bacon, por favor."

Marg looked up, her expression dazed. "Same."

Was she on anti-depressants again? Her skin was pale and even with the makeup and great hair, she looked worse than I did the morning after clubbing. A breakup with Manni must have sent her into a downward spiral.

As a psychiatric social worker, she was a firm believer in mood enhancement through drug therapy. Marg had taken Xanax during her separation for her depression and could hardly remember any of it.

Marg waited for the server to leave before she whispered, "I need a man."

I gasped. Marg was not the type to need a man.

"I really do, Adie."

Where had I heard this before? Of course, Carmelita had said the very same thing at Hemmingway's but unlike Marg, she was a big game hunter. Carmelita took the man she wanted with no hesitation.

"I could take you somewhere to find one."

Marg's eyes widened. She reached across the table and grasped my hand. "Could you, Adie? That would be fab. But you can't go to bars now that you're with Wolf, can you? He wouldn't allow it, would he?"

"He's not the controlling type."

"Oh, really? I doubt that." Marg raised a finely arched brow in disbelief. "Believe me, they all are."

At that moment the server arrived with coffee, juice and eggs, placing them carefully on the table. Then he stood and waited for us, not wanting to interrupt. "Anything else, señoritas?"

I shook my head. Marg said, "Sweetener?"

The waiter nodded and grabbed a bowl from the bar filled with yellow packages and set it on our table. "Well, are you allowed?"

I sighed. Marg was like a fifties housewife trapped in a time warp. Had she ever heard of women's rights? "Wolf doesn't own me. Besides we aren't engaged—just working on our relationship. He gave me a condo."

"Oh my. He's getting just like that user Alvarez."

I ignored her. I knew she disliked Diego.

"Wolf said when I'm ready, I could move my clothes into his place but with all this stuff going on—" My voice trailed off, remembering too late not to mention the whole Linda thing.

Marg leaned forward eagerly, nearly tipping her coffee. "Stuff going on? Spill, girlfriend."

I frowned, not sure I should. Marg was a great friend but had a tendency to have loose lips.

"Nothing."

I got the raised eyebrow again. I thought she was done with the subject when she calmly picked up her fork and knife to cut the eggs. From the way she attacked the breakfast I could tell she hadn't eaten much lately. She had this tendency to eat nothing or something strange like radishes for breakfast. Marg loaded her fork and swallowed a chunk of bacon. With a happy sigh, she lifted another load and brought her eyes to me. "I am your best friend. You can trust me not to tell anyone." She held her hand up. "I swear."

Slowly, I sipped my orange juice. "It would blow your mind."

Marg held her fork in mid-air. "You found a murder victim?"

Sometimes Marg knew me better than anyone. "I did, but I shouldn't say anything."

"Get out! I can't believe it, not again!"

I nodded.

Marg shoved in another mouthful and chewed more thoughtfully this time. "Are you in trouble with the police?"

"They don't know, at least not yet."

Marg whispered, "You're kidding! There's a dead body out there somewhere?"

"Um-m."

"Why don't the police know?"

"They didn't want to report it."

"Who didn't? How could they not?"

"It's complicated."

"Tell me everything."

"Wolf has a brother named Heinz. I hadn't seen him for years, but he's here in Cozumel now and manages the Erizo del Mar condo project. His ex was murdered in Heinz's condo."

"Eew!" she squeaked.

"Ssh!"

"Did he kill her?"

"Heinz was struck on the back of his head. When I walked in, he was semi-conscious."

"He didn't kill her?"

"Heinz only looked guilty because Linda was dead in *his* condo."

Marg perked up excitedly. "Then who?"

"Keep your voice down or I can't tell you anymore. I shouldn't have said anything as it is."

"Sorry, I was just surprised. I promise to speak quietly," Marg murmured softly.

"Linda was a beautiful woman—not a nice person, but she was attractive. I walked in and found Heinz on the floor. I didn't notice the body right away. When I did, it was awful. Linda was halfway into the fish tank, fish swimming through her hair."

"What! In an aquarium? You must be kiddin'?"

"No, I'm not. Her long red hair was floating around like seaweed. Her dead eyes were just staring." I shuddered, replaying Linda's demise in my mind.

Marg's jaw dropped. "Why didn't you call the police?"

"This is Mexico. The police are not like the police at home. They like throwing people in jail. They would probably have arrested Heinz in Canada too, I'd bet. The husband is the first one they look at for the crime. Once they make an arrest here the suspect ends up behind bars. It could take months for it to come to trial. Anyway, he was set up. He didn't do it and neither did I."

"The police would blame you?"

"Maybe. Hernandez doesn't like me and Heinz pointed out my fingerprints were all over the place."

"And Linda? Where is she now?"

I shrugged. "Diego's men took her away.

"What does Alvarez have to do with it?"

"I couldn't reach Wolf. So, I contacted Diego. He always knows what to do in a tricky situation. Besides, he's an investor. He didn't want me involved. The condo project would get bad publicity and I might be arrested."

"I should have known. That guy is unscrupulous, Adie. I don't care how rich he is."

"There's something else, Marg. He still wants to marry me."

"You'd be crazy to marry Alvarez. Sure, some consider him handsome, I know, even super hot and rich as Croesus but he's scum. I guess, though, in this case, he was trying to protect you. What about Wolf?"

"He believes Heinz is innocent. Mind you, there's more to this."

"Huh?"

"Heinz was attacked the other night. Diego's brother and I rushed in to help. Two thugs were beating up Heinz."

Marg pursed her lips. "Diego's brother, eh?"

"His name is Cy. He was my scuba master. That's how we met. He's a friend."

"Really?" Marg stared at me. "You can't pull the wool over my eyes. He's a person of interest."

"Huh?"

Marg pointed. "To you! I can tell when you think someone is sexy."

"Naw, he's a friend, that's all." I tore into my eggs. The bacon was just right—crispy yet tender but my breakfast was cooling down. Marg had to starting doing the talking or I would have a cold breakfast. "Enough of this. Tell me why you're not with Manni anymore."

"I don't want to talk about him. He broke my heart. End of story."

Her eyes blinked rapidly. Maybe, Marg needed to wear her glasses. Obviously, she was not motivated enough to adjust to contact lenses. Right now, she looked like a petrified bunny getting tested by a mascara company.

"What?" I asked, seeing her stare steadily in my direction, the flicker gone, at least for the moment.

Marg gobbled up the last bits of her breakfast and washed it down with the coffee. "You need help, right?"

"For what?"

"To find the killer."

I chewed my eggs thoughtfully. Wolf wouldn't want me involved in this, but Linda didn't deserve to die and then get bundled up like a bag of potatoes to be dumped somewhere like garbage. "Well, I am going to investigate but I don't know if you can help."

"You have a plan, right?"

"Kind of."

Marg pointed to herself. "I am your woman. I can work undercover."

It was an idea—maybe a stupid one. She could snoop around. Marge was a bullet when she wanted to be. Smarter than you'd think to look at her and the point in her favor was—no one knew her or would suspect she was looking for information. With my guidance she could ask the right questions, but first, I would need to prepare her.

After we paid the bill, we headed down the street. "What about going to a party?"

"Oh, I don't know. I haven't got any clothes for that."

"Or for a singles bar either, I suppose."

Marg shook her head sadly.

"I think I know who can fix that."

My hairdresser, Alejandro, had expanded his shop to include a clothing boutique with expensive gowns. He assisted Carmelita when she had a fashion show. This man could work miracles.

Believe me, Marg would stand out like a sore thumb the way she dressed. If she was to help, she had to blend in to the crowd of elitists coming to the party. The crème de la crème of Cozumel society would be here. No one would be wearing T-shirts and jeans or denim anything.

Our arms entwined, we set off to find the fashion guru. I wasn't sure where his shop was on Avenida 5 but I thought it was near the bakery.

On the sidewalk a woman with a towel wrapped around her neck wandered out of a doorway. Liquid blotches, like car oil were splattered randomly in her short hair.

"Hola," I said. "We are looking for a hairdressing salon, slash boutique.

The woman looked disoriented. "I'm getting my hair done." She pointed at the sign above the frame, "Confianza" written in fancy script.

I eyed her hair. "Color?"

"Yup, lowlights, but I forgot my wallet. My car is down the street. Sorry, don't know 'bout a boutique."

"No problem. This could be it." I scanned the sign above the door.

"What does *Confianza* mean, Adie?" Marg asked puzzled. She was at a beginner level in Spanish. I wasn't much better.

"Confidence, I think."

A heavy squat woman poked her head out the door. She had a broad face, a hooked nose, plump lips, big dark eyes and thickly tattooed eyebrows. "Come in señoritas, you will get plenty of confidence with a treatment from this salon." She gave us the once over. "I have time to cut." She gestured for us to enter the shop.

Marg nudged me. "I thought we were looking for your friend?"

"We are looking for Alejandro. Do you know him?"

"Dios mio! He is famous! I am Augustina. You are in the right place." Then she whispered, "Very few get the privilege of his cut. He is señorita Bolivar Alvarez's personal stylist." She twisted her hands. "I am not certain he will see you."

"I would appreciate if you would ask. I am Adie Sturm, a friend of Carmelita Bolivar Alvarez."

Augustina clamped a hand over her mouth. "Hah! I know who you are!" She smiled surreptitiously. "They say señor Bolivar Alvarez wants to marry and he has chosen you."

A lithe young man in tight black jeans and a fuschia short sleeved shirt came to the door. "What's up, chica? Did you forget you work here?"

The man had a girlish face, full lips, hazel eyes framed by long lashes and a fade with a blond high top. When he saw me, he was ecstatic.

"Adie, you're back! We must give you the full treatment so that señor Bolivar Alvarez swoons when he sees you next."

I moved in for air kisses and then stepped back. "That's what I need, a cut from the expert. May I introduce my friend, Marg. You gave her a makeover a while ago but now we need your help again."

Alejandro's forehead wrinkled into number eleven lines as he considered Marg and then his eyes shot back to me. "You need it even more, Adelina, since you have the heart of señor Bolivar Alvarez.

"Hair and clothes, Alejandro, for my friend. Styling and a trim for me. We need some of Carmelita's designs to choose from for Marg. There's a party at the villa tonight so we need to get right at it. Can you help?"

Alejandro gave Marg an appraising glance. "My boutique is in the back. It's only open for the select few. Who will pay for the dress?"

"Marg has the money."

"Oh, my! It's not in my budget, Adie."

"Come on, seriously? You have an inheritance and knowing what you're like, you haven't spent a dime yet, have you? It's all safely tucked in a bank account?"

"Yes, I dare not withdraw anything on that type of account." Marg's eyes darted away, frightened like a trapped bat. "I don't want to end up penniless and alone."

"You will if you don't buy some clothes. Alejandro will use your credit card. You can afford it."

Alejandro interceded. "I can rent a dress to you. How is that? Maybe $400 dollars for the night?"

"Wow, pricey!"

I nodded. "Marg, you only live once. I imagine this gown is worth a couple of thousand. Am I right, Alejandro?"

"True, all the gowns are $2000 or more."

Marg sighed. "Ok, but not the most expensive rental, okay, Alejandro?"

Alejandro wasn't listening. He shot out of the room for the boutique in the back.

Augustina spoke up. "Go follow him. He will select the dress, with your approval of course and then hurry back for a shampoo. Luisa will do that." She indicated the tiny slender girl standing by the sinks wearing a green apron over a white dress.

In the back room, Alejandro held up a gold lamé fitted dress, angled to mid-calf and then a pale powder-blue ballerina type gown, cinched at the waist. "Try these," he said holding them out to Marg, who grabbed them hastily, fumbled and dropped them on his ivory marble floor.

Augustina shot down on the floor like a startled deer. She gave Marg an eye roll when she retrieved the dresses, holding them gingerly like precious treasures before motioning Marg to go to the fitting room.

After ten minutes of waffling, I decided the ballerina outfit was all wrong. It made Marg look like she was pregnant and dumpy. It had to be the tight gold lamé dress.

"With hair and makeup, she will fit into the crowd, no problem," Alejandro said seriously.

A while later we were out the door, Marg carrying her new dress, a big smile plastered on her face like she was about to go to her high school prom.

***

Cars lined the circular driveway. Sleek, expensive European imports in unobtrusive shades of silver. Towering emperor palms partially obstructed my view of an ivory mansion with a red-tiled roof. On the right, a six-car garage was attached to the villa. Through the lime trees, there was a glimpse of tennis courts and the glint of blue from a pool. Diego owned a fleet of sports cars and there was a limousine for when he preferred to work in the car or had a guest. Luis or Churo would drive him.

Once we started walking the scent of bougainvillea in the garden wafted towards us in the warm moist breeze. From somewhere within the grounds, I heard soft guitar music and the garble of voices.

Multi-colored lanterns were strung into the palms, the fronds swaying with the ocean breeze, stronger now at night but pleasantly cooling on the skin. Moonlight reflected on the cobblestone walkway as I approached the villa on Wolf's arm while Marg rested her hand on his other elbow.

He was the perfect escort in an black tuxedo, formal white silk shirt and slim trousers. If he'd worn a bowtie, I would have mistaken him for James Bond, heading to the casino, his white-blond hair combed back from his forehead, a captivating smile on his full lips. Glancing up, the lighting lent mystery to his asymmetrical face. He was a head taller but with four-inch heels I was able to lift my head easily for a kiss if an opportunity arose.

Wolf usually wore a black T-shirt and jeans. He disliked the formal look but the opening of the Erizo was this type of event. Wolf could be a chameleon when he wanted to be.

"How kind of you to take me to this party, Wolf," Marg murmured shyly to my boyfriend.

"My pleasure. I hope you enjoy it. Alvarez has a good spread. No one goes away hungry."

"Take it easy on the drinks though," I warned. "Diego's bartender tends to be heavy-handed with the booze."

Wolf's lips curled up at the ends. "Have fun." He checked her out. "You will knock them dead tonight."

Marg smiled. "Thank you!" Then she whispered in my ear, "I will see what I can find out about the investors. I have pictures of them on my cell and their names for the undercover operation."

I hadn't told Wolf that Marg knew about Linda. She was smart enough not to blab, or at least I hoped so.

Wolf turned to Marg. "Please, enjoy the party. Excuse us."

"Sure. I'll go grab a drink."

Wolf waited for her to go. "You are super hot tonight, Adie. Red is your color."

I could feel the heat in my cheeks, something a drop-dead gorgeous man with a husky voice can easily do.

"And you are extremely handsome. By the way, how is Heinz doing?"

"I got a doctor to check him. He has a concussion, feels dizzy, and has trouble keeping food down. I still haven't got the whole story out of him." He stooped to kiss my lips. "I'll see you later. Stay out of trouble, okay?"

I nodded. Let him do what he had to do. I was eager to find out who was behind Linda's murder.

7

Marg didn't really understand. Heinz was the good brother but had turned evil, just like in the Mexican soap she saw daily. Apparently, Wolf was the good brother. That's all she gleaned from that conversation, except that was not so true now. Maybe it was never true. It was something Adie had told herself to justify falling in love with the wrong guy.

Years ago, Adie told her about Wolf, the bad boy—seducing women, being seduced, driving super fast and getting into a motorcycle accident that nearly killed him.

She sighed. Adie had been involved with him in her teens but it fizzled out before anything started. It was only a matter of time. When she met Wolf again, she fell for him. Her weakness was bad boys.

Never mind that. Adie had given her an assignment. Marg was to connect with the investors, basically a reconnaissance mission. She was thrilled. Her life had been so humdrum after she split with Manni, this was exactly the type of adventure she needed.

Marg and Manni were like hummingbirds that buzzed around dizzy in love but became disoriented only to fly off in different directions, never to mate. It was mishandled but it was so romantic. Marg missed the comfy times. They would watch the sunset on the beach, holding hands, eating assorted chocolates. Manni would drink deeply from a beer bottle just like a hummingbird sucking the nectar out of a hibiscus.

Still, she didn't mind being here, especially since she was on a mission. No one was a better friend than Adie. She always got her out of trouble and now it was her turn to help. This trouble Adie was in was serious enough for her to get arrested as an accomplice in a murder. It had to be something bad Heinz was involved in and he had managed to drag Adie into it. So what if Adie had Cy Bolivar Alvarez to assist her in the investigation? No one should trust a Bolivar Alvarez. Adie made her believe that Cy was different from his brother Diego Bolivar Alvarez. He was a filthy rich criminal, manipulating the law and all the individuals on this island.

Marg was a superspy or maybe Supergirl. She could see herself flying through the air, bouncing her powerful fists off bad guys and watching them splatter on the pavement below in a puddle of blood.

Marg scanned the buffet—sushi, chicken and lobster displayed in abundance. With a plate in one hand she scooped up tasty morsels to consume with the other, disregarding the butter that dripped on her designer gown. After she had downed two powerful margaritas, she didn't care about a stain or two.

It was like she had been let loose on a skydiving excursion flying solo into the wide expanse of sky. Marg wanted to trap some bad guys. They all thought they were above the law but she would catch the rogue player. It would be especially satisfying to find evidence to incriminate Diego Alvarez.

In her clutch purse she had photos of the investors. Each one had to be investigated, the evidence given to Adie for her friend to figure out. Who gained from killing Linda?

"Hola, chica! Can you put me on your plate, carino?" a tall man called out from behind her.

Marg gazed up at a dark-haired guy. He was a seven or maybe an eight on her scale that rated Wolf a ten. He had brown eyes, a short nose, and was clean shaven. He was attractive in his white jacket, over a white shirt, tucked into tan trousers. Neat and clean. She liked that. He hadn't gone all out like Wolf to dress in evening wear, yet he wasn't likely to be at a food truck getting his dinner. Maybe, this is what a really rich guy wore to an evening party. She could go for him. Come to think of it, Adie had a man that liked to wear white on her list of suspects, someone who wasn't Diego Bolivar Alvarez. Adie nicknamed this investor Mr. Clean. What was Mr. Clean's real name? She scratched her head, willing her brain to function.

"Is your name Luis?" Marg said the name quickly, remembering what she thought was Mr. Clean's first name. She could hardly pull out her cell and check with him standing right there staring at her.

"As a matter of fact, that is my name."

"Really? What a coincidence."

"Yes, my precious," said the stranger. "What should I call you?

You look like a Maria."

"Close enough, although I'm not religious anymore. For a while I was Catholic when my boyfriend wanted to marry me, but we broke up." For a few seconds she almost let her emotions take over. A tear flooded her eye. She sniffed. "My name is Marg."

"Nice to meet you, Marg. Short for Margarita, sí? Why do you search for Luis?"

Marg's eyes grew distant as she tried to focus. She wanted to help Adie without giving away too much information. "I heard he had some real estate on the island. Do you know about any condos, ocean front near Corpus Christi?"

"Oh, yes, I know of some. Many expats live in that area."

"Do you know of the condo building called Erizo del Mar? It looks grand."

"It is."

Marg peered at the man. He did look like the photo Adie had sent. He was dressed in white and was a trifle thin.

"Have you tried one of these?" He held up an orange-hued cocktail for her to sample. "I have a treasure to share with you."

"What treasure?" Marg inquired innocently, taking the drink he offered.

The sinewy man peered at her low-cut dress, tiny brown eyes bright as a bird's and said in a dramatic voice, "I will make you come alive. Come." Snatching up her hand he led her to the villa.

Marg went along a bit hesitantly but what could possibly happen in this fabulous place? It was so romantic with the palms swaying in the breeze and atmospheric lighting from the decorative granite Japanese lanterns, positioned along the mansion and around the pool.

Together they wandered down a wide hall painted white, skylights above, directing moonlight unto a polished marble floor. Their footsteps echoing as they headed to a lounge on the right. There a grouping of plush white leather couches was situated along with a heavy oak coffee table and matching end tables under dim lighting recessed into the walls and ceiling. The floor was covered by a thick woven multi-colored Indian area rug.

The paintings on the wall were signed Kahlo and Rivera, most likely very expensive originals. Marg knew nothing about art but the modernistic brilliant colored themes of a woman holding a naked man had her fascinated. Even Marg knew the jade statue on the coffee table, glyphs of Mayan gods around the base, was worth a king's ransom. Combined with the canvases on the walls she would estimate Alvarez had invested millions in art. This was outrageous, she fumed. The man was an evil devil that did not deserve a life of privilege.

The Bolivar Alvarez villa was loaded with antiquities, every corner and shelf displaying items that had to be real. Marg stood there and gawked at a bowl in red clay of mythical animals circling, holding each others' tails. She knew they shouldn't be in this room. She glanced around nervously.

What if the devil himself, Santiago Francisco Bolivar Alvarez appeared? He would be angry. Who knows if he knew Luis? It would be embarrassing if Diego caught her here. He could accuse her of casing the room for a theft. Nothing was beneath him. He disliked her as much as she detested him.

Unfortunately, he could wrap Adie around his little finger. Marg, on the other hand was more likely to give him her middle finger than talk to that self-centered rich slime, yet she had to remember she was on his turf. He had security guards. They could toss her out if he commanded it. That would put an end to her espionage. Adie would be so disappointed in her. She owed that girl her freedom from Boris. It was time to start spying but not to be stupid about it.

"I think we should go. We don't want to be caught in this room, Luis. Diego Bolivar Alvarez is a scary gangster. He has no sense of what is right. He could have us thrown into jail if he found us here."

"*Tranquilo, carino.* No one will notice." He plopped down on the leather sofa and spread his legs. "Make yourself comfortable and relax. Sit here on the couch beside me. You will enjoy this."

He leaned forward, busying himself at the coffee table taking out a small baggie of white powder and placing a portion of it on the table. He took out a ten-dollar bill from his billfold and rolled it up while Marg watched. "Here we are," he said, indicating the line of white powder on the table.

"What is that?" she said puzzled. This man was doing something they did in those TV crime shows.

He placed the rolled-up bill over the powder and snorted some up his nose. "Watch and learn."

The next few moments were ecstatic exhilaration. Marg was seeing colors. The room was spinning. She plopped herself into a high back blue-velvet wing chair. Luis finished the powder and sat on the armrest leaning into her. She felt his lips on her neck and his hand stroking her thigh. He was on her as enthusiastically as a colony of E-coli on room temperature Canadian beef. As his hand travelled over her dress, they were interrupted by a big hulk of a man.

***

"In here, señorita Sturm," a loud voice boomed. "This lady went into the villa with a man. I remembered she came in with you so I set out to search for you before throwing them both out. It is my opinion he was up to no good, possibly dragging her into his dirt."

"Thank you, Churo. I was worried when I couldn't find her."

"Look, there she is!" Churo saw the traces of white powder on the table. "We do not allow drugs in the villa, señor."

"Watch your tone, man. I am Leo Del Socorro. My cousin is in business with señor Bolivar Alvarez. I am sure you would not want to offend señor Del Socorro. There is a great deal of money involved in this project."

"I think I need to leave," Marg said softly. She stood unsteadily.

Taking hold of Marg's wrist as he got on his feet, Leo Del Socorro ordered her. "You will stay."

"Let her go."

Marg recognized the confident voice of her bestie. "Adie!"

Leo didn't give up. "We were enjoying each other's company, lady, when you and this giant rudely interrupted."

"Well, get this, buster, she's not available!"

I pushed Marg aside and kicked the man's knee lightly, unbalancing him. With his thumb in my grip I pulled him to the side, shooting him out like a cannonball back onto the couch.

Marg stood dumbfounded, her eyes blinking.

"Come on, Marg, we're leaving." I spun Marg about. "This way!" With all my power I directed her ahead down the hallway to the door. I shouted over my shoulder at the massive square-faced security guard. "Thanks, Churo!"

Sliding my heels as if I was ice skating, I skimmed the slippery marble flooring, propelling Marg out the door back into the buzz of the party.

I never expected to see Marg go into the villa for a snort of cocaine, especially with the skinny dude. She only used pharmaceuticals. This behavior wasn't like her. She was a straight arrow. "What the heck are you thinking? You have to be more aware. These people do drugs!"

"Okay, yes, I was foolish. I really didn't know what that stuff was. Sorry, Adie, but the cocktails were so strong. They left me befuddled."

"You can say that again!" I shouldn't blame her. Marg could never go undercover to find out anything. She was a psychiatric social worker from Canada. A babe in the woods, a naïve innocent.

I was the one who was stupid. Who was this Leo creep? He seemed to be acquainted with the villa and a certain investor by the name of Leon Luis Ruiz Del Socorro, the Texas oil man, costumed as a bad-boy rocker. This tool was the druggie's cousin. I was more than disappointed to learn that cocaine was being used in the villa. Maybe, Diego didn't know. Well, if he was unaware, I was sure Churo would tell him. No one protected Diego like Churo. He might be unappealing on the outside, with a face only his mother could love, but he had a heart of gold and the loyalty of a guard dog.

"Adie, I'm sorry. I got carried away. I'm not used to," Marg waved her arms around widely at the party scene, the bright lights, the dancing, the active buffet and bar, "all this glam! I'll focus on our targets. I promise."

I looked into Marg's eyes, dilated pupils in the light of the lanterns around the pool. "Stay away from the margaritas, okay? Drink water. Eat something. Do you want me to stay with you?"

"No, I will be more careful," Marg muttered.

I hoped Marg wouldn't get paranoid in her coked-up state. I vowed to keep an eye out for her before saying, "I'll talk to you later, but if you need me, call me, and I'll get you," I said, turning the volume up on my cell, before sticking it back into my purse and heading in the direction of the main bar.

Brick Shithouse leaned on the counter swishing a bottle of Sol in his hand, talking to the attractive Latina barkeep.

This guy was a player. Carmelita wasn't enough for him, obviously. When a tall Latina with an elegant neck and slender body, a diamond bracelet on her wrist, wearing a red off the shoulder gown appeared, he stopped talking to the bartender and cozied up to this new morsel of interest. Was she the art collector investor?

I took out my cell phone to refresh my memory. I pressed on my notes. Bingo! Yes, she was. This was Perla Bravo Gonzales, the art collector. A beautiful brunette, hair piled high on her head, coal-black eyes surrounded by long curled lashes and wearing a flattering red dress, different from mine. Where her dress was flouncy, and an expensive Carmelita gown, mine was a Victoria's Secret, backless, clingy, ruched on the skirt and a deep claret.

On the other side of Brick, a woman stood, her back to me, her auburn tresses curling down to her waist almost to the top of her enhanced butt cheeks tightly encased in a low-backed black satin dress. She was easily recognizable. It was that python, Daniella.

The body-builder's name was Ed, although I fondly referred to him as Brick Shithouse, last name forgotten. I scrolled down my notes on my cell for his surname. Ed Marion, the lawyer, from Cancun, defender of dubious criminals. I shouldn't judge the man. My recent involvement with Heinz and his dead wife was not something I wanted to be part of. If the police wanted me for the murder, I might need the defence of someone with the reputation of Ed Marion.

As I stood there watching, a soft voice whispered in my ear, "This is almost déjà vu, isn't it, chica?" Carmelita had stepped up beside me. She was giving the group a once-over. "Should I try to snatch Ed away? I think I fancy him."

"Only if you really want to. He's a player."

"Then he and I will have much in common. I hate to commit myself to one man at this point in my life. It would be interesting to get to know this man. I can see myself running my fingers down his chest, to his abs and then—"

"All right. I get the picture, Carmelita. You should indulge yourself. I, myself, am more interested in getting to know the other investors."

"Oh? Why?"

I pursed my lips. I had said too much. It wouldn't be wise to tell her but I needn't have worried she was honing in on the group, already forgetting what I had just said.

"Come, chica, we will get to know them, the men, I mean. I am not interested in the women." Carmelita charged ahead, eager to start over with Ed Marion. She waved for me to follow.

"I'll join you, in a bit." Just then a husky voice murmured softly, his cheek close to mine. "I have been waiting to speak to you alone, mi amor."

A whiff of his citron-scented cologne told me it was Diego. His voice, his slight British accent and his intimate gestures were all part of his persona. He had gone to Oxford for his law degree, coming from a wealthy family with no inclination to pinch pennies when it came to the education of their offspring. I was not immune to his tall lean body outfitted in a classic white tuxedo or his symmetrical good looks either. He was so different from Wolf yet interesting in his own way.

"Have you discarded him yet?" Diego's hazel eyes sparkled. "Are you ready to accept me into your life?"

"If you mean, did I break up with Wolf, the answer is no."

"Then, I'll need to persuade you." He handed me a goblet of dark red wine. "This wine is especially, for you, from my private cellar."

I put my nose into the glass and took a whiff of the bouquet. "Berries."

"And?"

"Of course, chocolate."

"Now drink it, Adelinita."

I swished the red wine in the glass and took a sip letting it coat my tongue. "A full-bodied cabernet."

"Yes, you are so perceptive. It is intoxicating, just like you." Diego's eyes swept over my body. "You are exquisite tonight, Adelinita. I don't think Du Lac deserves a woman as fine as you."

"Wolf is not like any man I have ever met."

"Oof!" Diego brought his fist to his heart. "That arrow pierced my heart. Surely, he has hurt you enough? Am I not your savior? What would you have done if I had not appeared to take her away?"

I bit my lip and looked about. I continued in a whisper. "Do you think the police will arrest me? I didn't have anything to do with her. I barely knew Linda. She went out with Heinz when I was a teenager but I haven't seen her in ten years."

"Yet, you have frequently visited Heinz Du Lac's apartment, am I correct? There would be fingerprints there."

"I have been there a couple of times. I suppose the police could find prints. I agree, I do owe you for this. It was an innocent encounter on my part. I heard shouting and came to help but I know the police wouldn't see it that way."

Diego smiled slyly. "They would think you were having a love affair with Du Lac's brother and she was jealous. You struck her on the head and pushed her into the aquarium to finish her off."

"Your imagination is running wild."

"Or perhaps you were having an affair with the brother and he killed her so he could be with you."

Adie laughed. "Which Du Lac killed her?"

"Whichever. One Du Lac is the same as the next. Now a Bolivar Alvarez is way more to your taste."

"You think?" I rolled my eyes. "Do you have any more possible scenarios?"

Diego moved in closer to my ear. "Only one. We are having a passionate love affair and you finally say yes to my proposal."

His breath felt warm on my skin. A fire coursed through my body.

My Hormone Voice got all excited. "Take him. You need to spread your wings and fly before you get hitched permanently."

Logical Voice stepped in to argue. "You are insane. Diego has dubious connections. Didn't he answer your cry for help a little too quickly? Linda knew too much and he had her killed. He wants the project to fail, then he could make his move and take you from Wolf."

I pushed him away. "You know Wolf and I are working on our relationship."

"And I am being patient. This relationship of yours has always been unstable. It could detonate at any minute, am I right?"

"I don't think so. We have a bond."

Diego smiled brightly. "And yet it hasn't happened since you broke up with Du Lac. No ring. No engagement."

I had enough of debating my feelings for Wolf. "What can you tell me about Ed Marion?"

Diego raised an eyebrow. "He can get anyone out of prison but at a price. Good man to have on your side."

"Is he married?"

"Divorced. Three times, I think." He winked. "Not your type."

"And my type is?"

"A tall dark handsome man crazy for you." Diego held his glass high. "A toast to my future."

"Only yours?"

"Ours—my lovely Adelinita. Whenever you say yes!"

"Let's drink to a successful party."

"Aren't they all?" He clicked his glass to mine. "Salud."

I studied Diego's face carefully, hoping he would be truthful. "Was Ed Marion having a fling with Linda?"

"Daniella, I thought." Diego rubbed his chin contemplatively. "However, the man was quite the stud. He might have dated Linda. I saw them together a few times."

"Anyone else?"

"It wouldn't surprise me. Marion is a player."

"Shouldn't you warn Carmelita about him?"

Diego shrugged. "What would be the use? If there are other women, she would be more enthusiastic than ever. She would want to win the competition even if the prize is a plastic ring."

"What about Orlando Keene? Is he here tonight?"

Scanning the patio, Diego's eyes stopped at the bar. He indicated with his chin the heavy man with the moustache wearing a white tuxedo. "The man beside Perla." His eyes narrowed. "If you'll excuse me, I have to go." He picked up my free hand and placed a kiss on my wrist. "The investors are having a meeting shortly. I shall see you in a while, mi amor. Enjoy and mingle. Everyone will want to speak with you."

The crowd parted to let the godfather of Cozumel through. I presumed he was back to wheeling and dealing this time with the gray-haired man, Orlando Keene, the bar owner from Cancun. Standing on Orlando's left was Marg with her back to Diego. Hopefully, she'd leave before Diego saw her. They would most likely argue, or Marg would, so strong was her dislike of him.

If it was time for the investors to assemble, Wolf was no where to be seen. Some of the others were standing around the bar with Diego. Perhaps, Wolf had already gone in. At the door Churo and Luis were motioning investors to enter.

"Buenos tardes." A woman positioned herself before me. Her

eyes twinkled like bright green emeralds. Her lips were full and shapely, beneath a slightly long aquiline nose. A high forehead and dark waves framed an attractive face, with only a few faint wrinkles at the side of her mouth. The lady appeared to be slightly shorter than I am but when I glanced down, I noticed her heels were barely three inches. She was older but I couldn't guess by how much.

Shapely in a green belted gown, draping elegantly to mid-calf, the dress was V-necked, displaying a discreet cleavage. She looked vaguely familiar.

"I am Felicia Francisca Bolivar Alvarez. You must be Adelina?"

Of course, she was Diego's mother. I should have clued in. Felicia's features had been passed on to all her children. Her nose was present in the faces of her sons and her eyes were exotically slanted like Carmelita's. Felicia was a very attractive woman.

"Nice to meet you, senora."

"Call me Felicia."

Her voice was low and husky like a smoker's yet her mouth didn't have smoker lines. Her breath was fresh and she had that Hollywood smile, the same as that of her son, Diego. Usually a smoker would have a yellowish hue to the forefinger and middle finger. Her hands had a French manicure and were extremely pale. She said quietly, "You are exquisite. Diego has good taste. No wonder my son admires you."

"Thank you, your children have inherited your beauty. I heard you were visiting from Mexico City." I added.

"Indeed I am." Felicia smiled. "Regretfully, Santiago needs my guidance in affairs of the heart. In fact, all of my children are regretfully unable to commit. I do worry about Amancio just as much, especially since he abandoned our Import and Exports business to waste his time scuba diving. I am here to steer them in the right direction."

"Carmelita was married."

"True, but it was a miserable marriage. I persuaded her father to find her a good family. His family was not the issue, he was." Felicia's eyes scanned the room. "I suppose it was fortunate there were no children. There is nothing worse than children taking after a selfish father. My husband was reticent but a kind and perceptive man. I wish my children to have a considerate partner who treats them exceptionally well."

"It is hard to find—an enduring love for life. You were lucky."

"True, but not impossible for those who put out the effort."
Felicia stepped closer, her tiger eyes meeting mine. "Are you the
woman for my son?" She pointed a finger up to the ceiling. "Don't
answer me now. Think about it. Diego loves women. He was with
a tall redhead on my last visit." She scanned the room. "I don't see
her here. Quite attractive. A fiery woman who wasn't afraid to
voice her opinion."

"A redhead? Long straight hair?" When Felicia nodded, I was
blown away. Diego had hidden this information. "Linda, Heinz Du
Lac's wife?"

Felicia laughed. "Yes, I believe her name was Linda, an
appropriate Spanish name for her striking good looks. Not Wolf
Du Lac's lady but his brother's, perhaps his ex now. I don't know
anything about her but they seemed close, yet now that you are
back Diego wants to renew your acquaintance, perhaps, even put a
ring on your finger." She glanced at my hand. "I see you haven't
gone that far with Wolf Du Lac, have you?"

Her words bounced like a boomerang in my brain. He never
mentioned he was with Linda. Interesting. Diego had an affair with
Linda and now she was dead. Did she know something about the
condo project that she shouldn't and had to be silenced?

"I would advise you to proceed with caution, whether it is with
Wolf Du Lac, who is quite the charmer or with either of my sons."
When she saw my surprised expression she added, "Carmelita
informed me and of course," she said with a smirk, "I have my
spies."

Felicia may have spies but somehow the murder of Linda had not
been shared.

My eyes shot over to the bar where Diego no longer stood
conversing with the heavy moustached fellow. The art collector
had her hand on his arm and he was smiling. What was up with
that? Was Diego making moves on Perla? Sure, she had a good
head of hair, beautiful thick waves but what did she have that I
didn't? I should get to know this Perla better.

"You see? My son needs to find himself before he picks the
woman who captures his heart."

"I'm sure you know him best."

Felicia smiled smugly. "I do, but do you?" With that she zoomed off into the crowd of partiers.

Was that a challenge from my potential mother-in-law? I shrugged my shoulders. Diego was as delicious as a dark chocolate truffle, which was excellent but my taste also ran to a creamy milk chocolate. No one set me on fire like Wolf. But it had to be more than that. It came down to trust, faith and loyalty in the man. I could appreciate the intelligence in both and each had his own mystique but for now, Wolf was my person.

When I scanned the bar, I noticed Diego and the moustached Orlando had gone, along with Ed Marion, Leon Luis Ruiz Del Socorro and Marg. Perla was having a word with Daniella. I should speak with her.

Setting my wine glass on the nearest waiter's tray I snaked my way through the crowd of elegantly dressed ladies in trendy evening wear. The men wearing tuxedos were just as stylish, the clothing tailor cut. I was impatient to cross this room when suddenly the band struck up a salsa and I was in the middle of the dance floor. A stranger caught up my hand and twirled me about to face him.

"Cy!" It was Diego's brother, and my former dive instructor. He wore a white tuxedo and a black shirt. What a shock to see him dressed up although those years he was CEO and dealt with the Exports end of the Bolivar Imports and Exports company, he must have acquired a formal wardrobe. Recently, he filmed shark activity in Malaysia for a documentary but something drew him back to Cozumel. It could have been anything but I had a feeling Diego had reached out for his help in this condo project.

Cy smiled, twirling me towards him and turned, keeping his arm behind my back. We stepped forward until I was once again spun around. I was a bit out of practise with salsa but with an excellent dancer like Cy, I got the rhythm, slowing down, taking the hint when he raised his eyebrow, frowning. I had to stop doing that— leading my partner. Most of my dance partners needed some guidance but not Cy. I decided I'd let him take the lead.

After a few minutes of rapid salsa, out of breath, I motioned to the bar. Not allowing me to trudge on by my lonesome, Cy offered his elbow and we zigzagged our way through the crowd until finally ending up at the long stand-up bar facing the ocean.

The fronds of the Emperor palms swayed slowly in the breeze cooling my face, pink from dancing.

Cy took my hands and said, "I took you out here to speak about Linda."

"And you think I know something about her death?"

"You are Adie Sturm, the famous detective, aren't you?"

"I am. Do you think I came up with the killer?"

"If not yet, you have some idea, right?"

"Motive, means and opportunity. I have a theory."

"Which you will share with your friend," he pointed to his chest, "me."

I raised my hand to pat him on the back. "Take it easy. It's only a theory. Not a lot of potential yet."

"Come with me. Let's walk. We need to compare notes."

I trod carefully on the uneven stone path in the dim light of the full moon. The lofty palms cast shadows on the charcoal and rose rounded quartz. In front of us the ocean rushed into the sand, white caps frothing as they reached shore pounding their force on the beach.

I reached out my hand to stop Cy.

"What?" he said.

"This place is so beautiful."

Cy stared at the sea, silently.

"When I look out there, I just want to breathe in the air and the atmosphere."

He gently took my hand. "I feel it too. The property has been in our family for decades. After a hurricane, many years ago, my great grandfather bought up land around the island. We built the villa here."

I turned to gaze at the three-story high mansion with the ivory walls, red tiled rooftops and the multi-car garage, surrounded by swaying Emperor palms.

"It's mesmerizing," I said softly.

I felt his hand move my chin upwards to his waiting lips.

It was obvious what his intentions were but I wasn't about to go any further. I dropped his hand and stepped back. There was a wrought iron and wooden planked seat for two facing the path. "Over there. Let's sit."

Cy grinned. "Okay, boss."

"First off, I want to remind you I am working on my relationship with Wolf, remember?"

"Oh, yeah," Cy muttered. "I was trying to forget that little detail."

"Okay, then. You'll need to remember." I gazed into his clear gray eyes. "What have you got?"

"Me?" Cy rubbed his chin. "I have the distinct impression you have something figured out."

"Not exactly. I found out Linda had lots of boyfriends."

"I can believe it. She was like a hunter when it came to men. She'd shoot them in the heart and drag them away to her lair to be eaten." He laughed at his joke.

"Really, Cy?"

"She's slept with all the condo investors."

"Even the fat moustached dude?"

Cy chortled. "Especially him."

"Why?"

"Because she had physical urges."

"Did that include your brother?"

"Why would he?"

"He has urges and he liked her body?"

Cy let out a hoot of appreciation. "More like he liked what she did to his body."

"You make Diego sound like a man 'ho."

"I call a spade a spade, but considering my brother is madly in love with you, he might have resisted her offer."

A husky voice called out, "Adie! Hey, babe." Footsteps sounded on the stone path past the blooming bougainvillea tree and a second later a tall blond Viking warrior appeared, or so he looked like to me. Of course, in the black tuxedo he was more Bond-like. Either way, he was chemistry on legs.

When Cy came into his line of vision he stopped in his tracks and remarked smoothly, "If isn't Amancio Bolivar Alvarez. I thought you were gone on another scuba adventure."

"No can do. I need to clear things up for the Bolivar Alvarez family."

"I see. Maybe you should stick to that. No reason to be bothering Adie, is there?"

Cy's eyes glittered. "Adie is the most interesting female here."

"Didn't anyone tell you Adie is *my* fiancée?"

"I don't see a ring on her finger, hombre. Maybe you need to get yourself to the jewelry store and spend some money."

I stood, holding my hand in the "stop" position. "Before you got here, Wolf, we were discussing Linda. What exactly happened to her after I left?"

"That would be better answered by Alvarez's men. I imagine the police should be on it by now unless—"

Wolf didn't say the rest but I imagined a huge cinder block attached to her legs before she was thrown into the ocean.

I touched Wolf's arm. "Hernandez found the body?"

"I don't know for sure. I didn't have the security guards roll up Linda in a rug, put her in a box and carry her out, but maybe," he shot a look at Cy, "your bro has the inside story. The police get their vacation pay from your family. He told them what to do."

I glanced at Cy. "Do you know? Has Diego heard from Hernandez?"

Detective Hernandez was the chief investigator on murder investigations in Cozumel. Personally, I was of the opinion he had it in for me, big time.

Whenever, there was a murder, it seemed I was the main suspect. Wrong place, wrong time. Unfortunately, in this case, bad luck gave me the opportunity to commit the crime but that didn't make me guilty. Try to convince Hernandez though. For some reason Hernandez liked me for the crime. Beats me why.

I glanced up at Wolf who was staring out at the sea. His voice was so soft I hardly heard him over the breakers. "Heinz was called in. Hernandez spoke with him."

"Heinz has history with Linda. Anyone could report his recent arguments with her to the Cozumel Police." I brushed a tendril of hair away from my eyes. "Do you think he mentioned she came up to the condo? That would for sure implicate him."

"I'm hoping he was sober when he went. Hernandez would not be happy with a jumbled account of when he last saw Linda."

"Heinz was borracho." Cy tapped his fingertips on the metal railing of the wooden chair. "Is your bro an alky?"

Wolf shook his head. "He was always the sober one—the one in control. I had some problems after my accident years ago but he was supportive and told me alcohol was not the solution."

Cy stared at Wolf. "And lately?"

"He's been hitting the bottle. Heinz has been a loose cannon since his split with Linda. Something bad went down."

I frowned. "Have you asked him what?"

Wolf shrugged. "I guess I'll have to." From the direction of the villa, the band started up. He took my hand helping me to my feet. "Say goodbye, Cy."

"See you, Cy."

Wolf took my hand and led me to the dance floor. "Tomorrow, lunch on my boat. Bring Carm."

"And Marg? Is it okay to invite her?"

"Sure. No problem. Now, let's dance."

8

The air was thick with steam rising from the fifty-foot pool. Couples wiggled to the salsa, hips swaying, arms stretched out in all directions, the strobe lights reflecting the faces shiny with perspiration, the colors of the rainbow in the sequins of the dresses. Laughs, screams and shouts reverberated in the midst of party music as the alcohol did its damage.

Usually when I danced, I couldn't think of anything else, especially if my partner was Wolf. The man moved his hips like a native. Rhythm was his middle name. What I liked about salsa is its emphasis on dancing with the lower body, much like horizontal dancing. When I swung around to face him, I had the added attraction of seeing his handsome face. My brain wasn't fully functional when his eyes sparkled blue.

"Your meeting was short!" I shouted above the music.

Wolf nodded. "Heinz didn't come. Hernandez has him at the station."

"Did you try texting him?"

"He must have his phone off. Not much to talk about without the manager to give his input. Alvarez called it off." He swayed behind me, speaking into my ear.

This was a problem. Heinz ran the condo business end. "The investors must be upset."

"No one was happy."

"Do you think he's still at the police station?"

Wolf shrugged.

"Are you going there?"

"I'm thinking about it."

"I want to help with this. A murderer is out there, Wolf."

Wolf nodded, mouth downward cast. He lifted my hand and set me in a double spin. It would have been fun if I could get the gory picture of Linda's head in the fish tank out of my mind, eyes staring blankly like something out of a horror movie.

"Let's find out what Hernandez has before you upset the applecart. I think they found her body."

"I think we should leave. I'll find Marg."

Wolf nodded. "I'll wait at the entrance."

When I surveyed the party, I was at a loss as to where my friend was. Fortunately, I spotted Carmelita. She was with Ed Marion.

Ed had one of those faces that could be handsome enough until you caught his glance. His dark eyes disguised his thoughts but if anyone had demon fire glowing in there, it was him. He was like an underwater predator, a moray eel, dressed up in a white tux, ivory shirt open to the chest, a few too many buttons undone. He was buff under that suit, the coat fitting tightly at the waist. He was built like a weightlifter, massive shoulders, biceps and a six pack. I knew this. I had seen him shirtless and wet at the beach club.

Carmelita was not the only female hot for his attention. Other women had that dazed look when an available steamy male struts his stuff.

Right now, Carmelita was lapping up his compliments, tittering at the right moments. Every once in a while, she squeezed his guns in a familiar manner, enjoying his salacious innuendos. She was cranking up the heat factor. Ed was lapping it up, like a lab eyeing a juicy steak on the BBQ.

The two cousins Del Socorro, aka the Clean cousins, were leaning on the bar near the end, partially obscuring my view, of Marg. When they separated to make a toast, I saw Marg joining in. One look at her and I knew she was shit-faced. I had to get her out of there.

"Hey, Marg! We are leaving."

"You go ahea'," she slurred. "Havin' a good time."

It was one thing leaving a sophisticated woman like Carmelita with the wolves and quite another to abandon an innocent lamb to the Clean boys.

"I need your help, bestie."

"But I—" Marg muttered.

Leo put his face into mine. "You heard her, chick, move on. She wants to stay."

I pushed past him and tugged on Marg's hand. "This is important. I can't do this without you. "You wouldn't bail on me, would you?"

"Fo sho, Adie. Ya need me, fo sho. Bye boys."

I breathed a sigh of relief. The last thing Diego wanted is for me to disrupt his festivities with an unplanned UFC match—Mr. Clean cousins versus Adie Sturm.

Marg started to sing off-key with the music. The band was playing, Guantanamera. "Did ya know this is a song from Cuba, girlfriend? I was told it's a patriotic song. Don't know all the words, Adie, but its classic Sandpipers." She started swaying to the rhythm and snapping her fingers.

"We need to go, Marg." Hurriedly I directed Marg across the floor towards the entrance, relieved that I got her away from the Del Socorro cousins. She was way too high to make any reasonable decisions.

"Are you okay, Marg?"

"Feelin' supa dupa!" Marg swirled around. "Lookit me!" She leaned in close and whispered, "Hey, I found out somethin' about those twins."

I patted her hand. "Sure you did. Come on, Wolf is waiting at the entrance."

"They thought I was so wasted they let somethin' 'bout a key slip."

Stopping abruptly, I asked, "What key?"

"Heinz has it. Leo said so."

"And?"

Marg clutched my arm. "It opens a storage space."

"What's in it?"

Marg blanked. "Don't have a clue but I'm guessin' it's illegal."

"Could it be linked with Linda getting killed?"

Marg swayed, her legs giving way. I grabbed her arm to hold her up.

"My head is spinnin'."

"Too much booze and drugs. Sit," I said, indicating a chair near the entrance. "Are you seeing double?"

"Seein' okay."

Through the crowd, I caught sight of Wolf. I waved him over. "I think we need to get Marg to bed."

Wolf checked out Marg's smudged mascara, smeared lipstick and ultra-white complexion. She looked like the Joker from the Batman movie. The only difference was the tight designer dress—rumpled, a few oil stains visible on the bodice of her gown.

"Marg looks totally wasted."

"She can sleep it off at my condo, so I guess—"

"I know. You can't leave her alone." Wolf grinned. "You take one arm and I'll take the other. We'll get this girl back to safety." On the way out I saw a bucket and snatched it up.

9

On the ride back to the Erizo del Mar, Wolf skimmed the Mexican speed bumps as gently as possible yet the Jeep not known for smooth sailing, thudded along causing Marg to burp and suddenly hurl. I halfway expected this to happen so I was prepared with the bucket held in front of her. This unpleasant episode was short yet painful to watch. The smell was horrendous. My stomach somersaulted.

Once she seemed more settled, I handed her the bucket to hold. This time she was ready for an episode when it came. Another vomit followed and then another. Just when I thought it was all out of her body, Marg upchucked again.

By the time we arrived at the condo building, Marg was wiped, paler than ever, energy depleted. She apologized to Wolf for the smell in the Jeep. His words were kinder than his expression. I think Wolf was glad I was taking care of her and not him. We said our goodbyes quickly before heading into the lobby. The lad at the desk hardly took note of our arrival he was so intent on the music piping in his earbuds. He was bopping up and down in his seat as the elevator closed.

"You okay?" I asked.

"Yes. Sorry for all that. I feel better now."

I patted her arm. "You aren't used to the lives of the rich and famous—drugs and alcohol."

As the doors opened, Marg hung her head. "I need mouthwash. My tongue feels like a rat died in there. Have you got any?"

"No worries." Peering down the empty hallway, I saw a maid's cart. I indicated it with my chin. "Over there. Put the bucket down on the cart for the cleanup staff." I glanced at the goods piled up and checked what was on each level. "I bet she has mouthwash, don't you? Let's look."

Setting the bucket on the bottom shelf, I found a small container of mouthwash amongst the soaps and shampoos.

Marg frowned. "Gross. Poor woman. I wonder what she'll think?"

"I am sure she's seen it all before. Maids are women of the world."

Marg nodded. "I guess so. There must be enough rich and famous condo owners in this place." She glanced at the ivory stucco walls. "Did you notice all the art on the walls? They look like the real thing but they're prints. Ya know Alvarez's villa has paintings, only I'd bet his art is original and pricy."

"Diego has paintings and sculptures from famous artists. Diego is—" My key card went into the slot and when it swung open, I held the door for Marg to enter, forgetting what I wanted to say about Diego.

"Sorry for all this, Adie." Marg trudged in, flopped down on the couch, and parked her feet up on the ottoman. She was white as a ghost.

Joining her on the white leather couch, I said, "If you're not too tired, I'd like for you to fill me in."

Marg sat up. "I told you everything though."

"Tell me again."

"Well, the boys didn't know I was listening. They thought I was out of it but I overheard stuff." She pursed her lips. "I suppose I was only half there but they underestimated me. I listened and retained every word." She pointed her finger at her temple. "In here."

It was hard not to smile at her earnest face. "What exactly was said?"

"Leon told Leo he got this envelope delivered to him at his condo by mistake. It had Du Lac on the outside written in cursive. Leon said he was curious. He could feel a key inside. He thought it was for something important."

"He didn't know what the key was for?"

Marg shook her head. "He had no idea. He didn't find a return address either. The envelope was slipped under his door at the condo. Once he checked inside, he figured it was important enough to return to Heinz, but it seems just as he was leaving, the Cozumel police arrived to pick up Heinz."

"What happened to the key?"

"Leon said that maybe they need to get into Heinz' condo and take the envelope before the police find it."

"Wow! So, they are worried about this key, huh?"

"I'd say. Leo broke out in a sweat."

"Listen, I'll get you some gym shorts and a T-shirt and then I want you to sleep here on the couch." I strode over to the linen closet and took out a pillow and a blanket." Handing them to Marg, I said, "Make yourself a bed and I'll get you the clothes."

In my bedroom I searched the drawers until I found clothes roomy enough for Marg to wear, and then bringing them out, I saw Marg had gotten her act together ready for camping at Chez Sturm's. "Good, you handled that great. You can wear these. It won't be cold. I leave the AC on, but barely. I don't like it too cold. It's nice to know I'm down south. Call me crazy but sometimes I open the windows and let the sea air in."

"Yes, that's weird, all right." She took the clothes and set them down on the couch. "Thanks, Adie." Then she scratched her head and stared at me suspiciously as I headed to the door. "What are you up to?"

"Just a little reconnaissance at the neighbor's place."

Marg's mind must have been clouded by her drug-alcohol experience. "I don't understand. What are you doing?" she said mid-point in undoing her zipper.

I hated to think what Alejandro would say when he saw the dress he had rented to Marg. It slipped to the floor in a pile, rumpled and stained. I knew they could clean it but he had entrusted me with his treasures and I had screwed it up by letting Marg loose in the A-crowd of Cozumel. *Como un elefante en una cacharrería*, came to mind. I had been taking Spanish on-line and ran across that one, translated into an elephant in a china shop.

"Going next door to look around."

Marg picked up the dress and hung it over the leather chair. "For?"

"The key, silly."

"How are you getting in?"

I dangled my key card in my fingers. "This card opens all doors."

"Huh?"

"It's a master key. Get some sleep, eh?"

Marg nodded. "Be careful, Adie."

"Yeah, sure. Anyway, enough chit-chat, I'm off." I left a dim light on by the door and entered the hall.

The ivory hallway walls were shadowy at night. I glanced about nervously as I came to Heinz's condo door. Willing my hands to work, the card slipped in the slot and a green light flicked on. I heard a click and swung the door open.

I was not keen on being inside this particular condo. The police might not know this was the scene of a murder yet, but I did. Clicking on the light switch, I walked into an extremely clean apartment. Nothing was out of place. It was neat and organized. Churo and Luis were better at housekeeping than the maid.

One look at the fish tank, and I could see it was running smoothly as if Linda's head hadn't ever been in there blocking the unsuspecting fish. As I watched, gold marble angelfish flit slowly about amongst the fake coral and skull now that the tank lighting was back on. I wondered what the murderer would have done if he hadn't found a fish tank to dump the body in. My mind worked in the macabre mode. Would Linda have been hung up in Heinz's closet or thrown off the balcony? I shuddered picturing each type of murder.

Taking a deep breath I cleared my mind. Where would Heinz have hidden the key? If this was important and he heard the police outside his door, he might have secured the envelope in an unlikely place. One thing was for sure, he had to have tucked it away quickly.

The safe was in the bedroom closet. If it was there, I couldn't open it. That safe had its own key. I forced myself to think. The linen closet came to mind.

Just inside, I found it filled with sheets, pillow cases and blankets. Checking in between the pillows and blankets I came up with nothing. Trekking over to the bedroom, I decided to go through each drawer of the dresser. Heinz liked his gitches—prints in checks, dog patterns, and Picasso slashes of blue and red. In the corner of this drawer there was a supply of Trojan condoms but still the elusive envelope was not to be found.

As I wandered back into the lounge, I examined every possibility. The area rug seemed out of place somehow. Kneeling down I pulled it until it straightened and as I put the edge down, a brown envelope slid out. Eagerly, I scooped it up.

Inside, was a golden key and a slip of paper with an address written in block letters. This was it! The address was near the airport. Something to investigate tomorrow. Rushing out, I raced to my condo, not keen on being alone in the hall after what happened to Linda. The key card went in and I opened the door. The light I had left on reassured me that all was well. Marg was softly snoring sleeping on her back.

Tiptoeing to my bedroom, I thought about where to hide the envelope. Coming up with nothing I placed the envelope under the area rug next to my dresser. Then I changed out of my gown, putting on a fluffy white robe. Not exactly ready for sleep, I slid the balcony doors open and stepped out to see the ocean and feel the sea breeze on my face. Sparkling lights from the cruise ship reflected on the water. This was the beauty of Cozumel; the place wishes came true. The exception was Linda. Her dreams had died with her.

10

I awoke to a loud banging on my door. I turned over and pulled the sheet over my ears, hoping that it would all go away. Someone was knocking and shouting in Spanish. It was a male voice so there was no way it was housekeeping.

"Adie!" a female yelled. "There's someone out here asking for you!"

"Who?" I screamed back. "Who is it, Marg?"

There was no answer. The commotion in the hall was bad enough for me to grab a robe and pull it on. Was there a fire? I hadn't heard the alarm go off.

I slept in the nude. Nothing was comfortable about clothing in bed, always rumpling up underneath my belly and waking me up. After splashing water on my face, I dabbed off the wet surfaces with a towel and applied mascara and lip gloss. Whoever was out there could wait.

Next, I pulled the ties on the inside of the robe snuggly together before I fastened the belt on the outside. Whoever was outside didn't deserve a free show.

When I entered the living room, I saw my bestie Marg cowering under the blanket on the couch. She eyed me apprehensively, the blanket pulled up over her nose. "Make them stop, Adie! Omigod, my head can't take all this noise," she groaned.

I wasn't eager to see who was causing such a ruckus but the banging and hollering convinced me I had to see who was disturbing my morning. Inhaling with a deep breath, I peeked out the peephole. Two men stood side by side. One of them was very familiar.

Swinging the condo door open, I encountered Detective Hernandez of the Cozumel police. He was medium height, had dark hair and eyes and sported a Hitler-like moustache. He wore a sports jacket in dove gray over beige dress pants. I knew him because we kept meeting whenever a murder crossed his path. It was not deliberate on my part but he'd had with me claiming my presence was deliberate. He had a vendetta against me. When I was with Wolf or Diego, he wouldn't harass me but they weren't there this morning and that meant he was out to get me. The other man he was with was tall, stout and mean looking.

Hernandez stood straight, chest thrust out self-importantly and announced in accented English, "Good morning, señorita Sturm. We need to speak to you." He turned to the other man. "Officer Iglesias."

Reluctantly, I let them in. Hernandez glanced curiously at Marg. "You have a visitor?"

"I do. She was sleeping."

"Sorry, señorita."

Marg babbled quietly from under the blanket, her words inaudible. I could see she was unsettled by Hernandez and his officer.

"My friend stayed overnight to get some sleep. She was ill." I frowned in annoyance. I didn't bother introducing him. He was too rude, waking me up like that. "Please sit," I said gesturing at the leather chairs. "You realize you disturbed our sleep."

I almost saw a smile but no, Hernandez didn't smile. He must have gas.

"Why are you here? My friend needs her rest, as do I."

"Señorita Sturm," Detective Hernandez glanced at his watch, "it is a quarter past the hour, a perfectly respectable time to make our inquiries."

"What hour?'

"Er, nine, señorita."

"Nine! That's a horrible time to knock on someone's door. We were up late last night."

Hernandaz curled his lips in disgust. "Our job starts at seven so you can see, I considerately let you sleep in."

"We are on vacation. We like to sleep in."

"I have a job to do. If you'd let me start, we will leave sooner rather than later."

"Nevertheless, it's rude not to call first. Am I right, Marg?"

Marg nodded, letting the blanket fall from her face. Her face was so pale, her freckles stood out like a speckled army on her nose. Her eyes had that frightened bunny in the lab appearance.

I continued, getting charged up in my outrage. "First off, I am not a morning person and secondly, we were at a party last night."

"Where?" He took out his notebook and held his pen up ready. "I need the details."

I leaned forward. "Really? Why?'

"It is part of my investigation."

"Investigation of what?"

Hernandez tapped his foot impatiently. "A murder inquiry. Your account is necessary."

"A murder? Who was murdered?" I had a sinking feeling I knew the answer to this.

"Never mind that. First, let's start with this party. Where was it?"

"We were at the Bolivar Alvarez villa. You must know of it?"

Hernandez frowned. "Oh, yes, of course. Everyone does."

I could see I had him there. If there's one person Hernandez was wary of, it was Diego Bolivar Alvarez, or as a matter of fact, anyone from that family. The police chief is Diego's cousin and I knew for a fact he did whatever Diego wanted. Cy ran the Import and Exports business with him in the past but for the last few years he had been scuba diving and making videos of his shark experiences, which the television stations in Mexico picked up on. He was becoming quite the celebrity.

"Was Heinz Du Lac present at this fiesta?"

I bit my lip. "I didn't see him but he might have been there."

"How well did he and his wife, Linda get along?"

I shrugged. "I don't know. I hardly knew her."

"Yet one of my witnesses said she had an altercation with you at Skyreef."

"Well, I'd hardly call it that."

"Was she pleasant to you?"

"No, I wouldn't say that either." I was being careful not to shoot off my mouth. The police love it when someone blurts out incriminating facts.

Hernandez persisted, crossing his leg at the knee. "They said she was shouting."

"Yes, I guess."

"To the point where señor Du Lac wanted her removed."

It was obvious Hernandez was trying to pin this on me.

"Something like that."

"What was that about?"

"She was upset because I was with Wolf Du Lac and she had

broken up with Heinz Du Lac."

"How did you meet her?"

I sighed. "Years ago at the Du Lac cabin in Canada. My family was visiting. Linda was Heinz's girlfriend. We went out on the Du Lac boat but I hardly spoke to her."

Marg's head shot up from the blanket. "Excuse me, officer. Sorry to interrupt but I need to ask Adie something."

"Sí, go ahead, señorita."

"Can I go lay down on your bed, Adie?"

I gazed at Marg's distraught face. "Of course, you can. You don't need my friend, do you, detective?"

Hernandez turned to Marg and bowed slightly. "You are free to go, señorita."

When Marg left the room, Hernandez leaned forward. "Tell me about your visit to Heinz Du Lac's condo."

Did he mean the first time after he had been beaten or the second when I saw Linda in the fish tank? "When was this?"

"There have been several occasions, am I right?" Hernandez met my eyes. "You and Heinz Du Lac were lovers, correct?"

"What? No!"

"That's why Linda hated you." He pointed his finger in the air. "She wanted him for herself!"

"Hardly. You know I'm in a relationship with Wolf Du Lac."

Hernandez rolled his eyes. "As you Americans say, this is not your first rodeo. You had sex with him, his brother and any number of other men, such as senor Bolivar Alvarez. I have also seen you with Amancio Bolivar Alvarez. You do get around, señorita Sturm, don't you?"

"Those are lies. There is no need to slut shame me, detective." I said, barely holding it together. I wanted to punch him in the throat so badly. I willed myself to stay calm. He only wanted a rise out of me so that he could justify arresting me. I'd be at his mercy then— stuck behind bars without a lawyer. "I am only involved with Wolf Du Lac."

"Really? What about the ring señor Bolivar Alvarez gave to you?"

"Did your spies also tell you I didn't accept his proposal and returned the ring?"

"Oh, sí, but you are still considering it, aren't you? You would be a fool not to, correct? The Bolivar Alvarez family is powerful in San Miguel and yet you are living in a condo provided by Wolf Du Lac. Are you seeing them both giving them equal access?"

"That is insulting."

Hernandez squinted at me. "And then there is the brother." He regarded the stuccoed ceiling. "Heinz Du Lac is also interested in you. He told me so himself. Heinz Du Lac said Linda was very jealous."

"That's the first I've heard of this. Señor Bolivar Alvarez will be upset with your insinuations." I stared pointedly at Hernandez. "He likes me to be treated with respect not implicated in a murder or shrouded with disgusting scenarios of imaginary sexual relationships."

"Perdón, señorita Sturm. I was just relating what I had been told."

"Well, whoever told you this garbage is an idiot. I have never been interested in Heinz Du Lac."

"Nevertheless, fingerprints were located in his condo. We could take some fingerprint samples."

I felt like I was descending into a sinkhole. Cenotes in Mexico were limestone caves all along the coast, the water in them often turquoise and the lighting magical. My particular sinkhole was not pretty. It was one of those nasty cenotes—gloomy, murky water, the air filled with flying bats.

"We could, Detective Hernandez, but we won't. I am not under arrest, am I?"

Hernandez shook his head and stood, motioning his officer to do the same. "This is merely an inquiry at this time. Linda Du Lac's body was discovered on the shore. It is my duty to investigate."

"Good luck with that then, detective."

Hernandez turned to go and then did an about-face. "You weren't in the least surprised by Linda Du Lac's murder or the discovery of her body. Why was that?"

I shrugged.

"I think you know more than you are telling me, señorita Sturm. We shall speak again."

The door clicked behind them. I felt like I'd swallowed a live flounder whole, my throat was so constricted. What had I gotten myself into?

"Omigod, Adie!"

"You overheard?"

"Yes. Are you in trouble with the police?"

"Mmm. Personally, I didn't know what to make of it." It had to be Heinz setting me up. Who else knew I was in that condo except Wolf, Cy and Diego? Why would they try to frame me? "I should text Wolf. "Excuse me," I said, padding over to the wall where my iPhone was charging. The text was short and sweet.

Where are you? I'm in trouble. Can we meet? Adie

I turned to Marg. "Let's get dressed and have breakfast. We need to return your dress."

Marg slapped her forehead. "Oh no, Alejandro will kill me! You saw my dress. It's hideous!" She paced the floor nervously. "Look Adie, can you return it for me? You know him. He'll forgive you, right?"

"Alejandro? He'll slap me all the way to Playa del Carmen. He's evil. So woman up and tell him yourself. What's the worst he can do, girl? Throw you out on your ass?" I nodded thoughtfully. "I suppose he could. Listen, Marg, he's a man of the world. He's seen worse than a little vomit on a dress."

Marg's lips twitched. "You mean like love juices?"

I smiled. "Maybe. Alejandro does get around. Anyway, you need to get ready. Come to my closet. There are some loose things in there that should fit you just fine."

In a few minutes we found a pair of track pants and a T-shirt in canary yellow that Marg could wear. Diego's housekeeper had picked out an assortment of outfits for casual, business and party wear. I was a queen with this closet. Glancing around the bedroom with the artwork and the matching turquoise duvet, I was energized. Diego and Wolf were wonderful men besides being eye-candy.

"Marg, I know someone who could calm down our boy Alejandro."

Bouncing up and down on her heels, Marg clutched her hands together nervously. "Who?"

"My friend, Carmelita, if I can get her to come."

I clicked on my cell just as a text chimed.

Babe. Come to my boat for brunch around 12. W

That was an offer I couldn't refuse.

"Can I bring Carmelita and Marg? I texted rapidly.
Sure. W
"Lucky you! I'm sure you will have a lovely time."
"You are invited too."
"How kind of your boyfriend, especially after I nearly ruined his Jeep last night." Marg's face fell. "Will you still go with me to Alejandro's?"
"Of course."
Marg's face fell. "What about your friend Carmelita? Can she meet us?"
"I'll text her."
Can you meet me at Alejandro's? My friend Marg needs your help. Afterwards shopping and lunch on Wolf's boat. Adie
A reply came a few seconds later.
On my way in twenty minutes. C
Picking up a tube of BB cream with 35 SPF I applied that and lip gloss before brushing my hair. Pleased with my efforts I searched through my closet and found a simple wine-red wrap-around print dress to wear that I had bought for my vacation.

Pleased with my efforts I decided to look in the jewelry box. I found a wide gold cuff bracelet decorated with a lizard relief. Iguanas are meant to be lucky. Slipping it on, I hoped it would ward off bad vibes. I should have had it on before opening the door to Hernandez.

A silver box held a pair of diamond tear-drop earrings in white gold. One clear round emerald surrounded by a circle of diamonds. It said Blue Nile on the box. I didn't know if I dared to wear these earrings. Were they from Wolf or Diego? If I wore them and they weren't from Wolf, would he be offended? My guess was these earrings were expensive. All the same, I took them to the mirror and put them on. I'd take the chance.

"Wow!" Marg exclaimed when she walked in. "I can see you are ready. Those look fantastic! From Wolf?"
"I have no idea. Guess, I can ask him when I see him."
"You mean they could be from Alvarez?"
"Seriously, I don't know."
Marg glance down at her T-shirt and track pants. "Glad I can go casual. Last night was too much for me." She held up the gold lamé gown. "Do you have a bag for this?"

In the double closet I found an ivory satchel, Michael Kors emblazed in gold. "Take this," I said gingerly gripping the costly bag. "Can you believe it!"

"Huh?"

"Michael Kors. It's a designer bag." I pointed to the satchel. "Big enough for a laptop too."

"Yes, nice. But Adie, I'm more concerned with Alejandro's dress."

"What about it?" I slipped on some red sandals and grabbed the red cross-shoulder purse, sticking some pesos and a credit card in.

"You don't think he'll ask me to pay for it?"

I shrugged. "Maybe, but Carmelita has him wrapped around her little finger." Grabbing my bag, I led Marg to the door. "I want to go shopping."

"What?" Marg's eyes widened. "With all this designer stuff you want more?"

"No, just something that is mine. I am not a kept woman. I have hard-earned money to pay for my own dress and I will find one."

Ten minutes by taxi we arrived at Alejandro's Styling and Boutique. Augustina greeted us at the door. After the initial pleasantries I pushed her for the intel. "Is senorita Bolivar Alvarez here?"

Augustina lifted one finely groomed eyebrow. "You were expecting her?"

"Yes." I waved to the pink leather chairs by the window. "We will wait for her there."

Before the formidable stylist could object, the door swung open and Carmelita entered.

Augustina zipped over to Carmelita, flustered, all but flinging herself at my amiga's feet.

I had to wait for Augustina to step aside before I could greet my friend with a kiss. In a whisper I said into her ear, "There's a problem." I waved Marg forward. "Have you two met each other? Marg, this is my friend, Carmelita."

"*Mucho gusto.*" Carmelita gave Marg the once over. "We must take you shopping, chica. There are some good stores here. You need something suitable for this hot weather, like a sundress, sí?"

Marg blushed. "Adie kindly provided these. Not my choice."

"What? You gave Marg these?" Carmelita curled her lips

downward disapprovingly. "Ay! Dios mío! This woman deserves better from her amiga, Adelina."

As Marg regarded me reproachfully, I said to her, "Sorry, but it's all I had in my closet that would fit."

"Oh-hh." Comprehension made her blush. "I understand."

Carmelita smiled brightly. "No problem, chicas. Marg can get an outfit from a shop. Alejandro will gladly help us out."

Marg squirmed uncomfortably. "Alejandro won't want me to rent anything again after the way this dress looks now."

"I think Marg needs you to talk to Alejandro." I turned to Marg. "Give me the dress, please." I grabbed the satchel from Marg's outstretched hand. Gathering the material, I pulled it out and held it high. "See the stains on the bodice?"

"Caramba! What happened?"

"It was a food spill." Marg ran her fingers through her hair nervously. "I'm so sorry, Carmelita. Can you help explain it?"

"It was an accident. No need to be concerned, chica. Alejandro can—"

The door at the back sprung open with a bang and Alejandro minced forward in tight black jeans and black silk shirt, open to the chest. A silver medallion in the shape of a jaguar hung between his pecs.

His hair was newly styled in blond streaks and shaved bald at the sides. He smiled brightly in greeting. "Señorita Bolivar Alvarez! It is indeed an honor. Señorita Sturm and lady friend, welcome!"

Carmelita bestowed kisses on Alejandro and then I had a go at him. He was beaming with pleasure. I hated to burst his bubble.

"We had an unfortunate incident at the fiesta." I handed the dress to him.

"I'm sure you can clean it," Carmelita said confidently.

Alejandro's arched eyebrows rose high as his eyes narrowed on the stains. "*Madre mia!* What is this? How did this happen, señorita?"

"It seems there was an accident at the fiesta."

Marg and I bobbed our heads in agreement.

Alejandro nodded and tossed the garment at Augustina who had rushed up to see what the commotion was about. "Clean this dress, please."

Shooting us a scornful glance, Augustina hustled off, muttering oaths under her breath.

"I am so very sorry, Alejandro," Marg said. "It was a crowded party. People bumping each other." The lie flowed off her tongue in a practised way. I had no idea Marg was so good at subterfuge.

"I suppose I am lucky the dress wasn't destroyed with acid or lit on fire. That we cannot rectify."

"So glad this has been resolved." Carmelita turned to us and commenced to lead us to the door."

Alejandro quickly followed us. "Forgive me for how abrupt I was but some who rent are way less reliable."

"Like who?" I asked, curious about the Cozumel society crowd.

Alejandro let out a big sigh. He whispered confidentially, "I really shouldn't say but she is new in this area and I am not impressed by her attitude."

"Who is that?" Carmelita asked.

Alejandro wiped an invisible piece of lint off his shirt.

Carmelita threw her head back in an arrogant model pose. "Surely you can tell me?"

"You can't tell anyone—"

"We won't," I said quickly, more inquisitive by the second. "We are your friends, Alejandro."

"I know you ladies are, but I must uphold client confidentiality, you see."

Stepping up, I pushed the issue. "Right, but you must know we wouldn't tell?"

"All right. Come closer. Augustina can't be trusted with a secret." Alejandro put his arms around us. We were so close, we were standing shoulder to shoulder.

"Honestly, Alejandro. Tell us!" Carmelita said impatiently, shaking him slightly with one hand.

He held a hand to his chest. "You forced it out of me."

Carmelita grinned wickedly. "It's no fun holding back."

Alejandro swept his arms out, palms up. "I give up, señoritas. It's that art dealer. You know her. She's already on city council and is putting the pliers on the mayor. She is so full of herself! She hasn't returned that dress from that very same fiesta and she didn't pay for the rental either. Augustina was bullied into giving her the dress." He eyed Carmelita. "If you are going down Avenida 5 could you do me a favor and stop by the gallery and give her a subtle reminder to come by and bring the dress?" He added hastily, "Don't anger señorita Gonzalez though, please. She can be malicious." He whispered, "It is like releasing the queen wasp—all sting, no honey."

"I am not afraid of that upstart," Carmelita said shortly. "Enough said. We are on our way."

After she air kissed Alejandro, she shoved us out the open door. "Gracias, my friend."

Alejandro stood at the door frame, his arms crossed a moment. Marg and I joined in to thank him. He waved his arms up. "*De nada*, señoritas. Just be careful with señorita Bravo Gonzalez."

11

"There!" Carmelita said, pointing to a shop two doors down. It had a green awning over a wooden door frame. The wall was a bright yellow and the roof red tile. The sign said Rosa's Ropas. "We will find a dress for you, Marg, and one for Adie's engagement party."

Marg squealed. "Really, Adie! Why didn't you say? Did that happen when Wolf took you away to speak privately last night? Did he propose?" Then she realized she had been left out of the loop. Marg hissed. "Why wouldn't you tell me? I'm your best friend—at least I was." She glared at Carmelita.

"Calm down, Marg." I patted Marg's hand. "Yes, you and Carmelita are my best friends in the world!" I lifted an eyebrow at Carmelita and said coolly, "So stop with the fictitious stories of my engagement. For your information my status has not changed. I am not engaged."

Carmelita smirked. "You will be, soon enough, amiga. Best to be prepared." Carmelita's glance shot over to Marg in her T-shirt and track pants. "We must find something for Marg, as well. She can't go to the yacht in those unsightly gym clothes!" She added hastily, "Not that they wouldn't do you well for a workout but drinks on a yacht?" Carmelita gave a thumbs down gesture.

Marg's eyes widened. "If you don't mind me saying so, you are really nice for an Alvarez." Her eyelashes fluttered like a captured butterfly in a jar. "No offence meant. You are so beautiful and have such a kind heart. That's rare. No wonder you are Adie's friend. I should be jealous but I could never be jealous of such an amazing person!"

"Gracias, cariño. I try to be a good person even if I am the sister of Santiago Bolivar Alvarez. But you know, Margarita, my other brother, Amancio is very sweet. He doesn't work in the Import-Export business right now. Cy's a scuba master and a hero. He saved Adelina's life once."

"Really? Maybe you should consider that brother, Adie. What's his name again?"

I remembered that time we had together. "He goes by Cy."

Carmelita smiled slyly. "Cy has a thing for Adie. She could easily start something," she lifted an eyebrow, "it seems they already started something a while ago. Too bad Adelina went back to the Sea God." She slung an arm around my shoulders. "We could have been sisters-in-laws. Wouldn't that be cool?"

"It would." The sister-in-laws part was stellar.

"And there's always, Diego. He has the ring."

"Sounds like he's hot to trot." Marg said sadly. "If Adie married him, he'd ban me from his house. I was lucky he didn't have me thrown out along with Leo."

I clapped my hands. "Attention troops. You all know what to do, right? Now let's get shopping!"

It was easier for Carmelita to assist Marg and look on my own for a dress. A turquoise silk dress appealed to me. Soon enough I trotted over to the sales lady and tugged out my Mastercard. The dress was everything I wanted, fitted at the waist and bodice and draped nicely above the knee. Oh, and yes, it was cut in a deep V-neck. That should charge Wolf's motor.

Just as I finished my transaction at the cash register, Marg, hair dishevelled, lipstick smeared, immerged from the dressing room a big grin plastered on her face. "Love this dress," she said to us, holding up the item.

Carmelita had found a flowing mid-calf gown in a rust brown print for Marg. I would have put her in ivory but it was obvious her clothing had a high mortality rate. Stains are less likely to be permanent with the darker colour. "Good choice. Thanks, Carmelita."

Marg turned around to fashion the dress.

I addressed the sales clerk, a painfully thin lady in an elegant fitted black dress, patent leather heels and a bun high on her head. She stood patiently waiting. "She will take the dress. Please cut the tags at the back. The lady will wear the dress."

"Sí," Señora Grafico nodded. "And these in the bag?" Her fingers gingerly touched the workout clothing Marg had tossed on the counter and dropped them in a plastic bag with the logo "Fashion Grafico" embossed on both sides.

"Adie, would you mind awfully if I went to Manni's hotel? I

might come to Wolf's boat after but it all depends on Manni. I want to tell him I still care about him. I don't want this relationship to end."

"Sure, but first let's fix your face." I led her to the counter and pulled out a tissue from the box next to the cash register. "There's lipstick on your cheek."

Marg stood compliantly while I did my best for her.

"There," I said, checking her face. "You look great. You want to stop in the art gallery before you head off to Moray's Eel?"

Her ex boyfriend was the desk manager at the hotel and I had the feeling she had dumped him after he cheated on her but maybe not. I didn't have the story from the horse's mouth. She might have decided against moving to San Miguel and they mutually broke it off, making him a free agent.

"Sure, I'll go in with you guys," Marg said excitedly, a spring in her step as she skipped down the street.

We hurried to keep up as Marg explained how she met Manni to Carmelita. I handed her a tissue when her eyes teared, listening as she elucidated how their passion was beyond any earth force. I was about ready to gag when luckily, we came to our destination. At the corner we saw the salmon-colored building under a flat red-tiled roof, a sign slung above the door frame reading Gonzalez Art.

She turned to Carmelita. "Does your brother buy from this woman? I noticed quite the collection at his villa."

Carmelita nodded. "Diego buys South American, Mayan and Mexican as well as European art. He spends profusely on these."

"He has a lot, probably worth a king's fortune," Marg muttered under her breath as she swung the door open.

Once inside I noticed the gallery consisted of three rooms, two displaying art and the third one, possibly for storage.

The room to the right was mostly Mayan glyphs and oil paintings.

A spiffy well-turned out young man, in tight white jeans, a rose shirt and slicked-back black hair rushed out to greet us. He had a moustache and a tiny beard, similar to a goatee. "Come in, ladies. I am Tomas Dunoir." His eyes crinkled at the corners appealingly as his hand gestured. "We have art for everyone." He paused to inspect his potential clients and decided Carmelita was the one with the money. "You look familiar, señorita. I am sure I have seen you before."

"Perhaps you have seen me at one of my fashion shows." Carmelita perused him up and down. "I am señorita Bolivar Alvarez and these are my friends," she said vaguely. I recalled I hadn't told her Marg's last name.

"Hola, I am Adie Sturm, and this is Marg Beige." I said smoothly. "What a fabulous gallery. Is señorita Gonzalez here?"

"I believe she is in the back room inspecting a new shipment of paintings from Guatemala. They are mostly Andres Curruchich, a painter of naïve art. Have you heard of him?"

"No, afraid not," Carmelita said, "We have Diego Rivera art in the villa."

Cha-ching! Tomas' eyes lit up. "Yes! Perhaps, I should notify señorita Gonzalez of your arrival, ladies. Please, look around whilst I find her."

That shouldn't be too difficult if he checked out the back room unless the Gonzalez woman had a habit of hiding behind boxes. When he rushed away to the back, I remarked, "He thinks he's got a live one."

"Do you mean like a fish?" Carmelita smiled. "He wants to sell us something. He's gone to get the shark."

"Huh?" Marg said, checking the nearest painting of Mayan dancers. "What do you mean?"

"He thinks Carmelita will buy. She's the one with the big bucks. We are her hangers-on, you know sycophants, in other words, the parasites waiting for handouts." I stared at the painting attracting Marg's attention. "I like that one. The painting has such warm tones." I closed in on the artist name. "This is an Andrés Curruchich, the Guatemalan painter. Simple style." I could hear Diego's voice in the back of my head, saying, yet *pleasing*.

"If you say so. I don't know anything about art," Marg said sadly.

Carmelita zoned in. "That one has got to be affordable. This artist is not famous."

Marg pointed at a modernistic piece in reds and blues. "Look at that price. They want two million for that one."

"That's way over priced," Carmelita remarked. "I know my art."

Scooting over to the next painting, my eyes went straight to the price tag of the Frida Kahlo oil of a woman and a man, seated side by side.

From behind me a soft voice said, "Buenos dios, ladies. I am

Perla Brava Gonzalez the owner. That painting is a Frida Kahlo. The woman in the forefront is Frida and that man in the hat is Diego Rivera. Notice the fine ochre yellows contrasting with the Mayan blue tones."

"Yes, it is very pleasing," I said, before spinning about to see a tall, striking olive-skinned beauty, long black waves caught up high in the back and let loose to spill onto her shoulders. Up close she was tall, about six feet and athletic. It hurt my neck to look up.

Dangly gold bracelets accessorised her muscular bare arms, her mauve shoulder-capped dress bringing out the amazing amethyst depths of her blue eyes. Perla Bravo Gonzalez looked down her rather long thin nose at us.

Carmelita commented. "It's rare to see that blue in paintings."

"Mesmerizing," I added. So, this was a painting by the beloved Frida Kahlo. "Frida Kahlo was as talented as her husband Diego Rivera."

Perla sniffed. "I'm surprised you know that about her. She was talented for sure. If she was a man who knows what fame she would have achieved. The world was a man's playground, even with her sharing the same bed as the famous Diego Rivera."

"Hey, cariña!" a man's voice called out from the back room. "This is way better than we thought we'd get. Come here, Perla!"

"So sorry for his rudeness. He is new. Excuse me, señoritas."

Marg's face blanched. She whispered, "I recognize that voice. It's Leo from the party. He lied that his name was Luis. He's related to Leon Del Socorro."

"Are you sure? I can't see why he would be here, do you?"

"No, but I could take a peek and check."

"Let's do that," I said, hooking her arm in mine. "Pretend we are strolling to see the paintings in the other room."

As quietly and quickly as possible we sidled by the supply room. The door was partially open. Perla was examining the back of a painting. The man brought another oil painting wrapped in brown paper over for her.

"Do you want me to take the backing paper off? We need to know how much is here."

"Keep your voice down, you idiot. The women in the gallery can hear you."

Marg's eyes widened as she caught a glimpse of Leo Del Socorro.

126

She mouthed. "It's him."

I put a finger to my lips and pulled her along to the next room. We stopped in front of an abstract jaguar painting glowing with dark and light reds. The jaguar was wickedly lethal; teeth flashing as it viciously seized and tore apart an animal resembling a deer.

I heard the click of heels and partially swiveled about to see Perla Bravo Gonzalez, her red lipstick dark and strong on her full lips now twisted in a fake smile.

"The artist used venetian reds and cadmium red washes to emphasize the bloody feast. See how he gave it a three-D effect with an undercoat of dry wall?" Perla said.

"A Mayan artist?"

"Yes, not famous as yet." She tilted her head disarmingly at me. "The Jaguar god is the most powerful one in the Mayan religion."

"I can see that."

"Underworld god by night and sun god by day."

"A fine painting."

"So glad you agree. This painting is a bargain—less than six thousand US." Perla squinted down at me contemplatively. "Are you interested?"

"Certainly worth my consideration, but I would like to look at them all first before I decide on any one artist."

Perla's forehead wrinkled. "Sí, I thought you looked familiar. I have heard of you, señorita Sturm. I saw you at Skyreef with Diego and Wolf." She threw her head back and laughed lightly, the sound like a tinkling stream. "I heard you are to marry one of them, but no one knows which one you fancy more."

"Rumors can be wrong," I said abruptly. "Perhaps you can show my friend señorita Beige some paintings? She has come into an inheritance and would love to start an art collection."

"Of course. I will be delighted. I love to speak to collectors."

I called over to Marg who had moved on to study some Mayan prints. "Señorita Bravo Gonzalez would like to show you some art, okay?"

"Sure, I like art." Marg pretended to take notice of the Mayan glyph of the rain and corn gods in a circular pattern. "What's this all about?" she asked Perla.

I made that my moment to exit and return to the front room. It was my opinion that Perla was not the most likable woman, attractive or not, her negative energy was suffocating me. Of course, I had enough of her insulting implications about my romances. She was just a busybody, sticking her nose into my life.

Carmelita scurried over. "You look upset, Adie."

"The druggie from last night is in the backroom. Leo Del Socorro. Did you meet him last night?"

"I might have. He's Leon Del Socorro's cousin."

I nodded. "The same."

"What does he have to do with Linda?"

"I'm not sure. Just puzzled about what his connection is with Perla. She's one of the condo investors."

Carmelita frowned. "Hmm. Do you think he's one of those hombres that killed her?"

"I don't know, but I want to find out more about this place, Carmelita. If you can help me, you could distract Perla when she comes back out. Ask her about the paintings. Make it seem as you are a potential buyer. Okay?"

"And you? What are you planning?" Carmelita's eyes narrowed. "Nothing dangerous, I hope."

"Not really. I'll be in and out of that backroom as soon as Leo leaves." Just then I noticed a man in a white shirt and jeans, dark sunglasses and a fedora leave the room carrying a box. "Look, there he is! Look away."

The simpering young man in the skin-tight white jeans and the chartreuse shirt, slinked up to Leo Del Socorro stroking his slicked hair down as he said, loud enough for us to hear, "Do you need help carrying this, señor Del Socorro?"

The square sunglasses perched on Del Socorro's nose shielded his eyes and my view. Did he have a stoner high right now or was he perked with meth or cocaine? His movements were erratic. I was sure he'd drop that box but he was very careful to hold on tight. There must be something very important in there.

Del Socorro didn't answer Tomas, indicating the door with his chin. Tomas rushed to open it for him and stood there watching him leave.

This was my chance to get a gander at the goods in the store room. I motioned for Carmelita to head over to Perla and I traipsed as quietly as I could into the room.

It was loaded with paintings and a few statues all wrapped in brown paper. What was Del Socorro all hyped about? Hastily, I surveyed the area, moving gingerly around careful not to knock anything down. One painting had been unwrapped.

It was a landscape, green palms swaying with the breeze, a turbulent dark blue sea crashing on the coral rocks in the background. Scraps of paper had been carelessly left on the tile floor. Something else was down there too, not brown paper but green.

My jaw dropped. A pile of stacked Ben Franklins, elasticized in a rubber band. Who has that much cash? What was going on here? All these questions ripped through my brain when I saw those bills. It was time for me to get the heck out of Dodge, so, cleverly, I slid one bill out of the pile and tucked it into my bra. I needed to get a closer look at Ben.

Glancing around I saw paintings on easels and a table littered with large stones half-carved. They were black, possibly obsidian and jade.

From outside the supply room I heard Carmelita, yell out, "Tomas, have you seen my friend, señorita Stum?"

Oh, no! I had to get out of here!

Scooting to the door I rushed out and collided into Perla Bravo Gonzalez. She was intense—her eyes like two brown circles, big black dots in the center. *Was she on drugs too?*

I stopped dead in my tracks. Perla pushed me back, impeding my retreat into the gallery, jabbering angrily, "What are you doing in my storage room?"

"Pardon me, señorita Gonzalez. I was looking for the washroom."

Perla curled her lips downward. "It is not in there. This is our room for paintings and such." She grabbed my elbow and led me like a disobedient child to her assistant. "Tomas will escort you to the toilet."

Tomas whispered, "Señorita you should have asked. Señorita Bravo Gonzalez has strict rules about entering this room."

"If it's so forbidden why wasn't the door closed and locked? It was a mistake, I assure you. I hardly want to see a supply closet."

Tomas's eyes flicked to the front door. "It's our fault, of course. I am afraid the gentleman doing the accounting left the door open by accident." He pushed my lower back, guiding me into the front room. Near the corner there was a door. "Here it is," he said. "It is normally for employees but as you are a buyer, you are welcome to use the facilities."

The first thing I did was carefully wash my face avoiding smearing my eye makeup. I felt like I had narrowly escaped Perla's tricky spider web. She was way too irate about finding me in there. What was she up to? A pile of those Ben Franklins could be several thousand dollars and who is to say there weren't more in that room? The brown paper on the floor had been ripped off the back of the painting. The money must have been hidden underneath. It was possible there was a lot more money in the wrapped paintings.

When I entered the gallery, Carmelita and Marg were waiting for me.

"Let's go," I said urgently. "Thanks so much for your time," I called out to Perla and Tomas. So sorry for the supply room mistake."

"No problem. Come again," Perla said her mouth drawn in a thin line. "There are many paintings to consider and I haven't shown you all of them yet."

"Chao!" Camelita said. "So, kind of you to share your paintings with us. Oh, by the way, Alejandro needs the dress you borrowed to be returned to the boutique."

Perlas's face flushed in anger but she held it together to hiss through her teeth. "I willl take care of that, gracias. See you again, ladies." She made a sound—deep throaty, an almost genuine laugh, much like the noise a cat makes in his throat before he chucks up some grass. "Perhaps you will buy a painting next time."

I sighed in relief as the door closed behind me.

In the street, Marg said, "Wow, she was mad about returning her dress, wasn't she?"

Carmelita sputtered, "Perla was seriously annoyed. No doubt about that. It was more than about that dress she needs to return. I'd say she was nervous about Adelina finding something in that backroom." Carmelita's face showed concern. "What was in there?"

"I might have discovered an illegal operation."

"No manches! We need to talk, chica."

***

Around the square there were several restaurants and shops. We traipsed along on the cobblestone street until we reached an outdoor restaurant with a yellow awning. It faced the park.

The centre had been renovated; the palm trees lined up in straight rows for a bigger dance area on Sundays when the bands played. Across from us, there were cement stairs leading to the grassy park sprinkled with trees and bushes.

The sun had made a powerful appearance, the heat coming up in waves from the stones. It was too unpleasantly hot for us to enjoy walking any further. A yellow dog lay sprawled out on the top step. I was concerned about the lab. Fortunately, the dog had some shade, a bowl of water someone had kindly placed nearby. He was ownerless, or at least appeared to be, but I had the feeling the restaurant workers made sure he was fed. I hoped he had enough people to look out for him.

There were several unoccupied tables shading us from the sun at Aguacates. We took the one closest to the park. From where we sat, we had a fabulous view of a cruise ship making its way out of the harbor. The water sparkled silver in the morning sunshine, palm trees swayed gently and I was relieved of my previous stress-filled adventure into the world.

When the waiter asked for our order we went with coffee. I could see Marg and Carmelita were fidgety, eager to talk.

Carmelita crossed her legs and picked up her coffee mug. "Perla had the *humor de perros*, didn't she? I wonder if she ruined the dress she rented and is afraid to return it? Or even worse, thinks Alejandro will tell people she can't afford to pay for that designer gown."

"Sorry, I don't understand. What's this about dogs?" Marg asked.

"Just a Spanish expression, chica. Perla was mad, like an angry dog."

Marg nodded her head. "If she was a dog, she would have bitten Adie, the way she looked when she saw her in the store room." Marg nudged me. "Come on, girl. Out with it! What was in there?"

"I can't show it to you now, but I'll tell you about it." I could feel the edge of Ben Franklin scraping my breast uncomfortably. "I have proof in my bra."

Marg tapped her fingernail on the glass table top. "Huh? Say this in English, Adie."

"Don't keep us in suspense, Adelina." Carmelita picked up her spoon and stirred milk into the frothy brown liquid. Her voice had a bored tone rich people get when they talk about money. "What did you find in there?"

"Money. US dollars bundled up into thousands."

Marg set down her cup so quickly it nearly tipped over. "You're kidding me. Where did you find that?"

"On the floor under some brown wrapping paper."

"No manches!" Carmelita stretched the word out. "You can't be serious?"

"I am very serious."

"What's that all about?" Marg asked.

"Listen to this. The same brown paper they were using to wrap the paintings was covering the money. I imagine they stuck bills under the backing paper and when it's delivered they tear it out, collect the money and then replace the brown paper, stapling it to the backs of the paintings."

"Wow! A shady operation right in front of our noses. Somehow, I should have guessed with Leo Del Socorro on the premises." Marg turned to Carmelita. "That guy got me high and was trying to force sex on me in your brother's villa."

"How shameful! How did you meet that pond scum?"

"At the party. He was most likely into the coke earlier that evening and after a few margaritas I," Marg frowned, "wasn't myself. Adie wanted me to investigate and I thought mistakenly Leo was Leon."

I nodded. "They do look a lot alike. The Clean cousins, both outfitted in white."

"Who?" Carmelita looked puzzled.

"The Del Socorro cousins. Leon, is an investor in the Erizo del Mar condo complex."

"What do you think this money has to do with them?"

I sipped my coffee. "I don't know yet, but I have other leads."

Marg leaned forward. "What do you have so far?"

"Money, art, drugs, maybe all of them connected to a murder. Linda Du Lac's killer."

"Anyone can have drugs in Cozumel," Carmelita said knowingly. "Drug money?"

Carmelita leaned back in her chair and in impassively gazed out at the dock where a ferry was entering port. "People come and go. This is an island. Cancun and Colombia are nearby. They are known for drugs."

"You can't be blasé about murder though, Carmelita. Hernandez wants to pin it on me. I need to unravel this mess or end up in jail." Tugging out my iPhone I checked the time. "We should be on our way. I want to update Wolf on this stuff." I jumped up, impatient to head out.

Carmelita signaled the waiter. He came with the bill, waving our money away, she paid. She squeezed my hand. "I know you had nothing to do with Linda's murder. If Hernandez hassles you anymore, I'm sure Diego will get you the best lawyer."

"Right. I have to find out who the real killer is before I get legal assistance."

"Ed Marion and I are close. I will ask him."

"No! Please don't. I don't want to sound like there's a conspiracy going on but there's more that I haven't told you yet. Don't talk to anyone about this art gallery money or the murder. I have to ask Wolf what Heinz told the police about me first."

Carmelita nodded.

Marg wriggled in her seat. "Thanks for helping me today," she said, "with the dress," to Carmelita.

"Glad I could." Carmelita stood and glanced at me. "Let's head out. I know you want to talk to Wolf."

Marg grabbed her purse. "Say, do you two mind if I go ahead? I want to get to Moray's Eel to touch base with Manni. I'm hoping to patch things up."

"I'll text you after our lunch with Wolf, okay? Or, you could always come and join us. We'll be at the new marina. The yacht is called Adie's Storm."

Marg giggled. "Ha, ha, Wolf is funny. He sure knows you."

"Eh!" I gave her the Italian gesture. "No smart-ass remarks, girlfriend. Wolf has the romance down just fine. Who wouldn't want a yacht called after her?"

Carmelita smiled. "Or buy a yacht and make it a romantic hideaway." She arched an eyebrow. "Are you certain I should come with you? Three is a crowd. Perhaps he wants to propose?"

"Not that I know of."

"Oh? Who would that be?"

"Wolf said he might ask Ed Marion to this lunch but not for sure."

"Oh, nice. He has a hot body that would be excellent for dessert.

"A chocolate dessert?" I grinned. "Those are delicious."

Carmelita sighed. "You should know. Wolf is sinfully delicious."

Marg tapped my arm impatiently. "Sorry to interrupt your fantasies, girls, but I need to sort out my life."

"You can come with us. We will drop you off at Moray's Eel. It's on the way."

From the café along the square and further on the left and right, the streets were pedestrian only. Plenty of shops selling souvenirs, jewelry and clothing. A vendor with a charming smile beckoned us with, "Come here, senoritas. Beautiful jewelry, almost free."

I waved, never wanting to offend anyone I called out, "Mañana."

We strolled towards Avenida Rafael E. Melgar, the main drag, and signaled a taxi. A husky middle-aged man wearing a beige shirt sat behind the wheel of a silver Kia sedan. He opened the door on his side and Marg slid in followed by me and Carmelita.

The seats were comfortable but not the leather ones Carmelita was accustomed to. Her nose sniffed slightly as she perused the interior of the taxi. Around the mirror hung blue rosary beads and a medallion of Mother Teresa along with an ornate silver cross.

The driver had dark hair, a bushy mustache and a plump face, just starting to wrinkle with the sun. The lines around his mouth, forehead and eyes indicated he was approaching mid-century. He looked like a friendly squirrel, nuts in his cheeks and a welcoming smile splashed on his face.

"Buenos dios. Como esta?" I asked.

"Bien. Where are we going, señoritas?" The driver said quickly.

"We would like to go to the Marina."

"The Caleta marina?"

I shook my head. "It's the new marina. I think it's called Fortune."

"Marina Fonatur on the way to the El Presidente."

"Yes, but first we need to drop my friend off at Moray's Eel."

"Bueno. I will get the lady there." He pulled the sedan out into the traffic and coasted to the corner where the traffic police were directing the rush hour vehicles. With several cruise ships in the harbor unloading tourists, it was a busy time.

Marg was chewing her fingernails on the ride to the hotel. I wasn't that positive she could repair the damage in her relationship. Last time I saw Manni he was having a close encounter with a dusky-skinned woman from my tour group in the dining room. She was not as attractive as Marg but she made up for it with sheer chutzpah. What she wanted, she went for. I never found out if they'd sealed the deal that night but the bulldozer from my tour group was a ballsy woman with an agenda.

"Good luck!" I called out after Marg when she jumped out. Marg raced to the front doors of Moray's Eel lobby like a speeding bullet, tripped over the rug at the door, righted herself and disappeared into the building. Luck is something Marg was badly in need of after a divorce and a new failed relationship. Manni plus Marg, plus ballsy woman, was a screw-up waiting to happen.

12

The driver jerked the taxi onto Avenida Rafael E. Melgar, motoring along at a brisk pace. We drove by hotels and dive shops, a flash view of the Caribbean, bright blue wherever a building ended. Finally, we passed the El Cid La Ceiba and the Hard Rock Café as the road became Carreterra Costera Sur. Veering to the right we entered the road that took us to the Marina Fonatur.

The water ahead was a brilliant cerulean blue speckled with white yachts and dive boats. At the dock there was a dive shop, palapas and lounge chairs as well as plenty of parking. The taxi let us off just as I received the ting of a text message. Tugging my iPhone from out of my purse, I left it for a minute as I paid the driver.

"Look, Adelina. There's Wolf's boat!" Carmelita saw my phone in my hand. "Is it a text from Wolf?"

Glancing up I saw the yacht "Adie's Storm". Suddenly, I was eager to see the Sea God. That man had the ability to light my fire in a way no other man could.

Dazzling bright sun sparkled on the crests of the waves. The Caribbean was a brilliant azure blue, the sky above, a soft cerulean blanketed with pillows of white. The sea waters lapped heavily on an elegant fifty-foot ivory yacht. It wasn't just any rich man's toy. It had my name in script next to the mermaid on the port side. *Adie's Storm.*

I pulled out my iPhone and read:

Don't go on board! Keep off the gangway. Dangerous. Will explain later. W

My glance caught a figure. I stopped in my tracks so suddenly my friend behind me, racing to keep up, tottered dangerously on five-inch stilettos. She bumped into me, nearly falling backwards. Clutching her arm, I righted her, asking, "You okay, Carmelita?"

"*Dios mio*, Adelina! What the heck is wrong with you!" Carmelita hissed out the last few words as her breath returned in gasps. "First you run to get here and then you stop like you've seen the Holy Spirit!" She patted the skirt of her green silk dress in place. It matched her sparkling eyes exactly, most likely her intention. Carmelita, the designer, knew what made her look outstanding.

"Sorry, I was distracted by Wolf's text. He said we need to stay away from the gangway and the yacht," I muttered, my eyes mesmerized by the tall muscular man I saw standing near the bow in a black neoprene suit, mask and scuba gear. I paused, puzzled. "I don't get it. He's going for a dive."

"So?"

"He knew we were coming. He warned us to keep our distance. He said it was dangerous and he'd explain later. We shouldn't go any further." My eyes shot over to the silver Mercedez SUV parked at the dock. It couldn't be his. Wolf drove a Jeep. "Why now?"

Carmelita glanced at her shiny Cartier watch; a pretty thing encrusted with diamonds almost as bright in the daylight as the sun's rays striking the Caribbean.

"The Sea God is being overly dramatic. I'm sure it's just another surprise he has planned for you. Logically speaking, we are forty-five minutes early, cariño. He isn't ready for us." She smirked. "Most likely he thought we'd be late after shopping. Probably thought we'd stop for drinks and snacks but, we were good girls for a change." She patted me on the arm, "And we found you a special dress for your party. Not that your little wrap-around red dress isn't cute but surely there has to be a soiree for the formal announcement."

I glanced at the paper bag in my hands. Inside, under layers of tissue was an incredible dress, fitted and short. It made me look svelte and long-legged. "The aqua silk is beautiful."

She clapped her hands in excitement. "I think this is where he wants to make the proposal and my bet is, he has decorators there."

I shrugged. "It hasn't gone that far."

She squeezed my hand. "I'm glad you two are moving slowly. You need to be sure. I know he's a hot guy but don't forget about the other fish nibbling on your line." Carmelita glanced around.

I stood silently hardly listening to her prattle.

Carmelita poked me with her forefinger. "Adelina?"

Ignoring my friend, I squinted into the sun. Wolf stood motionless for a few seconds before he shot backwards into the water in a perfect dive. He went under and then resurfaced again to clear his mask.

I debated shouting out to him but I figured he wouldn't be able to hear me from here. The gangway was in place awaiting our arrival. There was a bench on this side that would do if we had to wait. I would take Carmelita and head off for a while before I had another text clearing us to go on board. Marg might not join us. Carmelita was Diego's sister after all and even though Marg got along with Carmelita, she was not keen on Diego. Her last encounter with him had left a bad taste in her mouth. I took out my cell and texted:

Are you coming to the boat? Wait at the bench on the dock. Wolf said not to approach the gangway. Dangerous. Adie

I was worried about what would be so dangerous. I turned to Carmelita to make sure she knew this was serious. "Wolf thinks something bad will happen."

"Oh? Has he been to see a psychic? She laughed at her joke.

"This is serious."

Carmelita pursed her lips in annoyance, ignoring my warning. "What's a girl with a thirst need to do?" She grinned. "I should have brought my new houseboy. He is excellent at making drinks, among other things. Did I tell you I have a new one? Very nice on the eyes." Her tongue flicked over her lip reflectively. "I am so thirsty."

"We could sit on that bench in the sun while we wait or head out to a beach club. I need to wait for a text from Wolf telling me it's okay to board. Something may be wrong with the boat."

Carmelita's eyes shifted to the ocean. The breeze was gently lifting her long locks off her shoulders. I could feel the salt in the air. It was beautiful but a knot in my stomach was warning me of something to come.

Brushing a bang away from her forehead, Carmelita said, "You know, chica, I love the sea. I would adore living in your Sea God's condo building. The view is terrific and the condos have more square footage than mine. I am so weary of my tired-looking place. There's no ocean view or a beach like at Diego's villa."

"Luxury condos with tennis courts and a pool."

"I should buy one," she mused. "Does he have any left?

"You have a few million to spare?"

Carmelita shot me a look.

"Of course, you do. Pocket change for a Bolivar Alvarez."

"And you could have all that also if you decided to marry my brother."

I sighed. "Wolf and I are trying to work things out."

"How many times have I heard that before? Isn't it better to move on if you have to keep trying to make it work, over and over? Love should run smoothly, right?" Carmelita chuckled. "Listen to me, chica. I have a fine selection of brothers, all sinfully delicious, don't you think?"

I nodded. "The way you talk they could be chocolate truffles."

Carmelita grinned.

She was right about the handsome Bolivar Alvarez men being hot commodities but Wolf wasn't chicken liver either. "Come on, let's go sit on the bench."

We were almost there when it happened. A yellow flash, a rumbling vibration and an ear shattering bang rocked the air. Fiberglass parts from the gangway went flying helter-skelter. I pushed Carmelita to the ground. She shrieked as the gravel tore into her skin. Carmelita collapsed in a heap with me halfway on top of her. My body shook with the secondary impact from the explosion and the missiles of debris.

I was dizzy, my body sore from hitting the pavement and debris volleyed down on me. My eyes refused to open. A tinkle of a warm liquid ran to my lips. I tasted salty blood. Eventually, footsteps approached. Voices spoke in hushed tones. Spanish males and a single female argued. I caught something about us being dead. A foot prodded my hip. Who were these heartless people? They seemed in no hurry to help us. I could feel Carmelita under me, warm, breathing and still. I didn't want to speak. Talking might seal my fate. They could be the ones that caused the explosion. They might want to finish us off.

A moment later I was picked up by the feet and arms. I let myself sag. The skirt of my dress rid high to my waist and I heard an incomprehensible guttural remark, followed by a loud guffaw. The woman's voice scolded in harsh rapid-fire Spanish.

Sea breeze fanned my warm skin. They had carried me to the water, but why? Had anyone called an ambulance?

"Ono, dos, tres!" A man shouted. I felt myself being thrown. For a brief moment I was suspended in the air before I hit the water with a splash, my eyes fluttered open briefly before the salt water stung them shut. The lukewarm water jolted me awake but my brain was having trouble processing. My face scraped by coral brought my brain to an alert mode. I flailed in the waves momentarily, treading water briefly, my head spinning in a world of its own. I knew I was drowning, my lungs collapsing. I was in and out of consciousness, when strong arms gripped my waist and lifted me upwards. I breathed out bubbles, weathering my way back to the surface, sticking it out as long as I could.

Just as my lungs felt like they would burst, I made it to the surface. I breathed deeply, still only partially aware of what had just transpired.

"Babe." I knew the voice but couldn't quite comprehend how Wolf could have appeared in time to save me. "Lay back. I'll take you to safety. I am so sorry you got caught up in this."

It was beyond me why I had ended up twenty feet under without a mask and a regulator. In fact, I was not on a scuba excursion gone wrong at all, or was I? If only I could get my brain waves unscrambled. What had just happened?

13

My temples were throbbing. Flying debris had beat my body leaving me sore and bruised. The pounding headache didn't help with the confusion. I was overwhelmed by an experience that should have killed me.

My eyes remained closed and I used my senses, drinking it all in. Salt coated my face, arms and legs, nipping my skin in the process of drying. I was lying on a bed covered with a thin bed sheet but I wasn't chilled as I expected after being tossed in the sea for an unanticipated dive. Memories flooded my mind. The experience of being dropped like fish food into the water. The inability to breathe until Wolf pushed me back to the surface. I was sure it was the Sea God. Who else called me babe? Where had he come from? How had he known I was in trouble?

All these thoughts ran randomly through my mind with no answers.

The room was warm but not unpleasantly so. From outside I heard the chatter of birds and the low buzz of traffic. I let myself relax but I was very aware that I needed to stay alert. If someone wanted me dead, I wasn't about to make it easy for them.

Slowly, I opened my eyes, taking in my surroundings. The walls, the window frame, the sheets and blinds were all a sterile white. I was in a single bed in a room with one window, the venetian blinds open, filtering light through the slats.

"Buenos dias," a male voice said from the door frame. He was tall, had dark wavy hair and twinkling brown eyes. He wore a white jacket over a blue shirt and gray dress pants. With a wide smile exposing his pink gums and white teeth he explained, "I am doctor Santos. How are you feeling, señorita?"

Bringing my fingertips to my head, I murmured, "Beat up. Headache."

"To be expected."

What happened?"

"You were involved in the explosion."

"A terrorist?"

Doctor Santos shook his head. "We don't know. The police will be here shortly. They will tell you those details." He glanced down at the clipboard he was holding. "It is not clear how you ended up in the sea. Can you explain that?"

I shook my head. To be honest I wasn't ready to trust this doctor. For all I knew he was working for the men who tried to dispose of me in the Caribbean.

"Is my friend Carmelita all right?"

"Yes, she is, probably because of you. You protected her from sharp particles that flew in your direction. She says you saved her."

"Is she here?"

"I believe she is resting at the villa of senor Bolivar Alvarez. She wanted to see you but I insisted she go and rest, as you should do. Your recovery depends on fewer visitors."

I glanced about. "What is this place?"

"Clinica de Cozumel. We are a private clinic. Don't worry about the fees. Your novio is paying for the tests and care."

"Wolf Du Lac?"

Doctor Santos chortled. "You have more than one novio?" He patted my hand reassuringly.

"Yes, the one I speak of is señor Du Lac."

"Did I have other visitors?"

"Just señor Bolivar Alvarez."

"No one else?"

"Yes, there may have been, but the nurses shooed them away. I didn't ask."

"Oh," I murmured in disappointment. It would have been good to see some friendly faces if indeed these people were actually my friends. I mean, how many people did I know on this island? After almost drowning, I wasn't so sure those visitors were friends. Linda's murder had to be connected with this attempt on my life.

"Perhaps they were reporters. They would only upset you. It is better not to see them."

"Right, reporters are a nuisance." I was feeling a lot better. Not in the least bit dizzy. "Please, doctor, may I leave?"

Doctor Santos smiled. "No, I'm afraid not. Not for a while. You must rest. We are running a battery of tests to make sure you have no residual trauma. The tests are necessary to see how this accident affected your health. After such an experience, they are essential to see if you are having a swelling of the brain."

"I see."

"We have taken blood and there will be a nurse in to assist you with an MRI. Tomorrow we will run the EEG, so no tea or coffee today." He patted my hand again. "We will take good care of you. Enjoy the rest." He turned to go.

"Thank you, doctor," I said gratefully. He sounded sincere, no intention of doing me any harm, but I was a long way from trusting anyone in this clinic.

As the doctor was leaving, the nurse entered. She was a stubby woman in a traditional white uniform, white stockings and practical shoes. Her name, Renata Ruda, I knew from the pin on her pocket. She had short curly brown hair and a piggish nose. Her eyes were small, brown and squinty. She was pleasantly plump but her disposition wasn't, pleasant, that is. Nurse Ruda was more in line with a military general, ordering me around like she would a lowly soldier. There was no arguing with this woman. She was to be obeyed.

Nurse Ruda proceeded to give me a bed bath followed by the use of the bed pan. She stood there and watched as she ordered me to urinate on command.

After that she and an orderly whipped me up onto a gurney and took me to a room for an MRI. It was akin to being in a space ship with a disembodied voice telling me to breathe and then ordering me to hold my breath. This repeated a few times before they loaded me back on the gurney to my room.

Nurse Ruda took hold of my shoulders while Theo Sanctuario, the orderly, his name pinned on his jacket lapel, took hold of my ankles and swung my legs over to position my butt back onto the middle of the bed. He was attractive, tall with black hair and eyes.

"Has señor Du Lac come to visit?" I asked, as she pulled the sheet up, covering my chest.

"No one is allowed to visit. Doctor Santos' orders."

"Not even my boyfriend?"

Nurse Ruda's teeth drew back in a snarl. "No one!" Then her tone softened. "We will be back to bring you down for the EKG reading. That one will not take that long." She gestured. "Come." At that, she and Theo marched out of the room.

Of course, there was nothing to do in there, no magazines, books or television. Just as I thought I'd die of boredom; the door flew open and I had a surprise unwanted visitor.

The shouting had me alerted before Detective Hernandez entered, followed by Nurse Ruda. She tried to stop him but she finally relented and let him enter.

I picked up from that brief yelling match that he would be allowed a few minutes. Hernandez watched as she shut the door behind her.

Hernandez was wearing a gray jacket, black shirt and wrinkled gray trousers. His hair was buzzed recently but he'd kept the moustache. The exchange in Spanish must have made his blood boil, his face was so red. I suppose if he was to keel over from a stress attack, the clinic was as good a place as any.

"Señorita Sturm. Listen to me. I will get right to the point. A bomb was set off on the gangway near the boat belonging to Wolf Du Lac. What do you know of this?"

"Me?"

"Sí, this was a criminal act. I am interested in whatever you might know."

"I'm afraid I know nothing. The dock workers might have noticed something."

Detective Hernandez puffed his chest in indignation, his little Hitler moustache bristling. "It is not for advice I have come to see you. Why is it you were in the water and señorita Bolivar Alvarez was thrown onto the walkway? It seems to me you were a threat."

"I don't know anything. You would be more familiar with these people. I am as confused as you are."

Hernandez's eyes narrowed. "They targeted you. You must have knowledge of their activities. Is this possibly connected to señora Linda Du Lac's murder?"

I shrugged.

"Are you withholding information, señorita Sturm?"

"I am as anxious as you are to know why."

"They were coming after you."

I pushed my hair back thoughtfully. "You think they would plant a bomb to kill me?"

"You were the only one thrown into the sea. What do you remember of this?"

"They were men."

"Really, that's it? Did you not see them?"

"My vision was blurred. I was in and out of consciousness."

"You disappoint me señorita Sturm. I am trying to find out who tried to kill you."

"Let me remind you they could have killed any number of people including señorita Bolivar Alvarez."

"All the more reason to find these criminals."

"I would be getting at it if I were you then. Señor Bolivar Alvarez will not be pleased that his sister was hurt."

Hernandez growled, "He was not pleased to know you were here in this clinic either. I think he believes you are his future—"

At this point Nurse Ruda barged in. She shot out directives to Hernandez. He moved towards the door quickly as if avoiding a spitting cobra. Ruda was taking a no-nonsense approach to Detective Hernandez's invasion into her territory.

I did get the part of *vamos cabron*, having heard that one enough on television. *Cabron* translates as a goat but usually means idiot and *vamos* is similar to get out. Ruda made no bones about who was boss but this time she was on my team.

For the first time I was glad that I had a dragon lady guarding my room. It was unlikely they planted a bomb just for me but they certainly had the intention to kill me when they tossed me into the sea. What bothered me is that neither Wolf nor Diego had come to see me. I was hurt. I turned away so Ruda wouldn't see the tear escaping the corner of my eye.

***

The following day was a haze. Nurse Ruda had administered some heavy-duty drugs into my system before the EEG. I had been returned from the examination room and was almost asleep when there was a commotion at my door.

Nurse Ruda was as irate as a disturbed bumblebee, her nest invaded by intruders. She shrieked out some Spanish words that would have kept anyone at bay but she was no match for Wolf who barged in, deflecting her with his arm. What a sight he was—tall, blond, muscular and Viking fit. His blond hair was windblown and his eyes were blue like the waters of the stream where we had fished years ago. Wolf was wearing a black T-shirt over his wide shoulders and chest, the shirt clinging to his taut six-pack tucked into blue jeans.

"Get her clothes, Nurse. I have arranged her release." Wolf grinned triumphantly and winked at me. No one was getting the better of him. "I am taking her out of here."

"What? This lady stays, señor. It must be cleared with the doctor."

"And it has been. I have some clean duds for señorita Sturm. I would appreciate you assisting her into them. I'm sure she is weak from her experience." Wolf handed her a duffle bag.

"Well, if we must do this, you, señor, must wait outside and give the patient her privacy."

"See you soon, princess." Wolf winked at me before he strolled out of the room.

With no makeup, not even lip gloss, I was certain I was hideous, like a bag lady left under a newspaper for a week in the rain, definitely not like any princess Wolf knew. Of course, Ruda had to be unfamiliar with cosmetics as she wore none herself.

"Did they find my purse and cell phone?"

"I will look." Nurse Ruda headed to the dresser and dug into a drawer, pulling out a plastic bag filled with my possessions.

"Amazing that they survived the explosion," I murmured when I saw my red cross-shoulder bag and sandals.

Barely suppressing her lack of enthusiasm, Ruda assisted me in dressing. Wolf had brought me panties but no bra. Nurse Ruda frowned at that. The purple dress had built-in support and I wasn't bouncing the girls around, much to Nurse Ruda's disappointment. She was displeased with my unplanned departure. Her agenda relied on tight rules and regulations.

"I'd like my purse, please." Inside I found mascara and lip-gloss. Just what I needed to look my old self. There was a tiny mirror attached to the blush I used for all the makeup. At the bottom my gold cuff and the diamond earrings lay in a clear Ziploc baggie. No one had stolen anything! How about that?

One last thing. My hair needed help. I pulled out a small brush from my purse which I ran through my tangled hair. Not the best style but it would have to do.

"Wolf?" I called out.

My boyfriend strode in and gave me another bag. "I went out to the Jeep. I bought you these."

"What's this?" Not waiting for an answer, I took out a wide brimmed straw hat and a pair of dark sunglasses. "You knew what I needed? Wow!"

"I thought you might like to keep the sun out of your eyes after your head injuries. Hope they're okay?"

"More than okay." Wolf was the best. "Thanks, Sea God. I don't know what I would do without you."

"Anything for my mermaid." Wolf swept his hand in the air to indicate the wheelchair. "Your chariot awaits, princess!"

"I don't need this wheelchair," I protested, but Nurse Ruda insisted. "It is clinic policy."

She handed me a second bag. "They also found this," she said disapprovingly, taking out my newly purchased dress, holding it up gingerly as if no one in their right mind would want such a garment. It was an aqua dress with a deep V-neck. "I'm surprised this dress wasn't thrown out or taken."

"It's a very nice dress." That was an understatement. I'd fallen in love with that aqua gown, eager to wear it for Wolf.

Wolf grinned in amusement. "Can't wait to see you in it."

Nurse Ruda didn't qualify that with a comment. Instead she started steering me into the hall. "You must not exert yourself in the next few days to speed up your recovery. Understand?'

I nodded. "Gracias for all your care."

Nurse Ruda narrowed her eyes taking in the full essence of the Sea God. "You may be interested in knowing that sex can help recovery but wait for that." A flicker of a smile made its way to her lips. "You can take the wheelchair outside to your car."

"Thank you, nurse." Wolf gave her his seductive grin which had set many a woman aquiver.

Nurse Ruda nodded, as if she finally approved.

Wolf took me through the sliding doors and down the ramp into the heat of the Cozumel sun. I was glad he had brought me a sleeveless dress. I was feeling a bit faint. Too many drugs and a sore head did not make for a pleasant Adie Sturm.

14

Wolf unzipped the plastic window on the passenger side before
he assisted me into the Jeep. Even so, it felt very warm inside the
vehicle until Wolf pulled out onto the road and the wind fanned my
face.

"What a relief to be out of there. What did the doctor say?"

"You're A-Okay, babe. You know, you're like a cat with nine
lives, surviving what would kill most of us."

"I'd be dead without you fishing me out of the sea. How did you
manage to catch me before I drown?"

"I was diving around the area to check if there was another bomb.
I had dismantled the one I found on board *Adie's Storm* but I
wondered if they had placed another on the gangway." His glance
flicked to a box wrapped in sparkly paper. "That's for you."

Picking up the gift, I asked, "Can I open it?"

"Yes, you definitely should."

Wolf was looking very mysterious, his lips turned up at the
corners. Just then my iPhone trilled a text. Curious as always, I
tugged out my cell.

*Mi amor, where are you? I came to take you to my villa but you
had left. You are not safe with Du Lac. D*

"Don't tell me. It's Alvarez."

I smiled. "Jealous?"

"No, just wondering if this guy will ever let up on wanting my
woman."

"He's only concerned about my safety."

"Sure. The only safe place for you is his bed, right?"

I laughed. "Sure, but his villa is even safer. He has Churo and
Luis, remember?"

"He's pissed because I came to get you."

"Most likely. Diego hopes you and I won't work out."

"Let him hope. By the way, I did try to see you but they wouldn't
allow me to disturb you."

"Good to know. I wondered if you had deserted me."

"Alvarez is delusional. You and I will work this out. Believe me."

"Maybe, he and Carmelita have a point."

"Which is?"

"We tried before and—"

Wolf shot me a look. "It was hardly my fault."

I nodded. "Well, let's not talk about that then. Let's move forward. I want to know what Heinz said."

Wolf frowned. "He's full of shit."

"Oh?"

"He thinks you murdered Linda."

My jaw dropped. "He's been smoking too much whacky tobaccy."

Wolf frowned.

I glanced down at my dress which was crumpled under the seat belt. Not many of these Jeeps had seat belts but Wolf liked to be safe. He must have had them especially installed. "Why would he say that?"

"An affair. You were vying for the same man—him."

"You must be kidding. Sure, Heinz looks fine, most would say he's a ten, but he's no comparison to you. You are the Sea God! No woman can resist you," I said with a smirk.

Wolf grinned. "True."

"What did Hernandez say?"

"He thinks that jealousy story could be true. They found Linda down on the beach below the condo building. The bodyguards didn't take her far."

"Making it seem that she was murdered close by. Both Heinz and I are staying in the condo. Your brother's obviously trying to pin this on me, but why?"

"He's in trouble. Hernandez found fingerprints in his condo. Linda's, I imagine."

"I thought Diego's bodyguards, Luis and Churo wiped it clean. That's what they always do."

Wolf drove into the parking lot as the side of the condo. "Alvarez gets you out of these messes often enough. He wants your gratitude, wouldn't you say?"

"I can't think leaving fingerprints is very competent, do you?"

Wolf pulled the throttle into first and stopped the engine. "He wants to be the one to rescue you."

"And at the same time make the Du Lacs look bad, right?" I reached for my door handle.

"Stay. I'll help you out."

I was about to protest. I was capable of getting out if I jumped."
Glancing at the scrapes and cuts on my arms, numb wounds from
the drugs they had given me, I began to doubt my athleticism. That
was my pre-explosion self. I could just as easily miss landing on
my feet. The wave of dizziness I had would attest to that.

Wolf swung the door open and reached in to lift me out and set
me down gently on the pavement. "Alvarez will figure out who
killed Linda from his informants and hand that information to
Hernandez. He knows you didn't do it."

"Of course, he would defend me to Hernandez but what about
Heinz's story?"

Wolf took my hand and led me to the lobby door. "He was angry
and decided to kill her. Then he knocked himself out." His eyes
met mine. "You believe that version?"

I grinned. "Anything is possible."

Wolf shook his head. "Not in this case. Heinz is not a murderer."

"But he's pointing the finger at me for no reason."

"He's afraid. He's behind the eight ball."

"Prison?"

Wolf sighed. "Possibly, if he doesn't spill on what he knows.
Unfortunately, Heinz is a closed book. He won't open up to me."

"Keep digging. You have informants too." I stroked his arm. "I
don't want to go to jail either."

Wolf leaned in and hugged me closely. "And I don't want to lose
you. Do you want me to call Ed Marion to represent you?"

I was in a bad situation. If I didn't get killed first, I might end up
in a Mexican jail.

"He's expensive. You said he got the mob people off."

"He knows the ropes. No worries, babe. I'll take care of it."

"Thank you."

Wolf held out his elbow to loop my arm through. "I'll call him."

"Thank you. It's good to have you on my team."

"You're not having doubts about us?"

I grinned. "Not yet."

Wolf bent to kiss me. I stood on my toes and felt his pillow lips
press on mine. Liquid heat shot to my core. A man like this one
was hard to find. Intelligent, kind and extremely sexy. He made me
melt like butter on a cobblestone street in the hot Cozumel sun.

"Let's get you to your condo." Wolf placed his hand on the small of my back and steered me to the elevator.

By the time we entered my condo, I was tired. "Can you help me to the bedroom?"

"Sure, babe." Wolf studied my face before he hoisted me up in his arms and carried me to the king-sized bed. "But, I am guessing you need a nap?"

"Yup."

In a husky voice, his eyes heavy-lidded, he said, "Too bad. I've been missing you."

Dropping down on my king-sized bed, I shot him a sultry look. "Me too—missing you. I have things to tell you."

"About?"

"This condo project is turning into a nightmare for everyone. Maybe you don't want to find out anything. It would be easier if there was nothing going on, right?"

Wolf frowned. "I'm not like that. You know me. I don't hide my head in the sand. What is it? Is Heinz involved in something criminal?"

I shrugged. "I had a conversation with Hernandez but haven't connected it all yet."

"You know something."

"I do."

"And it worries you."

I nodded. "I don't want to be implicated in Linda's murder either."

Wolf sat down on the edge of the bed and studied me. "Do you think Heinz killed her?"

"Maybe." I straightened a pillow behind my neck. "Hernandez said they put Linda's body on the beach near the condo. I am sure Churo and Luis wouldn't bring her back to the Erizo beach. How did he connect Linda's killing to Heinz's condo? Why would the police check for prints?"

Wolf sighed. "Heinz."

I bit my lip thoughtfully. "Exactly. He's into something."

"Who else is involved? Did you find out?"

My mind flashed back to the art gallery run by Perla Bravo Gonzalez and to Marg's rendezvous with the Clean cousin. "Perla, Leo Del Socorro and possibly his cousin, Leon, your investor."

"I am impressed. How did you get this information?"

"Snooping."

Wolf laughed. "You haven't lost your skills, have you? Adie Sturm is a master snoop." He pulled me close to him. "Tell me."

I gave him a brief synopsis of my trek into the gallery with Carmelita and Marg. "I had a $100 bill in my bra but it wasn't in my effects when I became a patient at the clinic. Someone took the evidence."

"You think the money was real?"

I shook my head. "I have no clue. I also don't know if the clinic staff can be trusted. Someone could have taken the $100 bill."

Wolf nodded. "It's getting hard to figure out who is playing what game."

"I'm still on this. Getting clues. I know there's more," I rubbed my temple, "just not thinking too clearly yet. I'll work on finding the murderer."

"But don't do anything crazy." Wolf stroked my cheek. "These punks are dangerous."

I made a mock salute. "Got it, but seriously when have I not been reliable?"

"You are totally unpredictable."

"But not unreliable."

Wolf grinned. "Are you okay to be left alone?"

I nodded. "I want to have a nap but," I grabbed his arm, "are you coming back?"

"As soon as I can, if not I will arrange something for later." Wolf stood. "Do you need me right now?" His smile was seductive, oozing testosterone.

"We could eat those chocolates."

"I need to keep my hands off you for a few hours, at least. Have a nap. When you're better, we can have some wine, and a nice soft in the mouth Shiraz."

"Sounds perfect. Wine and chocolate."

"That should release those endorphins." Wolf stroked my cheek. "I think they badly need releasing but you need to heal. Sleep."

"And then?" I asked innocently with a tiny smile pulling the corners of my mouth up.

Wolf placed a soft kiss on my lips before he stood. "Rest up."

I watched him stroll out the door. Moments later the condo door clicked shut and I was left alone with my thoughts. The images of guilty parties lined up in my head before I closed my eyes and dozed off.

In my dream I was underwater surrounded by tangs, grunts and angelfish. Yellow brain coral mingled with white pointy bits from a brownish-orange seaweed. I reached out to touch it, knowing even as I slept it was not a good idea. Pain shot into my fingertips. This was not seaweed. It was the deadly marine organism related to the sea anemone and jelly fish. Divers called it fire coral for its agonizing sting. The needles hurt like hell. I screamed in my head, awaking with a start.

Was the dream déjà vu? Or was it symbolic for the mess I was in?

Somewhere in the recesses of my brain I had forgotten something. The key. The one that Heinz received in the mail. Where had I hidden it? I rubbed my fingers to my temples, rubbing them like a genie lamp, willing the hiding place to come to me. It was too much. The concussion had wiped my memory clean.

I shrugged it off. There was a murder to be solved.

Getting myself in gear, I propelled myself off the bed and padded over to the dresser. It was too hot outside to wear jeans. My search yielded denim shorts, a pair of black lacy bikini panties, a matching bra and a loose floral print top.

When I was dressed, I did my makeup and brushed my hair. It was then that I heard a clamor through the wall from Heinz's condo.

Perfect timing. I would confront him. He knew what this was all about. I wouldn't be surprised if he had seen Linda's killer either. If he did, we could go to Hernandez and let him arrest the murderer.

On the way out I snatched up my purse and a pair of sunglasses. The hallway was empty as I approached Heinz's condo door. I hesitated, but then summoning courage, I knocked.

More shuffling noises from inside. Finally, the door released a fraction. A portion of a face that looked like Heinz gaped through the opening before he clicked the door shut.

"What the—Heinz!"

I knocked on the door again, louder this time. There were no sounds on the other side of the door. Was he standing there like some dumbass robot?

"Heinz!" I yelled. "Open this door now!"

The door creaked ajar. Heinz stood there in a printed gitch and a blue T-shirt that had a white Maple Leaf logo printed on the front. The Leafs were a big-league NHL team. People from Ontario, where I come from, rooted for them if they were smart. Especially if they didn't want to get clobbered in the Scotiabank Arena by the Leaf fans.

The gitch and T-shirt were normal enough attire for a Canuck from the greater Toronto area, except most Canadians usually wore shorts over the gitch. He wore white sports socks and no shoes to complete his outfit. A quick glance at his face confirmed my suspicions. It was tough going at the police station. He was not looking good. His hotness rating went down to a three.

Dark shadows looked like makeup smears under his bloodshot eyes. Luckily, he had very little hair because what there was of it was unsightly—long blond strands hung slack and greasy on his forehead. There was a bruise under his left temple like he'd taken a hit from a massive fist.

"Did they rough you up at the police station?"

"It's nothing," he droned, making me wonder if his sparring opponent had smashed his mouth and left him incapable of lucid speech.

"Go away, Adie." He started to close the door in my face when he saw the abrasion on my temple. "What the hell happened to you? Did they arrest you too?"

"There was a little explosion at the dock. Wolf didn't tell you?"

"That's what this scrape is about?" With his finger he jabbed at my temple.

"Ouch! Get off me!" I took a step away. "We can't speak in this hallway, you idiot."

"I guess," Heinz mumbled, "but I have nothing for you. I know nothing—nothing."

"You have explaining to do," I said, pushing him back into his condo with both my hands on his chest, all the force coming from my legs and body weight. Although I'm a lightweight, I was able to force him to retreat into the condo. He was wobbly himself. I didn't believe that part about the police not throwing a punch in his direction.

The living room was the same as it was before, white leather couches, ivory marble flooring, paintings on the walls, minus

Linda's dead body disturbing the gold marbled angelfish. Heinz flung himself down on the couch, his legs swinging over the armrest.

"Right, let's get down to it."

"What?'

"You lied. You told Hernandez that I killed Linda and threw her in the aquarium." I sat down on the couch opposite his. "I'd like to know why."

Heinz rolled his eyes. "Do you know anything about the Cozumel police? Have you ever been arrested?"

"Well, no, not really."

"What are you saying? They decided you killed her because—"

"I had no choice. I'm the prime suspect as far as they're concerned. I was about to be her ex-husband." He gazed at the ceiling thoughtfully. "I guess I am her ex now anyway. Linda's dead, Adie." His lips curled downwards on the ends. "It's my fault. She should be alive and married to me." Heinz sighed. "I loved her, Adie."

"Are you saying Linda went off you? You mean like cream going bad?"

"Exactly. I lost my sex appeal." Heinz placed a hand over his eyes and threw his head back on the sofa, letting it rest. "I am so useless. I failed her. I wish I could go back in time and do it all differently."

"Like how?" It appeared as if Heinz was playing a sympathy card. He had taken a few hard knocks but nothing like what had happened to me. I wasn't in the mood for his pity party. "What did you do wrong besides throwing me under the bus?"

"I think she found someone more appealing."

"You mean rich and better looking?"

Heinz chuckled. "I am the best in the looks department." He glanced down. "I guess not right now, but normally women love me. I can't model any more. I'm too old and I need money, Adie. I'm almost broke."

"You're strapped for cash?"

"All the money I have is invested—it's not liquid, so to speak." He stretched out his arms. "I moved to Cozumel and put the money into the Erizo del Mar. Wolf had me go in on this deal with him. I'm still waiting for a return."

"So that's why you got involved in something illegal?"

Heinz sat up. "You're worse than the police. Questions, questions, questions. How can Wolf stand you?"

I grinned. "This coming from the husband of the psycho redhead. Why was she so in my face at the Skyreef?"

"I didn't know she was, but," Heinz scratched his head, "I think she was jealous that you had Wolf, the rich brother."

"And she had a loser?"

Color blotched Heinz's cheeks. "I made a decent amount modelling but that's over with. Wolf offered me the manager's position for the Erizo. That wasn't good enough for crazy Linda. She didn't want me anymore. I kind of think she hooked a fish of her own to get over the drought. A rich bastard."

"Why would she need so much money?"

"Linda had expensive taste. Liked designer stuff. And let's not forget that divorce cost her." He got up and strolled to the fridge. "Want a beer?"

I glanced over at him and saw a slight bulge in his middle. Was it bloat or fat? Was he drinking too much beer? It could account for the Molson muscle he was developing. He had Coronas in his tummy not Molson, our ever-popular go-to Canadian beer but that paunch was the beginning of a noticeable belly roll. "Sure, thanks."

When he handed me the bottle, we clicked long necks, and I said, "Are you okay?"

"Ya know, how it is here, eh?"

"Sure." I drank, staring at him from over the bottle. "What have you been doing since they released you?"

"Just out and about."

Glancing over at the bin beside the fridge, I spied at least a dozen Corona empties. "Depressed?"

"Yeah, a bit. Wasting my time in Margaritaville."

"I can understand that you got targeted by the police but why implicate me?"

"It was the only way I could get out of there and have a cold one."

I gritted my teeth. "That was nasty of you."

"I know."

"Listen, you can talk to me."

"I'm not sure you'd understand."

I tipped back my beer too suddenly and got fizz up my nose. I'm not one to drink beer but today I needed a drink and beer is as good as any in hot weather. That was my excuse. It was a rough two days.

"Say, you hungry?"

My ears perked up at the mention of food. I couldn't remember when I last had something decent to eat. The clinic food was about as appealing as cardboard on a plate.

"I have real Mexican food. Not Taco Bell. Got some of these tamales this old lady around the corner was selling. Good stuff, I kid you not!" He opened the fridge and brought out brown paper wrapped food, setting it on the granite kitchen countertop. "Mayan banana leaf chicken tamales." Slowly, he unwrapped his treasure and presented the product with a flourish. "I can heat them up in the microwave."

"Okay, sounds good. Thanks." I hadn't tried tamales yet but when the stomach needs a fill up it's my duty to oblige.

I wasn't sure about the tamales until the second bite. I could see why Diego had this thing for tamales. A little doughy but tasty. The corn tamale is good heated up like tortillas.

"Listen, Adie, I have to warn you, seeing as you are beat up enough right now. You need to stay away from the condo investors. You don't want to end up like Linda, ya know? Chill, eh."

My mouth was too full to answer but what he said made me feel guilty. I should be investigating before Wolf's deal blows up.

After I consumed the last morsel of my tamale, he told me I had to leave. He tapped his fingertips on the counter nervously, "I have to run an errand. Nice talking."

I nodded. Heinz didn't bother walking me to the door. I went out and made my way down the elevator without a fuss. One thing was for sure, Heinz was not telling me much. My idea was to follow him.

15

I waited around the corner of the Erizo del Mar. Heinz came out wearing the same blue Toronto Maple Leafs T-shirt and tan cargo shorts. He wore a pair of brown leather sandals. He looked considerably better with a beige fedora slipped low over his head, covering the ghastly greasy hair. Apparently, a shower was not on his list of priorities.

Heinz headed down Rafael E. Melgar at a rapid pace, dodging vendors and finally winding down a side street. I had to run to keep up which was not easy after lying in a hospital bed for a couple of days.

He stopped at a bar called Peligrosa and ducked in. From the outside posters of female legs clad in black fishnet stockings, garters and stiletto heels against a pink background greeted the customers. They advertised cerveza, liquor and dancers. My guess was that Heinz was hard up for female company. Hopefully, I wasn't wasting my afternoon. I would rather see him doing a drug deal so I could take that information to Wolf.

I gathered up as much chutzpah as I could wiping the sweat from my forehead before I entered the double doors. I was hoping my bravado wouldn't disappear as quickly as my cool demeanor had.

A short brunette, long waves past her shoulders, large brown eyes and two-inch lashes motioned me to a table. I kept my hat and sunglasses on, ordered a Corona, guessing a beer would be germless and appropriate for this type of scuzzy bar. The dusky-skinned woman on stage gyrating with a pole had a pink fuzzy bra on her barely-there boobs and a G-string on a butt that wouldn't quit. She must have oiled up her skin before her dance because her skin shone brightly pink with the strobe lighting. I almost expected one of those silver disco orbs to be rotating along with her but it was the reflection from her ass cheeks.

My body was sadly the opposite of the dancer in pink, bigger on top and smaller on the bottom. The karate training gave my behind a nice upward tilt that Wolf admired and I kept my tatas firm from workouts, an asset Diego appreciated. As for what Cy liked, I didn't give a damn.

Two delicious men like chocolate are enough for any woman unless she was Carmelita. She had a habit of gathering groupies. Diego said she used and abused men, discarding them as often as a woman changes her lipstick shades. It is my contention that he was a bit jealous. Diego gets his fair share of women but men, even a stud like Diego has to work to capture the heart of a woman and he was just too lazy to do that.

Once my eyes adjusted to the dim light, I spotted Heinz at a table next to the stage. Other men were at tables hunched over drinking getting a look-see at the scantily clad waitresses in bright red two-piece outfits. The shorts they wore barely covered their solid round bottoms. They dipped down when they served drinks so the clientele had awesome views of their booties at all angles.

I was feeling foolish sitting there in a girlie club, thinking I should be on the beach enjoying the sun and surf while it was still here to enjoy. I was worried the hurricane would hit Cozumel. Having never experienced anything but a severe storm in my life, it was stupid to be wasting my time spying on Wolf's brother, even if it was justified.

Suddenly Heinz was joined by a stout gray-haired man with a moustache. He wore an expensive fitted lightweight gray suit and a white shirt. His shoes were black leather slip ons.

I knew I had seen him before at Diego's party. This dude was Orlando Keene. He suffered from pale freckled skin which tended to burn in the Cozumel sun. To top that off, his bulbous red nose was shiny enough to light any sleigh Santa drove on Christmas Eve. Liquor was not his liver's friend.

Orlando Keene was famous for his cowboy bars in Texas as well as Cancun. He seemed to be friendly enough with Heinz, ordering a round of beer. Heinz and another man were the recipients of his generosity.

The third man sat down, facing away from me. He was a heavy-set bodybuilder, tat sleeves exposed in a muscle shirt. He had a shaved head, neck rolls and wore dark clothing. The top of his head was as shiny as the dancer's bottom, reflecting light from the pink strobes almost as well.

The discussion at that table was a serious one. No one was smiling even a little. The beer guzzling was almost as serious, although I think Heinz was in competition with the bodybuilder more than the owner, Orlando Keene. The empties piled up as I watched. Orlando Keene waved his hand for service and a tray of botanas were carried over by a buxom girl in a black tank and denim shorts.

Apparently, after eating the snacks, the talk was short and sweet. Heinz stood, ready to leave. The men shook hands with that extra arm clap to conclude the bonding, leaving the bodybuilder sitting on his lonesome. I bent my head down and hunched in the shadows as Heinz strode out the door past me.

I left some bills to cover the beer and charged after Heinz. He was unexpectedly fast. In no time he was on Melgar again. It was all I could do to keep up.

"Heinz!" I called out breathless, feeling the effects of my injuries. "Wait up!"

He stopped and turned. "What are you doin' here, Adie?"

"I have to ask you a question."

"I asked what are you doin' here?" He gawked at me. "You following me?"

"I have questions."

"About?"

"Did they find the murder weapon?"

"Blunt object. That's all I know. What does it matter?"

"Do you think it was the same object that hit you?"

"Could be." He stared at me. "Was it you with a baseball bat, Adie?"

"Me? You must be kidding, I don't play baseball, slugger. By the time I entered your condo you were out like a light and Linda was head first in the fish tank, with the angelfish feasting on her head."

"Yuk. That's gross, Adie. Have some respect! Some bastard killed her."

"And I am trying to solve that mystery. You can be helpful with this, Heinz. Why was Linda killed?"

Heinz stopped and wiped his face. "This weather is so freakin' hot." He glanced up at the sky. "There's a hurricane wrecking Puerta Rico as we speak. It might be here by tomorrow." He pointed at the cirrus clouds above. "That's what it looks like before a hurricane. See the black sky behind it? Maybe you should get a flight back to Canada today. Pack your stuff, girl, before they close the airport." He squinted at me. "You're not safe here."

I tapped his arm to get his attention. "You're avoiding the question. You did something the killer didn't like, didn't you?"

Heinz's eyes flicked away.

"Who had it in for you?"

"It's better to leave it alone, Adie. You don't want to end up dead, do you?"

"And you're happy that these criminals killed her?"

"No, of course not. It was meant for me—a warning."

"What are you saying? You didn't do what they wanted so you'll be next?"

Heinz frowned. "I didn't want to do anything illegal. When I didn't do what they asked they killed Linda."

"Why didn't you tell me that before? I suspected you were involved in a criminal activity."

"I couldn't. You'd tell Wolf and I wouldn't have a job."

"Do you know who killed Linda?"

"Kind of, but no, not exactly."

"Is there money laundering going on?"

Heinz nodded sadly. "They're bad people, Adie. They'll kill you if you interfere."

"There's a time to stand up to them and this is it." I stared up at him. "Agreed?"

"You're right. They'll probably kill us anyway."

I shook my head. What an attitude. Seriously negative. Heinz was a doormat. "The Erizo del Mar must have camera surveillance."

"Yup, it does. Every condo unit has cameras installed."

"And what did it have from your unit?"

Heinz frowned. "Not a clue. The guy at the lobby has tapes."

"We need to look at it, eh? Maybe the killer or killers are on tape."

Heinz pulled his hat further onto his forehead. I could see trickles of sweat roll down his cheek.

"You don't think Hernandez has done this already?"

"No, he wants to frame me or you. That would make his job easy. Blame a Canadian for another Canadian's death."

His hand shot up in defeat. "Mexico stays safe for tourists that way."

I nodded. "It's been done before. Linda's body was found down on the beach. I think someone or persons unknown took the body and put it right on the Erizo del Mar's beach. It's obvious we are being set up."

"That sneaky bastard, Alvarez!"

"I'm not sure he would do that," I said. "He may be the island's godfather but he has his own code of ethics. Anyway, I can't believe Diego's men wouldn't move Linda's body farther away down the beach."

"Yeah, it would be a colossal error for his muscle to screw up. The big Kahuna isn't known for his big heart." He shot me a glance. "Anyway, fill me in, girl. Are things getting serious? I heard he has a boner for you."

I felt heat rise to my cheeks and it wasn't from the weather. "I am working on a relationship with Wolf. As for Diego's men, they were helping. I trust them."

"They moved Linda, all right but not far enough. Hernandez said that they found Linda on the Erizo property."

"Then we need to check out the surveillance tapes for the beach too."

"I guess." He motioned to the street. "Let's cross here and head back."

We started on our way across when a black jeep shot out of nowhere and headed straight towards us.

I grabbed Heinz's arm and pulled him so hard I toppled over onto the sidewalk with Heinz beside me.

"What the—" Heinz rubbed his arm.

I looked up in the direction of the Jeep and saw only a couple of taxis and a Beetle. Where had it gone? "He was trying to hit us."

"Or maybe just you," Heinz pointed out as he stood.

Brushing off the dirt, I got on my feet. "I must be getting close to the answers."

"I hope so for both our sakes."

"Listen, we need to go check the tapes."

"Okeydokey. But don't expect me to do any more than that." He glanced up at the sky. "I don't want to be here during Hurricane Pandora. It might be a big one. I need to get out of Dodge while the going's good."

"Hola, stranger!"

A deep voice called out from the front of a jewelry shop. The voice was familiar. I swiveled around. "Cy!"

"In the flesh. Did I surprise you?"

"What are you doing here? Did you see the Jeep?"

"The one that nearly flattened you like tortillas?"

"The same."

"And before you ask what I was doing standing around while you struggled to survive, I was too far away to save you, but believe me, or I would have." Cy glanced at Heinz. "Not sure about him, though."

"So, you're following me too?" Heinz was furious but not as angry as I was.

"Can't come up with anything on your own?" I studied Diego's brother. He wore blue jeans and a white muscle shirt with the logo Scuba Shark Tours in blue letters across his chest. An octopus tattoo was on his bicep, tentacles reaching out.

"Someone has to find out why the Erizo is in trouble."

Heinz growled, "You mean this clown has been trying to implicate me in a condo scam? You've got nerve, buster. Why are you getting into my business?"

"In case you hadn't noticed your ex, Linda, was murdered. Have you found out why? Don't answer that, you know exactly why, Heinz Du Lac."

Heinz scowled at Cy. "It's not my fault Linda is dead."

"You sure about that, hombre?"

"Hey, you two, stop shouting. We've got surveillance footage to check out." I gathered up the two men by their elbows and started pulling them along to the condo. Heinz shook me off but Cy didn't mind the contact one iota.

***

Paco Herrera was a man past his prime. He sat at the desk in the lobby staring out the window and thinking about his youth. Years ago, he was a police officer. This security job was pitiful compared to what he had done back then but if a man wanted to get respect it paid to be smartly turned out. His white shirt with the logo on his shirt Erizo Del Mar was neatly tucked into navy blue trousers.

Heinz stomped up to the desk and snapped his fingers. "Wake up, fellow. I am Heinz Du Lac, the manager of this hotel. I want to see the surveillance tapes."

"Du Lac?" The little rotund man, his gray hair in a bowl haircut and the beginnings of a beard on his chin sat and glowered, looking Heinz up and down, and finally his eyes glued on the greasy strand hanging from under his fedora on his forehead.

Paco sneered derisively, "You are not señor Du Lac. El Lobo has the white hair of the wolf and he has good muscles." His glance examined Heinz. "He is clean and does not smell."

Heinz responded by getting his gitch in a twist.

Stabbing at his chest with his forefinger, Heinz growled, "I am señor Du Lac's brother, Heinz Du Lac, your manager. I want to see the tapes of 303 and the beach the night of the murder. You know about that, don't you?"

"I do.

"I would get those tapes on the screen if I were you or kiss your cushy job good-bye. I am your boss, the jefe, remember?"

Paco was taken aback. "Caramba! What really?"

"I sure am. Now, get your ass in motion. I want to see the tapes of the beach on the night of the murder and those from my place, 303.

"Sí, I do not recognize you. I know the owner, señor Du Lac and see him often. He is a kind man and respectful to his employees." Paco stared reproachfully at Heinz. "I want to see identification."

"Never you mind that. I told you I am in charge." He turned to me and Cy. "Besides, these two can vouch for me. They know I am Heinz Du Lac."

Paco gazed at us. "Is that true, señores?"

"Yes, he is Heinz du Lac," I said seriously. "I am señorita Sturm. My boyfriend, mi novio, is señor Wolf Du Lac, the other Du Lac with the white hair. This man is his brother and manager." I nudged Cy. "And this man is señor Bolivar Alvarez, brother of Diego Bolivar Alvarez. Tell Paco that," I pointed to Heinz, "he is the manager."

Cy nodded reluctantly, a smirk on his lips.

Paco hit his forehead with his hand. "Of course, señor Bolivar Alvarez. I did not recognize you either. You are strong looking, unlike your brother. Not that he is not handsome as well but he is like, a model, so slender like a woman." He patted his thigh. "He wears the tight trousers, not like those. I am so sorry for the mistake."

"No problem."

"Listen to me." Heinz said tersely, his jaw clenched, "I want to see the tapes. Are the tapes still here or have the police taken them?"

"They should be here, señor."

"Get at it then, man!"

Paco got busy and started rewinding the tapes, reluctantly playing back tapes of the murder night. Heinz and I grabbed chairs and placed them on either side of Paco. Cy stood behind us and we waited.

"This is from 303."

The surveillance tapes were not that clear—two shadowy figures on the screen. The slender female, most likely Linda, threw an object at Heinz. He ducked and they were at a standoff. Two more people entered the room and then it went blank for several screens until another figure opened the door. I was that figure.

"Someone blocked the camera," Cy said. "This tape is useless. Paco, we need to see the beach that night. Find it for us, por favor."

Paco switched to another tape. There was nothing.

"Fast forward," I said.

The tapes registered approximately five hours later. Two figures carried a long object between them. They were coming from further down the beach.

"What building is south of here?" I asked.

"Ah, señorita Sturm, it is a beautiful five-star hotel. The Hotel Palancar has five pools and also it has hot tubs." He sighed as he mentioned the hot tubs.

"Did Diego know about this?" I asked.

Heinz shrugged.

I touched Cy's hand. "Find out, Cy. Call Diego."

Cy retreated to an alcove to make the call. He spoke softly in Spanish for a minute.

"May I speak to him?" I called out.

With Cy's Samsung in my hand I spoke to Diego. "Hola, Diego."

"How pleasant to hear your voice, mi amor. Cy has filled me in on the problem. I assure you it was not Churo or Luis who brought the package back to the Erizo."

"So you don't know who did?"

"Unfortunately, no. Do not be alarmed. My cousin is the chief of police, he will tell the police to leave you out of it. Someone is obviously setting you up."

"Heinz was called down to the police station. When they threatened him with jail, he said it was me."

There was a pause. "Is this man out of his mind? He is making a mess out of the situation. I thought Du Lac wanted his brother to check out the situation. I thought these Du Lac brothers were smarter than this."

"Wolf is a good business man. He sensed something was off. That's why he called in Heinz to find out. Heinz has gone through a lot lately—the death of his wife, you know."

"Don't worry about him. I will fix this. But tonight, we will think of nothing but the party."

"What party?"

"Didn't Du Lac tell you about the pirate ship cruise? Dinner, drinks and a show. Your costume has already been delivered."

"What?"

"Carmelita picked all the female pirate garb herself. She knows your size. You will love this. Everyone has a great time. Beautiful Adelinita, I am sending you kisses! Sweet slow long kisses."

"Oh." He was a hot guy but he wasn't Wolf. I didn't want to offend him but I didn't want any kisses from Diego. "Hugs to you too."

Diego's voice was husky. "I will give you more in person."

I handed the cell back to Cy who was standing by grinning.

"You'd better let him down easy. He's gone loco for you."

"Oh, shut up."

"Hey, you two." Heinz yelled from the desk. "There's no more on these tapes. I need to go up and shower. I'll see you later, eh? On the ship."

"You're going too?"

"Have to. Someone is framing me," Heinz paused and pointed, "or you, Adie Sturm."

16

The pirate cruise was quite the event. A crowd gathered below on the pier waiting to board an ominous clipper ship flying the Jolly Roger. Carmelita, Marg and I were pirates decked out in net stockings, low-cut white blouses, black vests, leather hot pants, high boots and a wide-brimmed black buckled hats. Carmelita had a red scarf tied under hers, sparkles on her lids and bright red lipstick and she made sure we had the same. Sexy, but not slutty.

This excursion was the most excitement Marg had experienced in more than a year. Last year, she and Manni were in love and attached at the hip, and now who knows? Marg was hyper, like a toy poodle on stage prancing around performing in the high boots Carmelita had arranged for her to wear. If she kept that up, her feet would be useless in an hour and I'd have to get one of the pirates to carry her off the ship, especially after a few drinks.

The point of this party was not just to try out the mojitos, margaritas and tequila shots. I had spread the word to my besties about eavesdropping on conversations. Someone could get lucky and hear something about who had it in for Linda.

Every time I thought about her hair whirling around in the tank with an aerator bubbling around her dead eyes, I felt like vomiting. Why was she killed, I kept asking myself? It had to be about Heinz. He had been beaten and today he was almost a hit and run victim. I desperately needed to talk to Wolf. After that head injury I couldn't remember what I had told him and what happened to the money in my bra. Had I imagined that?

"Carmelita, did you see that hundred-dollar bill in my bra? I showed it to you guys at the café, didn't I?"

"*Que*?" She seemed focused on a particular brawny pirate with a Superman body and a grim expression holding onto a rope standing next to a mast, posed perfectly for cell shots as he waited for the tourists and expats to board. Carmelita's eyes were eating him alive.

I nudged my friend. "When we went to that café on the square, did I show you what I found in the gallery supply room?"

"Umm." She turned to me. "Yes, you did. It was a hundred-dollar bill. You thought they were up to something crooked at the gallery."

"I saw it, too, Adie," Marg chirped, "but I was so worried about Manni, I didn't exactly listen to what you said. How did you get it?"

I rolled my eyes. Talking to Marg was like explaining something to a distracted Labrador retriever puppy. Right now, she was only one degree below Carmelita in her attention deficit disorder.

"We are talking about a money laundering operation in the gallery. Does anyone see a connection?"

Carmelita's jaw dropped. "I do. The paintings. Diego has some like those Riveras we saw. You don't think—"

"Yes, he would," Marg said. "I had dealings with your brother and he is a shady guy."

"That's because you don't understand these things, Marg. Besides, Carmelita is his sister. You can't just accuse Diego without knowing the law." Marg still felt resentful for what she thought Diego had done when she first came to Cozumel. "That isn't fair. Besides, Carmelita has nothing to do with Diego's business dealings."

"You're right. Sorry, Carmelita. I was being insensitive," Marg said. Her eyes suddenly flicked to the gangway. "We can board. Omigod, I am so pumped! Let's go, ladies!"

Marg was like a toddler released from preschool, and just as unsteady on those high-heeled boots.

As I tottered on board behind her on my high-heeled boots, I remembered the key I had taken from Heinz's condo. Unfortunately, I couldn't for the life of me recall where I had hidden the envelope with the address and key inside.

A long table on the starboard side of the ship was reserved for us. There were also some empty seats for latecomers.

The Clean cousins and Brick Shithouse took seats opposite us. I hoped they'd say something about Linda because I was at a dead end.

The music started up and pirates came by holding trays to distribute the booze. The drinks weren't spectacular but there were plenty of choices. Couples got up to dance but since I didn't have a dance partner, I took a mojito, keeping my eyes on the Clean cousins.

Leon Luis Ruiz Del Socorro was watching me like a hawk. When his cousin started to talk about the investors, he nudged him. Leo must have been on some recreational drug, his eyes were bleary and his movements sluggish.

I took that opportunity to whisper to Marg. "Maybe you can get Leo to talk about Linda. He is drugged up on something. Weed, most likely. Just stay in the open so he doesn't get any ideas."

"Sure, Adie. I owe you."

Leo waved to Marg. She waved back and the next moment she sprang up, waltzed around the table and the two of them danced unsteadily with the ship rocking against the waves. At certain times it seemed like the two of them would tumble and roll instead of swish and swing with the beat of the salsa music.

This was as good a time as any to make a bathroom run. The liquor would make it worse as the night went on. When the music stopped and the pirate show began, I circled my way between couples until I was close to the bow of the ship where the washroom was located.

It was dim in the hallway when I brushed against a tall pirate coming out of the shadows. Had he been waiting for me? He wore an open black leather vest over a bare chest, tight leather pants and knee-high boots. A wide brimmed hat slanting down over his forehead, covered most of his pale blond hair. I couldn't help noticing his powerful biceps and forearms and his large strong hands. He was like chocolate—creamy rich and sinfully delicious.

My Hormone voice whispered, Take him. He's your fantasy man.

The pirate stopped and took hold of my shoulders. Brushing my hair aside, he lightly stroked my neck before kissing my throat, capturing my skin with his warm lips. His tongue trailed to my shoulder, silken and hot. I threaded my fingers through his thick clean hair, smelling of soap and balmy ocean breeze. From his broad shoulders to his muscular arms, my hands explored. This pirate was all natural, untamed and wild. The intense passion in his eyes filled me with longing. Wolf desired me as much as I wanted him.

His eyes sparkled a clear vivid blue between black eyeliner. Their glint gave me a jolt. Wolf took that moment to press his mouth on mine, lips moving firmly until my lady parts quivered with longing. My hand crept up to his cheek. My hand stroked his firm manly jaw. I felt myself melt as fast as spilled ice cream on Cozumel's hot cobblestone streets.

Those lips were meant for delightful nibbles. I pulled his head down and bit him gently. Softly, he groaned. A rush of endorphins shot down to my core and I clung to him wanting all of him.

His lips seared my skin with their heat. Lightly his hand slid along my thigh and teased me with his light touch. My hips moved in response—every nerve ending sparked, igniting into flames.

"You know how to rev my engine, babe." Wolf said, his large hands stroking down past my hips over every curve.

"I really do." He was good to touch and I enjoyed every second. This was not a time for conversation. I had an agenda. My hands undid his belt, taking control but not for long. Wolf had his own course of action.

Somehow, we moved to the back wall past the bathroom and Wolf lifted me up on a shelf. He started at my neck kissing his way down. His hands massaged my breasts and every part of me responded.

"I need you," I whispered, my voice hoarse with desire.

Our bodies sprung together like magnets. Steamy heat pulsed from my skin. Passion pulled him closer, my fingers entwined in his hair, and we vibrated to the rhythm of the waves slapping against the boat. I felt a rush that shot me up into a cloud of euphoria. Our hot juices mingled. The moans that tore out of me turned into screams, camouflaged by the music in the open area of the ship. I remained suspended high in a dream cloud. His lips drew me in one last time and he let out a groan. When our dance ended, I grew limp in his arms. He murmured, "Princess."

From the passageway male voices carried, ending our union. Dragging my skirt down with one hand I rearranged my blouse with the other.

Two men strode by us unsteadily, intent on finding the men's bathroom. I hid my face in Wolf's chest, catching my breath and taking in his scent. His skin was damp. This unexpected interlude had consumed my energy. I was still weak from my stay at the clinic. Now, I really did need that bathroom.

I gave Wolf a quick smooch, jumped down and trotted over to the washroom. Good timing on my part because a few women had finished dancing and were heading my way. I locked the door and opened my purse. It was hard to control my smiling lips when I applied lip gloss. The Sea God had done it again. This was my fantasy man in action. There was no one who could do it better.

When I walked out, with a pleased as punch grin on my lips, Wolf was nowhere in sight. Navigating my way past the waiting women, I walked into a writhing crowd pulsing to the blasting Cuban salsa.

At that moment my hand was seized and I twirled around to gaze at a devastatingly handsome man. He was athletic and trim. He wore a white shirt on under a black leather vest open to the waist, hinting at his perfect six-pack. His shapely butt fit perfectly in the tight leather pants, tucked into high boots. He, too had on a wide-brimmed black felt hat, his hair dark wavy brown flowing down to his neck. What caught my attention the most were his eyes, a mesmerizing hazel tinged with green.

I knew he was Diego even with the pirate getup and eye makeup. His dazzling Hollywood smile was a dead giveaway and the way his athletic body moved naturally with the salsa beat.

I freed his hand and wiggled my hips towards him. He snatched both my hands and I stepped under the bridge he created and released a hand, standing still. The pace of the music was so fast I quickly lost my breath. As karate brown belt I was slightly ashamed.

"So sorry, Diego, but I am not quite recovered. I took a hit to my head. I think I need to sit."

"Of course. It is I who regrets tiring you out." He pushed a tendril of my hair away from my face. "You are pale. It hasn't been long since that horrendous explosion. Did the doctor tell you anything?"

"I should recover with time. I hate the lack the energy for a simple dance. I trained for karate for years and it seems as this dance has done a number on me unlike anything in my classes. My endurance level right now is pitiful."

"No problem, Adelinita. I know we can dance again." Sidling up, he closed his hand around my waist. "That is something we both enjoy, isn't it?" He led me to the long wooden table. "It looks like we are about to be served our lobster and steak." Diego eyed the pirate waiter and waved him over. "Bring us six bottles of the

Australian shiraz I have reserved for this table."

Diego took a seat across from me and surveyed the crowd dancing. "Where are Du Lac, Ed and Perla?" He scanned the partiers. "Hmm, seems Orlando isn't here either." He pushed his hair back from his forehead. "Leon must be dancing. Quite the crowd."

"Heinz is sitting over at that table." I jerked my chin in the direction of the other table.

Diego nodded. "Yes, I saw him but what about your ex? Have you parted ways again?"

"No." I smiled up at him. "What about you? Have you found my replacement?"

"I think you know the answer to that. No woman is like you but until you wed Du Lac don't expect me to quit my pursuit. You have always been a challenge and I'm up for it. Eventually, you will tire of Du Lac and his secretive ways."

This was a classic case of the pot calling the kettle black. Who was keeping their lips shut on this mess? My guess was that Wolf and Diego were not telling anyone anything in case people stopped buying the condos.

Carmelita and Marg, came back from the facilities and squeezed in beside me on the bench.

"Hola," Carmelita called out. "I see you found Adelina."

"Yes, we danced." Diego smirked at Carmelita. "Where has Ed gone?"

Carmelita surveyed the dancers as the pirate server came to the table with plates of lobster and steak, done to perfection, setting them down on the table.

Carmelita was genuinely confused. "He was here and we danced but now who knows?"

"I was hoping to speak with him," I said. "Wolf wanted Ed Marion to represent me if Hernandez decided I was a suspect in Linda's death."

The music stopped while we ate when suddenly someone screamed. A moment later, one of the pirates yelled out, "Man overboard!"

I rushed to the starboard side of the boat and peered out into the dark waters. Someone threw a life buoy in but the person who needed to catch it was no where in sight.

"Who was it?" I asked the pirate on my right. He shrugged but the female pirate with the slutty corset, torn net stockings and short skirt spoke up. Her eyelash extensions and blood red lipstick fit perfectly with the big hair, piled high on her head, tumbling down her back. Pushing back her teased fringe hanging in her eyes she readily contributed her two pesos worth.

"His said his name is Ed. We danced earlier. Got up close and personal." Her tongue came up to lick her lips. "So fit. The guy trains regular like. Ed works up a sweat in the gym most days. I've seen him in there myself doing dead lifts."

"This guy wasn't Ed Marion, the lawyer?"

"I can't say for a fact. I don't know what he does for a living. All I can tell you is he is a big man, six feet tall for sure, if not more, and built like a—"

"Brick Shithouse?"

"Yup! You could say that. I wouldn't mind getting him in the sack."

"They'll be lucky if they ever find him." A voice said from behind my shoulder.

Cy's beard was a biker's black bush. He wore pirate clothes, like Wolf he was shirtless under the leather vest which he wore with leather pants and knee-high boots. A black hat covered his head, slanting wickedly over one eye which was blocked by a patch.

I swivelled about. "Cy! I didn't know you were here." I studied his face. "The man who went overboard was Ed Marion, wasn't it?" I glanced over to the table where Carmelita was sipping a margarita. "Carmelita will be very upset. I know they dated a couple of times. What a sad ending to their romance." I frowned. "You think he was pushed overboard to keep him quiet?"

Cy nodded. "You were counting on Ed Marion to protect you from Detective Hernandez and his force. It's too late now. That hombre won't survive the water without a wetsuit. Did you get a chance to speak to him?"

I bit my lip. "Unfortunately, no."

"I think someone made sure you wouldn't. You need to watch out, Adie Sturm. Whoever did this thought you knew too much."

"You mean about Linda? What about Carmelita? She will be devastated."

"She will be disappointed, no doubt but you," Cy stared

searchingly, "have found out more about the Erizo del Mar condo developers, haven't you?"

"That's why I need to follow a lead." I wasn't telling anyone about the money or the key. Not yet.

"You mean this is about Diego and Wolf?"

"Yes. If something turns up, I'm sure the police would want to know as well."

"I'll go with you. I can provide you protection."

My eyes shot down his body. It was strong and powerful. "All right. I will text you tomorrow morning around nine. There's something I need to check out before we can get anywhere with this."

"And that is?"

"You'll find out. I have a feeling."

17

I slept soundly with Wolf's arm around me, no thoughts of drowning. He had to get up early; way earlier than any normal person should get up, maybe half past seven.

"Stay inside today, babe. You need to recover from your concussion."

"Sure."

"Do I have to remind you of what happened to Linda? You don't fool around with these people, babe."

"I hear you."

Wolf pulled me close. "There's a hurricane coming in, anytime now."

"There's food and water in the fridge."

"I'll text you if we have to move to the cottage. The ground is higher. We'll need to evacuate if it's a category three."

"I get it. Don't worry. I know where the cottage is. I can take a taxi if I have to."

With a warm goodbye kiss and another cautionary warning to lock the door, Wolf headed out to work out on a new job.

Ed Marion was most likely dead. I was still breathing and alive but if I didn't put this puzzle together I wouldn't be for long. Whoever killed Brick would make sure I wouldn't see tomorrow. I had been missing bits of memory ever since I got back from the clinic. I knew the key was in the bedroom, but where?

The bedside clock read eight o'clock. Sitting up, I closed my eyes and let myself go back in time. Where would I hide it so the maid wouldn't find it?

As I opened my eyes, I let them wander, finally settling them on the area rug. It was slightly askew. Eureka! When I jumped off the bed, I let my fingers slide over the surface, realizing there was something buckling the rug. Years ago, I had a cat named Sensei who stole my paint brushes and hid them under a rug, taking them out to play with whenever he wanted a toy. A rug was perfect for hidden treasures.

The envelope was in exactly the same spot where I had

discovered it in Heinz's condo. Once again, I was amazed at how good I was becoming at sleuthing. What a perfect hiding place. Well, I guess I couldn't take credit for Heinz's subterfuge. It was his idea in the first place. Peeling back the flap, of the brown envelope I found an address on a slip of paper and a gold key.

This was the break in the case I had been looking for! Laying the items carefully on the bed, I searched the drawers for a top and pair of shorts. I settled on a sky-blue sleeveless cotton print that draped over the waist of the denim shorts and a pair of metallic flip-flops, and hastily tugged them on.

Finally, for luck, I fastened a pair of jade earrings. Jade was for the Mayan nobility and the silver cuff in a Mayan design of Ixchel was to give me fertility. That part was better put on hold. With no definite partner in sight, the goddess could give her pregnancy to someone else more deserving but I still liked her strength on my wrist. After taking time for personal maintenance, I was ready to roll.

I texted Cy.

I'm ready. You?

A few minutes later there was knock on my door. Through the peephole I saw it was Cy. I breathed a sigh of relief. Cy was a good person to have as a wingman on this mission. I could trust Cy to have my back.

I swung the door open and before I could speak, Cy said, "Hola, chica, you're lookin' chill!" He led the way to the elevator.

"I am? What do you mean?" I pressed *L* for lobby as Cy stepped in.

"Considering how your legal defence left you high and dry, you don't seem at all worried." The elevator shuddered as it reached the ground floor.

"Ha, ha, so funny," I said dryly. "Poor schmuck is fish food."

"Seems to be a theme here."

That made me think of my own involuntary underwater dive which almost ended my life. If it hadn't been for the Sea God, I would be there on the sandy bottom sixty feet under along with Ed Marion feeding the barracudas.

Cy's motorcycle was parked in the small lot adjoining the condo. He climbed on and waited for me.

"Wait. Where can I put my purse?"

"Give it here. I'll put it into the pouch."

Before he revved the bike, he told me to hang on to his waist. I knew that much having been on a motorcycle before but never with Cy. He was amazingly trim but I knew that already. Those Bolivar Alvarez men take care of their bodies.

Like a pro, he swung his Harley into Rafael E. Melgar and headed north.

"How do you know where we're going? I haven't told you anything yet."

"Hold on tight!" he said over his shoulder, before we flew over a speed bump.

Cy's eyes remained on the road. "If you are going to be of any use to me, I'll have to fill your belly first to get your brain to work. After that accident you need to eat. I don't want you looking like Carmelita's models, all skin and bones."

"Really? Carmelita's models are very attractive!" I said into his ear.

"Only if you look at their faces," he shouted back. "I like my women with meat on their bones." He chuckled. "Something to hold on to in the heat of passion." He eased in between two Jeeps and opened up his motor to a loud roar.

Shaking my head, I said, "I may not have big hips but I have muscle. I train in karate, Cy." After a grueling four-hour karate grading, I had recently made brown belt, limping out of the dojo with purple bruises and a broken toe. It took days for me to feel mobile again but I was pleased at my success.

"Hardly a plus, being the karate kid, Adie. My plan is to put some weight on you, girl."

Cy didn't know this but I loved to eat. Wolf was a witness to my fascination with food. My gluten allergy put a wrench in my plans at times but Mexico's food was based on corn which means no gluten.

"So where should we go?"

"Have you been to Diego's?" he shouted back.

"No." I said into his ear.

"It's great," he said over his shoulder.

"Let's go for it!"

Our conversation came to a halt as Cy swiftly wound the Harley into the town going towards the airport. San Miguel isn't a huge place so driving anywhere only takes a few moments.

It turned out that Diego's Tacos was a little outdoor place a few blocks from the airport. The energy of the place was positive—red plastic chairs and red tables, some covered in blue and white striped tablecloths. Casual and friendly. I got the feeling the food would be good from the clientele, mostly expats or locals occupying the tables. The smiling owner gave us our choice of tables. He explained he was Diego's son, and his mom did the cooking.

The menu mentioned shrimp, fish, chicken and veggie guacamole tacos. I choose three chicken tacos mostly because the fish was coated and now that I knew I was celiac that was a no-no. Cy decided on the shrimp tacos.

I didn't get to eat more than a couple bites before Cy started grilling me.

"Where are we going?"

"Wait." I pulled out my cell and checked. "It's near here." I gulped down some of the taco before I said, "It's on Google maps."

"And what exactly will we find when we get there?"

"I'm not sure what but I have a feeling it's something illegal."

Cy sighed. "I hope you know what you're doing."

"I do," I said confidently, leaving money for the bill on the table. "Gracias," I called out to the owner. "Let's go check it out, partner."

A short ride brought us to a large white building topped by a red tile roof. Off the beaten track, on a back street we arrived in less than five minutes. Cy parked the motorcycle on the opposite side of the street and we hid behind a flowering bougainvillea tree to observe.

A hunched-over older woman, gray hair flying around her face, wearing a floral dress to her ankles hobbled along assisted by a cane. Seeing us, she gave me the evil eye like witches do to curse people.

"What's up with that? We weren't doing anything," I whispered to Cy.

"She thinks you're a hooker."

"Thanks a lot." I glanced down at my shorts. "Hardly hooker hot pants. Don't they wear skirts her in Cozumel, like mini skirts?

Hasn't that come to San Miguel?"

Cy grinned. "Sí, the locals do. Doesn't matter if the women have grown too plump to wear them. They like their clothes sexy and tight. Never mind the crone."

On the other side in front of the white building a few young men strolled by, checking out the young skank passing by.

"That's the place. I can go in and you can be at the door in case of trouble."

Cy frowned. "Maybe I should go in with you."

"I'm the one who's in trouble here if I can't find out why Linda was killed." Opening the passenger door, I stepped out onto the cracked sidewalk and strode to the entrance.

By the time I was at the door of the storage building, Cy got out of the Jeep and was heading to the door.

There was no one in the long narrow hall of the building. It had five doors on each side, each storage unit locked with heavy padlocks. When I reached door number seven, I took out the key from my cross-body purse and inserted it into the padlock. I heard the click pulling down on the release.

The heavy steel door creaked as I swung it open to a room about twelve feet long and six feet wide. What I saw was puzzling. Two rows of black wet suits, inserts in blue, gray, and pink were hanging up on racks. The Cressi label was on the front of the wetsuits. For the life of me I couldn't figure out why these wetsuits would be something a person wanted to hide in a locked storage room. Sure, they weren't cheap, about two hundred each, depending on the thickness.

It all looked perfectly innocent to me. A scuba shop was getting a shipment of wetsuits and decided to store them. But why there? Were the wetsuits stolen goods?

I guessed there was more to this or Heinz wouldn't have been given this key. What was he meant to do with the wetsuits?

Cy was a scuba master. Maybe he'd know.

Leaving the door open I ran down the corridor to the front door. When I peeked my head out, I saw Cy.

"Psst!" I hissed.

Cy saw me and sidled over.

"Come in here," I whispered.

In the hallway I told him he had to come and see the contents of the storage unit. We made our way to number seven and stopped.

"There's a smell in here. Nasty," I said. "See those little black things? Mouse droppings. They haven't chewed up the suits because they're high on a rack far enough out of reach of the little critters."

"Okay, but there's something else smelling in here."

I nodded. "It's a vinegary smell like cleaning chemicals." The odor permeated the floor and walls. "What could that be?"

Cy strode to the rack and felt one of the wetsuits before he bent his head and sniffed.

"Eew!"

"What is it?"

"I think they're soaked in a drug, maybe liquid heroin."

18

It might be time to take this to the police, although I had my doubts if Hernandez could be trusted. He liked to make me his prime suspect and Heinz had given him a green flag with the Linda murder.

I texted Wolf to keep him in the loop.

I found wet suits soaked in a chemical in a storage unit. The key to the unit was meant for Heinz. Ask him what he's playing at. Adie

What are you doing out and about, babe? You are to be resting after a concussion. Go back to the condo and lock yourself in. There's a hurricane coming. Go back. I'll be there soon. W

In my hands I carried a wet suit in a black plastic bag to bring to Carmelita's chemist friend. My friend was picking me up outside the Erizo Del Mar. Cy had given me a ride there but he had a dive group to take out in his boat for an afternoon trip to the Palancar Caves. I told him I'd text him what I found out.

I checked my cell for text messages and found one from Diego.

Mi amor, we must go out to dine. Tell Wolf you're too tired and I'll take you to a romantic restaurant. xxxx D

Not sure I can. A

I await your text that says YES. My heart pounds for you, cariño. Tomorrow then? D

No, sorry. Thanks anyway. A

A white limousine approached and parked. It was beautifully classic. The Rolls Royce symbol on the hood gleamed with polish as did the vehicle, the Phantom.

The Spirit of Ecstasy is the bonnet ornament sculpture on a Rolls-Royce car. It is in the form of a woman leaning forwards with her arms outstretched behind and above her. Billowing cloth runs from her arms to her back, resembling wings. My first thought was royalty and I suppose Carmelita was Cozumel's only princess.

The lines on the edge of the curb were painted red to discourage any parking but I guessed Carmelita's driver didn't care. I'm sure the cops were paid plenty to ignore any traffic violations by the Bolivar Alvarez family.

Carmelita rolled down her window, yelling out to her driver, "Open the door for Adelina, Roberto! Hola, chica!"

"Hey, Carmelita!"

The limo driver hopped out and raced over to open the back door. He was tall, had jet black hair of medium length, and dark wrap-around sunglasses on a square face. He wore a gray uniform, elegantly cut styled like a pilot's uniform.

"Can you put this bag up front with you?" I held out the plastic bag.

Roberto flicked his eyes at the bag, disgust written on his face. "Perhaps, the trunk is a better place, señorita Sturm."

I wrinkled my nose. "Good idea, Roberto. Sorry about that smell." I slid into the plush leather seat while Roberto locked the wet suit package in the trunk.

"Thanks for doing this." I scanned Carmelita's long lacy top and tan leggings. She wore a comfortable pair of beige sandals with a two-inch heel, not her usual stilettos.

Her hands swept her clothes. "See, how I dressed to do some detecting with you?"

I smiled, amused by her enthusiasm. "Good job!" I gripped her hand. "So sorry about Ed. I know you liked him."

Carmelita cast her eyes down. "It was horrible news. He was my lover, Adelina. I hardly expected this. I was excited about our relationship." She sighed and a tear slid out of the corner of one eye.

"I am sorry," I said, bringing her close for a hug.

Carmelita drew in a breath and appeared more composed. "I need to turn his murder into a positive thing, He would be glad we are fighting for him. I can solve this murder with you. It will be just what I need. Honestly, it is an abomination! Here I found a good man. I was finally dating, having fun with Ed," she paused, squeezing out another tear, whether from sadness or self-pity, wasn't sure.

"Someone killed him in front of us all. Drown him like a rat. Some bastardo had it in for him." She threw her hands in the air, "In the water, just like Linda. Ay caramba!"

Carmelita glanced out the window at the shops as the limo moved down Rafael E. Melgar. "I should be used to it by now. Diego tends to dirty his hands and I get the fallout."

I mulled it over. Within a minute Ed Maron was dancing and the next he was in the sea. Worse still for me, he was to be my defense attorney." That was selfish on my part but I really did need a great lawyer. The Cozumel police wanted to throw the book at me, which meant a miserable existence in prison, possibly for years if I survived, the Mexican government having abolished the death penalty.

"This is another murder for you to solve, chica." Carmelita's voice trembled. "We need to bring his killer to justice. I beg you urgently to find this *hijo de perro*."

I nodded, translating "son of a dog" in my mind. That was true. If he was Linda's killer, that was one wicked psycho. "There is nothing I would rather do. Let's see what your chemist can find out. How do you know her?"

"Ana Diaz Zapota is a friend from school. She was one of my group way back. Ana owes me. I saved her from unwarranted attacks from the jealous *brujas* at the school."

"The mean girls stuck it to her?"

"Sí. Ana is a sweet girl, reminds me of you."

Roberto made a right turn and drove down calle 4 away from downtown. He stopped at a regular Spanish style house with white walls and a red-tiled roof. The house was surrounded by an ivory stone fence, red and orange bougainvillea hanging over the sides. The gate was wrought-iron about seven feet high. Carmelita had just finished texting her friend when Roberto pulled up and the gate opened. He parked behind a closed garage.

Carmelita barked an order to Roberto after he swung the door of the Rolls open and helped her out. I was next.

Once again, Roberto was instructed in rapid-fire Spanish while we scooted up to the door, Roberto holding the nasty-smelling plastic bag.

A short young woman, with glossy black hair in a bun, wearing a white maid's uniform opened the door. In halting English, she told us to enter and led the way to the lounge. She told us señora Diaz Zapato would join us shortly.

Carmelita led the way to the living area down a marble hall. It was attractively decorated with bright abstract paintings and coral walls. The lounge itself was down a few steps, a sunken living area vivid with cushioned print pillows and rattan chairs.

We settled in while Roberto remained standing impassively holding the offensive object.

A voice carried into the room from the hall. "What is that odorous thing you have brought with you, Carmelita? It simply reeks with chemicals." A trim petite red-head with long wavy locks took us in with large brown almond eyes, almost Asian in appearance. They were thickly lined, the long black lash extensions adding to the beauty of her expressive eyes. She was casually dressed in skinny blue jeans and a capped sleeve Guess T-shirt. White Nike sneakers completed her outfit.

Carmelita giggled. "You haven't changed, chica. Straight forward and offensive as always."

The woman stood, hands clasped staring enthralled at us. "A mystery to solve. Intriguing. Love it!" She clasped me in her arms and gave me the double kiss salute. "I am Ana Diaz Zapato and stop," Ana lifted her palm, "you must be the famous Adie Sturm, engaged to the handsome Wolf Du Lac or is it the charming Diego Bolivar Alvarez?"

Carmelita grinned. "I think it may be either, or so they want to believe it. How are you, chica?" She leaned in for kisses. Hollywood couldn't have done it better, the air kisses just missing the skin.

"I am happy with my work," Ana said cryptically.

Carmelita snorted. "You know I am not referring to work, chica. How is your love life?"

"I am living with my lady love, Dolly, a Texan. Although we have no children as yet, we are looking for a healthy specimen to contribute the donor sperm."

"So, you decided on a woman after all?"

"I love both sexes, amiga," she chuckled, "but Dolly is my special lady. I am fortunate she wants to settle down with me. How about you? I'm always hearing about your fashion shows and your men."

Carmelita looked down, her mouth down at the corners. "That is one reason we are here. Two murders and a suspicious storage closet. One of the victims was the man I was dating."

"Oh, no! How awful!"

"Yes, it was devastating. Listen, Ana, I know you as an outstanding chemist. For that reason, I am asking for a favor."

Ana's furled her forehead and pointed a finger to her chest.

"From me? Surely, you have others at your disposal? I can't believe Carmelita Bolivar Alvarez needs my assistance?"

"Don't be modest, chica!" Carmelita snapped. "Everyone knows you are the best. We bring you a problem to solve. It involves chemistry. Are you able to go to a lab to figure this out or should we drive you there?"

Ana grinned. "No need. I have a lab right here in my home." She waved us forward. "Come follow me."

Carmelita gestured for Roberto to join us and we proceeded behind Ana down a long corridor. The house was larger than I imagined. The bedrooms were up a staircase; Ana explained but led us further past several rooms until we came upon a steel door. Ana clicked in a code and touched a pad with her thumb and looked at a camera. "I have cornea identification. Many businesses hire me to research for them. It has become my ticket to fame and wealth."

We followed Ana into a large laboratory with steel tables and bottles of chemicals on shelves on a counter.

"Impressive," Carmelita said. "I hope you have the chemicals we need here."

"If I don't, you will need to send your package to Cancun."

I shook my head. "Not possible. This is urgent. We can't wait."

Ana looked startled. "Why?'

"There could be another murder depending if we don't find out what this is." That murder could be me. I set the package on the steel counter. "I want you to check for liquid heroin."

"Or any type of drug," Carmelita added.

"Is the cartel involved?"

Carmelita shrugged her shoulders. "Diego will make sure you are protected. I promise you that. He's always fancied you."

"He did?" Ana pouted. "I wish I had known that. I had a crush on him."

"You were too young. He liked older women then."

Ana squawked as if she had been punched in the solar plexus with a big fist.

"Shall we leave you to figure this out?" I motioned towards the door.

Carmelita nodded. "We'll come back in an hour?"

Ana nodded.

I locked arms with Carmelita in the living room, whispering in her ear, "Well played. If your friend is any good we'll know soon. Let's go eat!"

Roberto helped us in the limo and we decided Otates was in the neighborhood. It was situated on Avendia 15 between Calle 3 and Rosada Salas, so not that close but when you've got a driver and you're in San Miguel, nothing is far away.

Los Otates' name had been changed to Los Tacotales but was the same as I remembered. Out of the touristy area, the prices were cheap and the food was excellent. An outdoor restaurant it got busy in the evening when people wanted beer with a snack. Wooden tables and chairs, yellow walls, and a peaked roof sporting a Mexican flag, all looked familiar. The chef was busy cooking when we arrived. Los Tacotales had everything we needed along with a friendly waiter.

They were famous for white pazole, a dish invented by the Mayans in Chipata Guervera and of course everyone loved the tacos originating in Jalisco.

Carmelita ordered the pozole, a hominy broth soup to maintain her slim figure and I decided on a power lunch of chicken tacos and a side of guacamole. The way things were going I needed some strength to complete my investigation.

"Amiga, check your text. It might be important."

"Yeah, sure," I said hesitantly, thinking Wolf might be chewing me out for disobeying his bed rest advice. I dug in my purse and snatched up my iPhone.

Listen to me, babe. You can't fool around with a head injury. I want you to stay alive. Go back to the condo. Now! I will deal with the situation. W

I decided I didn't care. I needed to clear my name and that meant solving the mystery. I turned off my phone. Wolf wouldn't see reason and we'd be text fighting.

"Well?"

"Just Wolf. He thinks I'll die from a brain swelling if I'm out investigating. Better to ignore him for now."

"Are you feeling all right?"

"I will be once I eat my tacos and down this Corona." Friends told me that Dos Equis was a superior beer but having found I have to eat and drink gluten free, I switched to Corona. This beer was not totally gluten free but it was low in gluten. I ate slowly, restraining myself from chowing down like my chum Marg. She was an odd girl—starved herself all day and then goes hogshit wild over food. I like to think I am more restrained, sticking to tiny bites and giving myself time to chew before devouring a man-size meal.

"I don't know how you can eat so much, Adelina. Doesn't it throw off your men when you have an appetite like that?"

I grinned. "No, Wolf says, a woman that likes to eat likes to—"

"He doesn't, really?" Carmelita smirked. "Well, well. That must be what Diego likes about you too. I don't know if I should ask but have you done it? I mean with Diego?" She leaned forward on the table. "Tell."

"I don't kiss and tell, girl."

"You are such a tease."

"Never mind those men. We are investigators not hookers. Text Ana and see if she found out if that is," I lowered my voice, "liquid heroin or not."

Carmelita nodded. "Yes, we must know." She grabbed her cell and texted.

I waited anxiously for a reply, consuming another taco to pass the time. A few moments later Carmelita's cell made a noise.

She read the text and then showed me.

"I can't read Spanish, or at least not well enough. What does it say?"

Carmelita grinned widely. "We were right."

"It's heroin like Cy said?"

"My brother is correct in his assumption." She lifted her spoon in the air in a circular motion. "Why would he know about drugs?"

"He was involved in the Bolivar Import-Export Company."

Carmelita frowned. "You mean Diego imported drugs?"

"Not necessarily but he must know of others who do."

"Cy is equally knowledgeable as they ran this business together for years before he decided to scuba dive for a living." She fluffed her hair thoughtfully. "It is ingenious to bring the liquid heroin in this way. How much do you think it is worth?"

"I imagine the wetsuits are worth a few mill."

"But how do drugs tie into two murders?"

"Crime does. Heinz is into it up to his eyeballs. That's why they were beating him into submission. He had to do what his bosses wanted."

"That means Diego and Wolf—"

"No, don't say it! Neither of them is bent." Nevertheless, I was worried. "At least, I can't think that Diego would sell drugs or hire Heinz and I don't want to believe Wolf has become a criminal either. Unfortunately, if I text Wolf and ask what he found out from Heinz, he'll tell me to back off and go to the condo and lock myself in."

Carmelita's eyes narrowed. "I could text, Diego."

"You could, but I doubt if he would tell us anything worthwhile. He is very secretive about his business." I tipped back my beer. "Does he know who the killer is? I doubt it, unless he was the one who hired the killer to off Linda because he was protecting himself." I shook my head. "No, there's no use asking Diego."

"And my Ed? He was murdered like Linda. He wasn't a threat to anyone."

I nodded. "I know, right? He was my only hope of getting cleared when Hernandez arrests me. You've got to know; the Mexican police like to pin murders on tourists. Tourists kill each other in Mexico. That's what the newspapers are told. No way does the island want bad publicity with cartel killings."

Carmelita crossed her leg. I couldn't help but notice a beautiful pair of five-inch platinum heels, encrusted with a diamond strap she was wearing.

"Off topic but I love the heels."

"Jimmy Choo, thank you,. Got them in the States."

I didn't want to ask how much they were but I could estimate a few thousand. What a life style she had. All of the Bolivar Alvarez family members lived like royalty—and indeed they were the Cozumel elite.

Carmelita leaned in. "Did you hear of the famous cartel woman, Dame of Death? She was killed a couple months ago in a shoot out."

I pushed my plate away. "She was only twenty-one. I saw the arrest on YouTube." A waiter came along to clear the plates. He told Carmelita something in Spanish.

"What?" I asked when he headed away to the kitchen.

"They're closing as soon as we leave. They want to secure everything in case of high winds."

"Hurricane Pandora is definitely hitting Cozumel?"

"It is. Looks like a category three. Let's finish our investigation and then, let's head over to Diego's villa. The land is high and he has sea walls. We should be safe. Wolf can come too."

I bit my lip. "Not sure he would. He said we are going to stay at his cottage."

"As long as you're safe. It's up to you, but Diego would want me to persuade you."

I dug out my cell.

Pandora is coming in. Carmelita wants us to stay at Diego's villa. I could meet you there? A

No, babe. We will stay at the cottage. Tell Carm thanks but no. W

"I have to stay at Wolf's cottage in town. I'm sure it will be fine. Thanks for inviting us."

"No problem. I love your company and Wolf is always a pleasure to see." Carmelita eyed the restaurant. "They want us out. We need to get going. Now what?"

"I have another lead to follow up."

A ping sounded from my cell. I pulled it out of my bag.

Tonight. Dinner with me at the villa. You will be safe and snug. Let Du Lac take a chance with flooding without you. It will be candlelight when the hydro goes out.

"What is it?"

"Just Diego, wanting me to snuggle with him at the villa."

"There you go. You have to come now."

"No, Wolf wants me at the cottage."

"And you're following orders? Seriously?"

"No, this is different. I have an urge to be with Wolf."

Carmelia chuckled. "You are so funny. I love my urges too." Suddenly, she appeared sad, tears welling in her eyes. "I so wish I could turn back the clock. I was falling for Ed, Adelina. I can't believe they killed him."

I dug a tissue out from my purse. "Use this. Rest assured we will find the killer."

Carmelita nodded solemnly. "Now what?"

"We need to pay a visit to Perla Bravo Gonzalez."

19

Roberto drove us back to the Gonzalez Art Gallery and let us off. The wind was strong and the rain had started to plummet down. On the sidewalk in front of the gallery Carmelita stepped under the awning for cover. She turned to me. "She will tell us everything. I'll make sure of it."

I wasn't so certain. Perla was a conniving diva. It was hard to tell what story her eyes told beneath those fake two-inch lashes. Even if she was getting cash with each painting sold, paying cash was legal with large transactions as well as for buying houses and paintings. Money payments were legitimate enough but why would there be cash hidden behind the brown backing paper?

I had a few theories which involved the other condo owners and Heinz. He was the tool of one of the investors and had gone rogue after he was beaten into submission to follow orders of a killer. Refusing to commit the crimes had led to Linda's death. I felt pity for him. Where had the good Heinz gone? Why hadn't he told Wolf when the shit hit the fan? Wolf would have helped unless he was involved. Wolf wasn't a saint though, nor was Diego. Neither one of them could be behind this, or could they?

The Ed Maron murder was also a perplexing situation. Ed was one of the best criminal lawyers around. Wolf had hired him to represent me when things went sour. Unfortunately, I hadn't had that private conference with the famous attorney to solve my police problem. It was still a riddle to me why they would kill him. I was being set up by the killer for a fall-guy probably because I was a tourist. I had to rely on Wolf or Diego to get me the "out of jail free" card. I hated having to rely on others. I needed to solve this mystery and fast!

On the street the locals were taking in patio furniture and closing up shops and restaurants. A few brave souls scurried down the street, umbrellas over their heads. Good luck with that. The umbrella would not work for long with the wind increasing in velocity.

Across the street, the bakery looked deserted, as did the chocolate shop where Wolf had bought those sinfully delicious truffles. Going back to ride out the hurricane at the cottage brought back some romantic memories we shared when we first met in Cozumel. That was where I first thought I was falling for the Sea God.

Stop, I told myself. This is no time to be thinking about Wolf. A hurricane was fast approaching and there was a killer on the loose.

"Adelina!" Carmelita nudged me out of my reverie. "The lights are on inside."

"Good, let's pay Perla a visit."

A tinkling chime was set off when we opened the wooden door painted in a soft pastel pink, a stained-glass insert of angels in the window. The building itself was salmon with a red-tiled roof.

The dim front room was gloomy, the sole light shone brightly on a painting of a bowl of fruit, consisting of apples, grapes and a banana. Smoke billowed in the air, a sickly-sweet smell covered up by a peach room deodorant.

A wispy voice spoke up behind us. "Beautiful, isn't it? Delicious enough to eat, so to speak. Oils. So lovely." He sighed longingly. "So sad. Art is often done in acrylics. An oil has so much dignity."

Behind us stood Perla's lithe fashion-conscious assistant. He wore narrow white trousers, a mauve long-sleeved shirt and suspenders with a delicate floral pattern. His hair was gelled to a peak and shaved bald on the sides. His cut was the same one worn by the military during WWI. He had removed his facial stubble and moustache to go with the retro look. "Welcome, ladies."

"We came to see Perla Bravo Gonzalez."

"How pleasant." The assistant's eyes were unfocused. "I am Tomas Dunoir." He bowed slightly as if he had just played a magnificent classical piece of Wagner at the concert hall.

"I remember, we met," I said brusquely. "Hola, can we speak business? Tell Perla we want to talk to her."

He continued as if I hadn't spoken. "Many enjoy a fascinating still-life. This fruit painting is especially pleasing. Notice the textured 3D effect in oils achieved by this very talented artist."

This guy was wasted. It didn't take a detective to deduce he had recently indulged in a fine quality cannabis. Strong too—his clothing reeked of the pungent sweet smell. By the appearance of his pupils I'd say the substance he smoked had a high THC content. The average person familiar with the product knew it fondly as weed. My guess is he knew the substance exceedingly well.

"Astounding work, wouldn't you say?" Tomas droned.

"It is," I said placatingly patting his arm, "as I mentioned before, we'd like to speak to your boss?"

Tomas waved his hand lightly in the mist of smoke visible surrounding the painting. He gazed with yearning on the fruit. "Have I mentioned how satisfying it is to see a fruit bowl painting in one's living area? A good buy for you, ladies." He peered at me, checking me out from top to bottom. "You two are a couple, am I right?" He studied my chest intently. "You ladies are scintillating. Hopefully, you haven't given up on men altogether? It would be such a waste."

Carmelita brought her arm around my waist, grinning mischievously. "We are pansexual. And you?"

Tomas chortled in amusement. "I like a good romp, as any man does. My tastes vary but I find you two very alluring."

"Hmph!" Carmelita said. "If I were in need of a romp, I would pick a virile buff man."

"True," I said. "Sorry."

Wandering over to the other room, I had a peek in and saw only a single black sconce attached to the ivory white wall turned on at full capacity over a painting of a prancing white horse. I turned back to him. "I seriously have enough activity in my life right now."

Tomas let out a deep breath. "That is unfortunate, but all is not lost. I can see you admire that painting. Such a delightful horse, wouldn't you say? See how lively it frolics! A masterful work demonstrated in acrylics. Powerful, isn't it?" He cooed into my ear, "Are you a fan?"

"Yes, horses are fine subjects for a painting, right, Carmelita?"

"Certainly, they are. How much is that one?"

Tomas perked up. "I would love for you to have that one but only señorita Brava Gonzalez knows how much it is truly worth."

"Where is Perla?" I said.

Tomas ignored me and squinted at Carmelita. "Ah-ha, I know you now. You are the carefree wild sister from the Bolivar Alvarez family. Correct?"

Carmelita's mouth twisted and she hissed, "Never mind that, cabron, my friend is asking where Perla is?"

Tomas rubbed his eyes. "I am not at liberty to divulge that information. She told me— "

Carmelita drew herself up to her full height and peered maliciously at Tomas. "She told you what?"

I pointed a finger at him. "Spill, Tomas!"

Tomas waved his arms around as if he were striking back at invading moths. "No need to get upset, señoritas."

"I don't wish to remind you that I am a member of the powerful Bolivar Alvarez family. My people can make you regret—"

Fear poked into his blissful state of euphoria. Tomas brought his hand up in a stop gesture. "Please, say no more. I need to keep my cojones. I hope I did not offend you, señorita Bolivar Alvarez?"

"Just tell us if she is here."

Tomas rubbed his chin with his forefinger. "Ah, I wish I could but she does not want to be disturbed."

"That's ridiculous!" I grabbed his arm, noticing how thin he was, his arms almost skeletal in their boniness. "We are here to speak business." I twisted about, letting go of him, afraid I had hurt the poor man. "Come, Carmelita, let's check out the backroom."

"No!" Tomas let out a squeal. "No one goes there except señorita Brava Gonzalez or with her permission, señor del Soccoro."

So Leo did have a hand in the shady art sales! I dashed over to the supply room where I had found the Franklins on my last visit.

When I turned on the light switch by the door, the room illuminated the stored paintings and sculptures, untidily arranged on three wooden tables. On an easel rested a half-finished painting of fruit, almost identical to the one we had just observed.

"Does Perla paint?" I inquired innocently.

Tomas nodded enthusiastically. "And she sculpts too. A gifted woman, señorita Perla.

"How talented and fortunate to own a gallery that sells paintings. How much does she ask for her paintings?"

Tomas chortled. "Whatever she can get."

Glancing about the room I spotted a table with large chunks of green rock. "Is that jade?"

Tomas zipped over to the table in question and covered everything with a tablecloth. "Señorita Perla doesn't like anyone to see what she is creating."

"Is she sculpting glyphs?"

Carmelita picked up the tablecloth at the edge and had a look. "I'd say, these are almost Mayan in appearance, looking exactly like the ones in the other room. Reminds me of the factories in Florence making all those fake artifacts. They sell them to unsuspecting tourists."

Tomas was distraught. "Never mind this. Forget what you have just seen. No one wants any trouble. You ladies need to leave. As you can see, señorita Perla is not here."

"Getting back to what we were asking you before. We want to speak to her. What is her address?"

Tomas shrunk back to the wall. "I am not allowed to give out personal information."

Carmelita strode over. "I can get my security men to extract that address from you but I must remind you it may be a bit painful if you don't tell us now."

"Please don't!" His face paled and he laid a hand protectively his trousers covering his jewels. "Señorita Perla is at her beach house."

"Where?" I grabbed a pen and a gallery card from a small table. "Write it down."

"She will be displeased," he muttered. "I might lose my job."

"Better your job than your cojones, eh?" I stared at his groin. "Churo and Luis wouldn't want to cause you pain but they are very loyal." I handed him the pen and the card. "Write."

Tomas' hand shook as he scrawled the address.

***

Outside the gallery the rain was fiercely plummeting down as the wind blew viciously, worse than any El Norte I've ever seen. The road was deserted.

"I texted Roberto. He should be here any second." Carmelita held her hair back from an aggressive storm that was blowing her hair helter-skelter to gaze searchingly down the street.

"There!" I pointed at a white limo a block away. "He's coming!"

A moment later we swung the door open, not waiting for Roberto to do his chauffeur duty, and slid onto the leather interior of the luxury vehicle.

Carmelita took the card I handed her and explained our plan to Roberto. He was not happy but knew better than to argue with his boss.

We headed north through the town towards the hotel zone. I was concerned when we came to an open area, palm fronds breaking off the trees, objects flying about. The rain pounded on the car and I was wondering how Roberto could see to drive let alone avoid flying vegetation but he was calm in the face of the storm having experienced many such as this on the island. Carmelita was relatively serene as well.

I grabbed my cell and texted Wolf giving him Perla's beach house address, just in case. Carmelita did the same, contacting Diego.

"This way they can't be angry, right, chica?"

I nodded, more nervous about the strength of the storm than the situation. The limo crept up the road swinging out of the way as tile roofing flew across the street, followed by a beach umbrella. The hotels along the way were too far back from the road and closer to the ocean to see what was happening there but from the ferocity of the gale and the damage, I wanted to get this over with as quickly as possible and retreat to the cottage with Wolf.

"Perla better be there." I stared out at the rain. "This rain is heavy. We should really be in a sheltered location but I want to know the truth."

"You must ask and I will observe. If she lies, we'll know from her eyes."

The limo slowed down as Roberto's GPS located Perla's beach house. He drove up a winding road finally coming to a halt at a gate. There was no one in the gatehouse; probably the security guard had gone home. Roberto shouted into the speaker in Spanish. No one answered from the house either but Roberto managed to operate the bar manually and lift it high. The bar stayed up as we drove into the driveway of Perla Brava Gonzalez' extensive property.

Palms and flowering bushes flanked the interlocking brick road to the villa. As we arrived I noticed Perla had wanted to distinguish her residence from the Spanish-styled villas in Cozumel. Hers was built with Roman Ionic columns at the front like a southern plantation house and had only a three-car garage as opposed to Diego's larger one, housing his fleet.

We left Roberto in the limo, parked in the circular driveway facing the road back in case of a quick getaway. Carmelita gave me a hooded rain cape from a drawer in front of us. It also held water bottles, tortilla chips and champagne.

When we were both garbed in rain gear, we ventured out the short distance to Perla's house. I shook my head when Carmelita gestured to knock and instead tried the door. It wasn't locked. We rushed in expecting to see Perla but the place seemed deserted.

The house itself was dark, the lights flickering in the hallway. Whoever built this seaside beach house couldn't make up their mind whether it was constructed to be in the Spanish style or a southern Louisiana plantation design. Paintings decorated the sterile ivory stucco walls; oak accent pieces were situated horizontally on the ceiling.

I tapped Carmelita's arm as I put my finger on my lips. We tiptoed quietly down past two closed doors. I shouldn't have cared about how much noise we made as the storm was whistling loudly outside.

Stairs connected this floor to an upper level. I motioned for Carmelita to follow me. We avoided the stairs and went straight down the corridor.

It opened to a kitchen with an island marble countertop, swivel chairs in tan leather on one side and on top a wooden cutting board flanked by Henkel knives of a variety of sizes. Two slabs of beef sat on the cutting board as if Perla anticipated chopping them into small sections. One large knife lay at the side of the beef.

"Where is she?" Carmelita whispered in my ear.

Off to the side I noticed a door. The noise of a flushing toilet. Perla strode out patting a scented plum body butter on her lacquered red hands. She was not pleased to see us.

"Who let you in? This is my beach house, my private residence."

"We have questions for you, Perla," Carmelita said.

She arched a brow. "Oh? Come to the gallery tomorrow and I will be pleased to answer anything about your purchase."

"These questions are about your purchases." I stepped forward putting myself in between Perla and the counter. If things got worse and she really was a killer she might try to stab me. "Expecting a guest for dinner?"

"That is my affair."

"Sit down, please," I said indicating the chair.

She shook her head. "I would advise you to leave, immediately. The hurricane is growing stronger. Listen!"

The wind was blowing as hard as a steam engine and then it whistled ear-piercingly. The beach house trembled with the blast of the wind.

Perla stared down at me. "You are an annoying pest, Adie Sturm. I am surprised the police haven't arrested you for the murder of Linda Du Lac yet."

"Because I didn't do it. I could hardly hoist that woman into the fish tank, could I, Perla? If she was out cold, I could drag her but I hardly think I am capable of hauling her up to cast her into the tank." I studied her slowly. "Well, well. It is noticeable you are as tall as Linda. I suggest you knocked them both out with that cudgel you use for sculpting the fake glyphs. You are," I looked at her muscular arms, "strong enough to lift and shove her into the fish tank."

Perla smiled fakely. "That's absurd. Why would I do such a thing?"

"Linda was your rival. She seduced your lover, didn't she?"

"She was a bother but I didn't kill her."

"To you, the more serious crime was how Linda seduced your lover. You were jealous but he wouldn't stop. He liked her action. You had no choice but to kill her."

"I deny that."

"Come on. Admit Linda had him in her bed."

"You want me to confess to murder? "I don't drag dead women anywhere, Adie Sturm! How could I possibly drag her down to the beach on my own? I may work out in the gym but lugging that wicked red-haired she-devil down to the beach? Not possible."

"How did you know she was found on the beach?"

"Common knowledge. Friends tell me things."

"Don't play with me. You know exactly what happened. Churo and Luis put her on the beach onto the next property but you and your thugs dragged her back to the Erizo del Mar beach." I stepped in front of her face to block her view of the knives. "Who helped?

197

Was it Leo del Soccoro who did your dirty work?"

She flipped her long tresses back disdainfully.

"Protest all you want but I know you are a jealous woman. You don't mind killing someone who took your lover, do you?"

Perla laughed derisively. "I had no idea Linda Du Lac was interested in anyone I spend time with."

"So Leo is not your man?"

"I think not, Sturm. For your information Leo is hardly worthy of my attention. He works for me."

"And what about Ed Maron, my lover?" Carmelita shouted. "I'm sure he rated highly in your books."

I grabbed Perla's arm. "You haven't an alibi for that, do you, Perla? The condo investors were all on that pirate ship. You were there."

Carmelita glared at Perla.

"You were angry with him because he wanted me."

"Or was it that he had the know-how to get the police off my back? Ed knew I was being framed."

Perla sighed. "You two with your stupid allegations bore me. Just leave."

Carmelita smirked. "He was a sensational lover, wasn't he?" She tapped her fingers on the countertop thoughtfully and assessed Perla. "Adelina, this woman isn't Ed's type. She's tall but seriously, she is nothing compared to me. I surmise he didn't care for you after he had the best. I mean, he knew you were nothing compared to the Queen of Cozumel, a Bolivar Alvarez. He ditched you, didn't he?"

Perla's face flushed. "He didn't know how to keep it in his pants." Perla stepped around me and added, "Now if that is all, I want you both out. I will call my security now."

"No use doing that, he's gone and I don't think we're going just yet. You have questions to answer."

"Questions?"

"What about the money in the backs of the paintings?"

"What!"

I pulled her close. "You know about that money as much as you know about the fake paintings and glyphs."

"I don't know of what you speak."

"Lying comes easily to you, doesn't it, Perla?" I had a powerful stare but it becomes more aggressive if someone is below me. This was not the case. Perla was a good six inches taller. Being vertically challenged has its downside.

"*Puta madre!* Get out, Carmelita!" Perla was angry as a Medusa, her hair spinning wildly from her head like snakes coiled to strike. "And take this little midget with you." She tried to shove me out of the kitchen but I grabbed her hand and swung her around in a police grip. "You have more to say."

"We want answers. Make her tell, Adelina!" Carmelita urged, putting her hand in her bag. I saw her fiddle with it; hopefully, she was clicking on record on her cell. "Admit it, Perla. You framed Adelina and killed Ed."

"No, you are wrong. Now, let me go. Leo, help!" she screeched at the top of her lungs, struggling as much as she could but with my hand pinning her arm there was very little wiggle room.

The slimeball slithered in as easily as a viper snake in a lush Mexican jungle. He wore a black jacket over a loose white shirt, perfect for carrying a concealed weapon. Leo held his hand up and intoned calmly in a rational voice, "Ladies, ladies, no more histrionics, please. It is so unpleasant." He stared at me gripping Perla. His eyes narrowed. "Let her go, Sturm."

"No problem," I said, throwing Perla towards him. He caught her before she hit the floor. "I think we have enough information to go to the police anyway."

"You have nothing!" Perla hissed.

The lights flickered on and off. I stared at Perla. "You sold forged paintings and glyphs."

Leo scowled. "You have no proof."

The howl of the wind almost drowned out her words "Shut up, Leo. Don't say anything." Perla sidled past me and stood side by side with Leo.

The screech of the gale outside took on an inhuman tone. When water hit the kitchen window I was suddenly aware that the ocean was high enough to pummel the walls of the beach house. My attention bounced back to Perla and Leo.

"Maybe we should all go," I suggested. "This house is unsafe."

"We have weathered hurricanes before. I was assured this house would withstand the elements. We will finish this now," Perla pronounced. "I will sue you for these unfounded allegations. You don't know what you are talking about."

"Oh, yes, we have proof." I moved my hand to the countertop where the knives were encased. "I found bills in the supply room at the gallery."

"And I saw it," Carmelita nodded to confirm. "There were bundles of hundreds."

"*Pinche!* I don't believe it. How did you get in there?" Leo's face turned red. "This is a lie. There is no way she got in there and found the—"

"Shut up, you fool! That idiot Thomas let her sneak in." Perla's jaw tightened and nerve in her cheek ticked.

"Money laundering!" Carmelita shouted. "You absorbed it into rentals, purchases or condo repairs. Your game is over. My brother will be made aware of your schemes."

My eyes fixated on the kitchen window, dark and blurry with water. Turning to Perla Brava Gonzales, I said, "It's scary, isn't it, Perla, when you're caught in a web of your own lies?"

"I didn't do anything. It's all Leo and his money-grabbing plans. He needs cash to buy his drugs." Perla glanced scornfully at Leo. "He stole some paintings and glyphs but I forgave him."

"Why would you let a thief stay on?" I rubbed my lip thoughtfully. "Unless he has something on you?"

"There is nothing to hide. You are mistaken. Besides, I like this hombre. He is my friend," Perla's hand embraced Leo's waist under his jacket.

Carmelita moved in front of Leo and Perla. She was blocking their line of vision when I grasped the kitchen knife and pulled it into my raincoat.

"I will make sure both of you are arrested for Linda, and Ed's murders and the attempted murder of Adelina. As a Bolivar Alvarez I have influence with this police force. The captain is my cousin."

"How misguided you are," Perla pulled out a gun from the back of Leo's waistband and held it in a two-handed grip, her arm straight in front of Carmelita. "A dead Bolivar Alvarez is sadly inconsequential. Now, step back."

Carmelita scowled. "Put that toy down. You don't know how to use a gun."

"I know all about this pistol. FYI, I have had lessons from a master and I practise regularly in a range." Her right hand gripped the gun, the web of her hand over the barrel and a finger on the trigger.

Perla's stare was icy. "This is a semi-automatic Glock 17. See how my hands are holding it to steady it from the recoil?"

Leo smiled. "I loaded one round in the barrel, and there are seventeen rounds in the magazine. Even if you run she can kill both of you in seconds."

The psycho was about to kill us. I had to make her talk. "Stop right there, Perla. Killing us makes no sense and is totally unfair."

"What, are you crazy?" Perla cocked an eyebrow. "That's ridiculous, Sturm. There is no reason to be fair when people need killing."

"Yes, there is. You are the brilliant mastermind. You owe us an explanation," I said, inching over to Perla and pushing Carmelita to my right side. "Tell us everything."

"You made up a killing rule? Okay, so why do you think?" Perla gritted her teeth. "Ed betrayed me with this puta and so did Linda," she said, pointing the semi-automatic in Carmelita's direction. I made sure Ed ended up in the deep blue sea, where you were also headed with the assistance of my men and now I have no reason not to finish off this Bolivar Alvarez bruja."

I had to raise my voice to be heard over the storm outside which made a whistling sound like a high pitched steam kettle. "Which makes me wonder why you would want to drown me?"

Leo's eyes gleamed with malice. "You were trying to sabotage the entire operation. You tried to turn Heinz. He was ready to make us money but you wanted him to remain loyal to his brother. You, Adie Sturm are trouble. Go ahead, kill her, Perla."

"Shut up, idiot! It is my operation. I give the orders." Perla waved her pistol from Carmelita to me, her lip curled in dissatisfaction. She glanced down at her dress. "I don't want to shoot into their heads. There will be too much blood." She waved the Glock. "Step back, putas!"

"Wait!" I called out. "Tell us about the liquid heroin in the scuba suits? That's worth millions."

Perla laughed. "Wasn't that clever? Another way to get richer."

"Now, you have it all. It was brilliant." Leo puffed up his chest. "Are you satisfied? Can you die in peace?"

"I think it's all over. Your time has come." Perla pointed the pistol at Carmelita.

"No! There's no use killing us." Carmelita stepped up close to Perla's face. "We aren't the only ones who know about your activities."

"Wait." A gruff voice from the doorway growled, "Who else knows about this?" Orlando Maderia, the moustached bar owner from the strip club poked his head in.

Perla acknowledged him with a smile. "Did we wake you, cariño?" She didn't bother to introduce us or explain why he was there in the house.

The oversized older man grunted. "Water is seeping into the bedrooms. We need to evacuate immediately. You too, Leo, but," he stared at us with dead eyes, "first tell me who knows about the heroin."

A bang brought all eyes to the window. A palm frond smacked the glass, leaving pieces of bark and vegetation behind, cracking the glass. The wind howled eerily, shaking the walls, and tumultuous rain pounded on the glass. Debris from the trees flew by and a loose pink roof tile struck the window with a wallop. A large crack from top to bottom spread into tributaries across the pane.

Gathering my wits about me, trying to forget the storm and create a credulous story to take them off balance wasn't easy. Straying from the truth would end with us winding up dead. These people were sociopaths. They liked killing.

I shouted above the storm, "Who do you think knows? The Bolivar Alvarez men and Wolf Du Lac. They know the whole story." I hoped they were on their way but there's no use counting on a maybe. It was up to us.

Perla was itching to shoot. Her finger cocked and I heard a click as I stepped over on an angle my left hand on her hand and my right hand around the barrel, swinging it up. On the twist and yank down, the Glock fired. The round released as the Glock fell into my possession. Leo waivered a moment before slumping down on the floor, his upper body hit, blood seeping out on his shirt.

A roundhouse kick struck Perla's knee. She screamed and hunched over. A jab to the chest brought her down. I aimed the pistol at Perla when I felt a big arm capture me in a rear choke hold. I dropped the weapon as his arm tightened. Instinctively, I put my head down to avoid being strangled and sunk down with my body weight. When he loosened his hold on my throat, I stepped forward with my right foot and kicked back with my left connecting with his groin. I felt his pain when he groaned loudly. This was my chance to grasp his hand and pull him off balance. He fell but was getting back on his feet when I remembered the knife in my pocket. I pulled it out and made contact with his arm. Just as I thought this was the end, Carmelita came to my aid, a frying pan in her hand. She whacked him soundly on the head.

A sudden crash brought the window pane down and a flood of water with it.

"Come on!" I pulled Carmelita with me into the bathroom and swung the door shut as the water poured into the kitchen. I leaned with my back on the door to keep the water out. Carmelita joined me on the floor as the lights went out. I could hear her praying into my ear above the noise of the wind.

***

Time stood still as we waited out the hurricane thinking each shudder of the walls would break our shelter and let in the sea. Hours later I heard what sounded like voices. To respond might be dead dangerous.

A man called out my name. His husky voice was familiar. When a second man joined in with Adelina, I knew we would be all right.

I nudged Carmelita. "It's Wolf and Diego."

"Gracias, Dios mio!" Carmelita whispered. "I never thought I would find religion but I think it has found me." She hugged my shoulders. "You are my most treasured friend. I owe you, chica."

"The same goes for me." I grinned. "You are handy in the kitchen— a wonder with the frying pan."

"It helps when there is an assistant to cut up the meat." She laughed. "I admire your technique."

Carmelita hugged me. "So glad we are alive." She leaned to the door and shouted. "Diego!"

"In here!" I shouted springing up. Carmelita was a bit slower to get on her feet as she took off her leather heels, holding them up just in time.

The door yanked open and water and debris flooded in. Wolf and Diego waited for us to come out. It was incredible how a near death crisis got me all emotional but I wasn't the only one. The guys looked a little weepy too.

Awkward. Quickly I hugged Wolf and then Diego. Carmelita got her share of attention next. She was a little miffed at that.
"I expected Wolf to ignore me but you," she pointed at Diego, "are my brother. I am your only sister, remember?"

"Certainly, but Adelina is my future." Diego smiled surreptitiously. "I want that for us, cariño," he said, directing his gaze at me.

"Not if I can help it," Wolf sneered at Cozumel's godfather.

They were getting into it again. Would they ever accept each other? No matter. I was used to the tension. At this point there were more important considerations.

Perla's formerly pristine kitchen had been ferociously ravaged by the hurricane, chairs overturned, a toaster and a blender on the floor and cupboard doors open randomly as if a crazed burglar had ransacked the room. Glass covered the floor.

Carmelita's eyes glazed over. She was staring at the interior of the room. Tapping her arm, I said, "Put your shoes on, Carmelita. The window broke, remember? There is glass everywhere!"

"Wake up!" Diego snapped his fingers impatiently in her face. "What are you waiting for?"

Carmelita stared at the shoes she held in her hands. "They are precious. The water will ruin them."

Diego grabbed the shoes from his sister's hands and yelled, "Put them on! Do you want to damage your feet?"

"Hold on, Alvarez, take it easy. The girls are in shock." Wolf righted a chair and then gathering Carmelita in his arms, set her down. "Please, you need to wear your shoes."

I figured the guys could handle this. Shoes were my thing but nine hundred for a pair would pay for most of my rent. There was no way I had that kind of money to throw away. It made more sense to see if Perla or the men were still in the house.

Diego started to shout in rapid-fire Spanish as I wandered down the hall, stepping over a tree frond that had made its way into Perla's beach house corridor. Water was several inches high on the floor where the tiles slanted. The wall was stained in rivulets as it started to dry. Down the hall, I opened one door and found it a worse mess than the kitchen—sea water had seeped in another broken window. Quickly, I slammed it shut. There was no use bringing in more water but the house had to be searched. Besides the bits of furniture, seaweed and sand, I was at a loss to find Perla or her cohorts. Diego followed me letting Wolf deal with his sister.

"What are you looking for, mi amor?" Diego put an arm around my shoulders. "I will help."

"Perla Brava Gonzalez, Leo del Socorro and Orlando Maderia were all in the kitchen before the window caved. Leo was bleeding from a gunshot wound and Orlando had been injured. I want to know where they are."

Diego took my face in his hands looking deep into my eyes. His hazel eyes sparkled golden. "How did this happen?"

"Perla was about to shoot us. When I stopped her she accidently shot Leo. Orlando tried to choke me. Carmelita hit him on head and I stabbed his hand." I glanced back at the kitchen at the wet floor and got an idea.

"Come," Diego took my hand gently, "let's go back to the kitchen."

"No, not yet. I want to check the hall. Did you bring a flashlight?"

"I did not but perhaps—"

"Wolf," I called out, "did you bring a flashlight?"

From out of the kitchen a light beamed in my eyes. Wolf sauntered up to my side and swung the light to the floor. "Alvarez should be with his sister. She's traumatized by this."

Diego nodded. "I'll go talk to her. Thanks."

I waited for Diego to be back in the kitchen. "Really? That's a slight exaggeration, Sea God. Carmelita is kickass. She saved me. The frying pan whacked Orlando on the head."

"I suppose. Carmelita iss a contender." Wolf scrutinized my face. "Why the flashlight?"

"To check for blood stains. Orlando and Leo were bleeding. Leo might be dead. Not so much Orlando. I thought a blood trail might explain where they went."

On the way to the front door there was red tinge on the floor where the floor was dry. Another one was on the door handle. "There! I think they left." To open the door I had to pull with all my strength. In the driveway the limo was gone.

From behind Diego approached. "What's going on, Adelina?"

I shook my head. "Let's go to the kitchen."

Once we were back, Diego pulled out a chair. "Adelina was about to explain what happened here. Sit, cariño. We will listen, right, Du Lac?"

"Of course. I am open to listening, are you?"

Diego grunted. "I am at your service, Adelina."

I held up both hands and sighed.

Wolf nodded. "I'm sorry. Go ahead."

With Carmelita's assistance I ran through the events occurring before the hurricane. She played them the sound track from her cell.

"Looks like the police would want this," Wolf said. "And we figure they might have gone out the front door and hijacked Carmelita's limo."

"With Robert in it?" Carmelita's face grew ashen. "She might kill him."

"Let's think positive. Perla might have told him to drive. Orlando had the pistol. He probably had no choice." I looked at Wolf. "We need to locate him."

"Or they might have tossed him out. He might be hurt. Either way we need to search for him."

A banging in the hall put us on alert.

Cy, Churo and Luis clattered down the hallway.

"Are you all right?" Cy asked, staring at me.

"Yes, and so is your sister." Diego said pointedly.

"Of course, she is. Carmelita's a Bolivar Alvarez."

Carmelita rushed up to Cy, her shoes on and tears gone. "Can you go outside with Churo and Luis to look for the limo and Roberto? He might be in the bushes, beat up or worse."

Cy nodded. "And if he's not there?"

"After that," Diego said, "if he's not to be found, we need to search further." He spoke to all of us. "Our vehicles have GPS tracking devices. The cell towers won't be working so Luis, I want you to go back to the villa and find out where the limo is. Churo go to Herandez and tell him to search for Roberto. Give him the details. He can put out a bulletin."

"Has anyone searched all the rooms here at the house?" I asked.

"Let's do that now." Wolf indicated he would take the first five rooms to the right and motioned for Diego to take the ones on the left. Since this was a beach house there was no second floor.

There was nothing, just debris, broken windows and sea water. Some of the walls and colonial pillars were gone, swept away by the sea. It had been a beautiful house and now it was a ghost of its former self. Perla would not be pleased.

***

In a couple of hours we met at Diego villa which seemed to be amazingly in one piece. The town of San Miguel was also doing well although it was flooded with a foot or two of water in places and the hydro was still out. The big news was that the hurricane was in Playa on its way to Cancun. It had been downgraded to a storm.

Hernandez was not happy about the drugs and money laundering. They found Leo dead, having bled out from the wound. Roberto had been shot in the head. The abandoned limousine had been left on off the side of the road on the north part of the island. There was no sign of Perla or Orlando.

Wolf and I said our good-byes, confident that Diego would know the perfect way to deal with Hernandez, exonerating me of Linda's murder. With a kiss and a hot sweep of his eyes that told me he was still very much interested in being my husband, Diego walked me to the door of his villa. Not to be forgotten, Cy gave me a hug saying we must dive together soon. I nodded. The Erizo del Mar had been ravaged by the hurricane and would need a few weeks to be repaired.

The town's people had started the clean up after the hurricane. Tomorrow we would do our bit too but for now we headed south in Wolf's Jeep to Wolf's cottage in the central San Miguel.

20

The flame glowed a vibrant red, springing alive with the addition of a log that Wolf threw in. I sat on the comfortable old fabric couch in shades of turquoise in front of the roaring fireplace. The fire lent a glow to the room, moving like shadows of salsa dancers, bouncing on the walls rhythmically.

It was a nippy night in Cozumel, the lingering effects of the rain and wind had cooled down the land. Outside, a palm tree had been damaged but Wolf's cottage had been lucky. When I gazed at the living room it brought back memories of other nights we had spent together.

Over the black lace bikini underwear, I wore Wolf's extra-large black T-shirt, which unlike the ones I had at home was missing the fuzz of Minnie's long gray cat fur which always adhered to the cotton like a powerful glue. I missed her and the boy cats. It was time to return home.

Right now I was caught up in the charm of Cozumel and the magnetic man who captured my heart, but it was torn in two. Not by the Diego and Wolf. It was more complicated. Half of me was in Canada with my family and furbabies and the other here with Wolf and my friends. Diego and Cy were persons of interest but hadn't progressed to the point of explosive fire I felt with the Sea God. Although to be fair I had to admit those Bolivar Alvarez men were steamy to the touch. I had left those relationships unexplored for good reason. My life was difficult enough. I wasn't Carmelita juggling three men simultaneously. I had a conscience.

"Deep in thought, Mermaid?" Wolf stroked my cheek. "Why?" He took the bottle of red wine sitting on the coffee table and poured two glasses.

"There are things we need to talk about."

"To figuring it out," Wolf said, raising his glass.

I clicked mine to his and drank. "Figuring it out!" I tasted the rich taste. Shiraz?"

"I know it's your favorite, Yellow Tail from Australia, vibrant, smooth and easy to enjoy. Not the most expensive wine—"

"Money doesn't matter when it comes to delicious red berries. They are so soft in the mouth and this shiraz goes perfectly with—"

Wolf pulled out a square red box from behind the pillow. "Chocolates for you."

"For us. I will share the treasure." Attacking the box I snatched up a truffle and placed it in my mouth, my teeth wedged in the middle and offered him the other part held in my lips. Wolf's eyes flashed enticingly. I moved closer and he joined me in a kiss, taking in the chocolate.

"Are your endorphins running wild yet?" Wolf's ruffled hair fell over his forehead, his eyes were a clear blue, and his body rivalled Sean Connery's in the Bond movies. He was untamed. It was like encountering a wolf in the wilds, luring me in to believe he needed me to initiate the taming process.

"Mmm, getting there. First, a refill." I offered him my glass.

Wolf smiled enigmatically. "Are you sure? I know how wine hits you."

"So do I, and I like the feeling."

Just then his cell buzzed. Wolf lifted a finger to signal me to wait before he answered. The person on the other end had a lot to say after Wolf said hello. Finally, Wolf asked, "You're sure?" There was a pause as someone answered. After a moment Wolf said, "Thanks, I will," and pressed the end icon.

"What was that about?"

"Some news."

"What's happening?"

"Heinz is packed and ready to go home to Canada."

When I lifted an eyebrow, Wolf said. "Hernandez agreed we don't want any bad publicity for the condo project or to upset the apple cart. Heinz had no choice. He signed a confession to be used if he returns without permission."

"And that's it?"

"Heinz will never be tempted to wash money again." Wolf laughed. "Heinz is scared shitless they will put him in jail. He'll stay clean."

"And the others? Have they been found?"

"Orlando's still missing but a woman who matches Perla's description washed up on the beach near her house."

"Someone killed her?"

"Or something did. Hurricane Pandora."

"We were lucky not to be swept away. Thank you for coming to get me."

Wolf placed his glass on the table and took mine and placed it beside his. "Yeah, you're safe for now." He laughed. Swooping in closer he caressed my neck and then my lips, the tip of his tongue teasing me.

I laughed. "Hurricane Wolf is just as powerful."

In answer Wolf's hands found their way to my legs, gliding up my thighs to the edge of the T-shirt I wore. In a joint effort we removed it, his lips kissing my body sensuously and then we tore off his. Our bare skin sparked electrically as his chest touched mine.

Wolf tilted my chin upwards. "How does it feel to be with me again?

I smiled. "Just the way I like it—dead dangerous."

About the Author

Anastasia Amor , a university psychology graduate, a mother and pet mom, writes suspense. She researches the location of each series thoroughly to allow the reader to feel part of the story.

In the Adie Sturm Mystery Series, the heroine is an intelligent martial artist, and tour guide. Adie Sturm actively solves murders in steamy Cozumel.

The Sommerville Suspense Series heroines are fearless and relentless when they encounter paranormal suspense in romantic southern locations. The books are set in Cuba and New Orleans with another one in progress set in Savannah.

Amor has also written an erotic romance set in Puerto Rico.

www.AnastasiaAmor.com

https://www.facebook.com/Anastasia.Amor.author

Anastasia.Amor@hotmail.com
http://anastasiaamor1.blogspot.ca